Clouds Over Markota

Kathleen Hegedus

Cover Design by Jamie Anne Haiden

Copyright © 2015 Kathleen Hegedus
All rights reserved.
ISBN-10: 1511862734
ISBN-13: 978-1511862738

With love, in memory of Lajos Hegedus

CHAPTER ONE

"Do you want to hear the Bells of Dusseldorf?" he asked.

She knew that twinkle in his eye meant mischief but she could deny Lajos nothing. "Sure," she said.

Grinning slyly, he picked up the largest stone he could lay his hand on and, channeling all the might of a twelve-year-old boy into one well-aimed throw, he launched it at the metal lock on the backyard gate. The loud clang shattered the morning stillness.

"Oh, Lajos!"

But the little boy was delighted. "The Bells of Dusseldorf!" he declared.

"The war!" she scolded. "People don't like to hear sudden loud noises."

"Lajos!" Uncle Vince's voice thundered from the next yard. "Stop fooling around and finish your chores."

"Gotta go," he said, already bolting off.

Ilonka smoothed her shapeless house smock and pushed her long, dark hair back behind her ears. The dusty road was empty. People were staying close to home. Her eyes scanned the sky, but there were no planes today, at least not right now. There seemed to be so many more lately. She wondered if it were true that the Allies were winning the war, but peace was all she hoped for. With so much lost already, she just wanted it to end.

Her eyes fell on the basket of wet clothes and she remembered what she'd been doing before Lajos stopped by. Picking up a clothespin, she went back to hanging the wash on the line.

All the young men were gone away to fight, but the soldier she had worried most about was Jozsi. Her older brother wore his uniform proudly. He looked so brave that day they waved farewell to him at the train station. She tried to be as brave as he looked. For a year, she wrote letters to Jozsi and clung to every bit of news that came back from the Soviet front, until the day the horrible news arrived: Jozsi was killed in action. Young men were dying every day, but not her big brother. Sometimes she still caught herself thinking that the war would end soon and he would come home.

Ilonka didn't want to hear any more names of men who would never return. When Jozsi went to war, her younger brother Sanyi and his best friend Lajos were still only little boys – children to be protected – but if the war went on much longer, soon they'd be young men to be drafted. She reached into the basket for a pair of Sanyi's pants and clipped these, too, to the clothesline.

Out of the quiet morning sounds, she heard the steady clopping of a horse's hooves. Uncle Vince waved to her as he steered his wagon out of his yard onto the street. She watched him until he turned onto his sister's road and her thoughts turned to her friend. When the war started Mariska was a young bride, newly married to Lászlo. They were barely settled into their house when Lászlo was called up for duty. It was around the same time as Jozsi. Mariska lived from letter to letter. What a cruel way to start a marriage, thought Ilonka. Would they ever have a chance to live their lives together? Or would today be the day they would hear news of Lászlo... no, she wouldn't let herself think about that.

How long could this war go on before all the husbands and brothers died? Would there be any young men left? She brushed the thought aside. Even thinking about her own marriage prospects seemed selfish. People were dying; what right did she have to think about her own happiness? It is not a happy world we live in, she reminded herself.

Such gloomy thoughts could pass through Ilonka's mind, but they couldn't lodge there. Practical matters were far too pressing to indulge in non-productive wallowing. She picked up another clothespin and her mother's well-worn apron, and finished hanging the wash on the line.

Emerging from the cloud, Captain Endre Kovacs took a quick 360-degree survey and was relieved to find himself all alone in the sky. The Focke Wulfs that had pock-marked his fuselage were making their way back to Germany just as surely as Endre was checking his compass and aligning his course towards England. The thunderous rumble of the fighter's engine filled the sky as the P-51 Mustang full-throttled its victory declaration.

Endre felt the exhilaration of a job well done. The B-17 Flying Fortresses he was sent here to protect had unloaded their ammunition on the targets and were halfway home by now. The fighter planes stayed behind to cover their tails and continue the battle with the Luftwaffe, high above Munich, but by then the mission was accomplished. Targets destroyed.

Once more he surveyed the sky, just to make sure. His heart was still pounding. Only seven minutes ago, he'd made a quick turn to port and found himself head-on with two Focke Wulfs. Pulling into a steep climb, he'd managed to avoid the first round of incoming artillery, but the Focke Wulfs were not so easily dissuaded. When the Mustang levelled off, they came diving down from the sun, ready to deliver their dangerous barrage. Endre heard the bullets pinging off his wing as he dove for cloud cover. With minimal visibility, he navigated westward by his instruments until he ran out of clouds.

Fortunately, the altocumulus cover extended far enough to bring him out of the danger zone. His pulse was on its way back down to normal. A check of the altimeter told him he was at eleven thousand feet. He noted that the engine kept a steady rhythm. The pelting from the Focke Wulf had dinged up the metal some but failed to inflict any serious damage.

While scuffling with the Germans, Endre separated from the rest of his squadron. Straining his eyes westward, he occasionally caught glimpses of them. Intermittently, their movements angled them just right to flash back reflections from the rays of the setting sun. Maintaining full throttle, he estimated that he would catch up to them by the time they entered Belgian air space. The P-51 Mustang was a one-man aircraft; that was fine with Endre. When not dodging bullets, flying was blissful. He reflected on the gaping incongruity between fighting for your life one moment and inhaling the serenity of a pink sunset the next.

With a multitude of other young Americans, Endre went to the recruiting office on December 8, 1941, the day after the Japanese bombed Pearl Harbour. At nineteen, Endre was not well versed in international politics and the complexities of military alliances. He believed he was off to Japan, not Europe. Three years later, he was considerably wiser. Still, Endre admitted, politics was not his forte – flying was.

Alone in the ebbing sunset, safe in friendly skies, Endre let his mind wander back to England

and the cute little British girl waiting for him at the pub. Sally was her name. Sally had turned her bright blue eyes on Endre last Saturday night. "Hello, handsome," was all she said before Endre was offering to buy her a drink. After several drinks and some distracting conversation, Endre led Sally to the dance floor just in time for a slow song. He congratulated himself on his great timing and pulled her close, as the lazy tempo demanded. Holding the pretty blonde and moving slowly to the pulse of the seductive beat, Endre caught a wink from his buddy. Sally was Jimmy's dance partner a week or two ago. This week, Jimmy was buying drinks for Nancy.

The sultry beat played on and Endre's hand continued to wander from Sally's waist, a little lower and a little lower still. Finally, Sally reached behind her, clasped his wrist and placed his hand back on her waist. All done with a teasing smile, like she really didn't mean it, Endre hoped.

The up-tempo trumpet blasts launched into the Andrews Sisters' rendition of *In the Mood*. The couple let go of each other and kicked up their heels. Setting down her drink, Nancy shouted, "I love this song!" as she grabbed Jimmy by the hand and dragged him onto the dance floor. Nancy and Sally started horsing around, singing along with the Andrews Sisters and laughing at themselves when they forgot the words. The boys applauded their little act and Jimmy called loudly for an encore. Sally giggled and went on dancing. No hard feelings. Jimmy was nothing more than yesterday's newspaper to her too.

When the music changed again, to *Good Night Irene*, Sally waltzed into his waiting arms. Endre knew he wasn't the first pilot to fall into those eyes, but what the heck! Pretty girls are a pilot's privilege, he reminded himself with a smile. That's why, at the pub, every man in uniform is a pilot.

Endre's sweet reminiscence was interrupted by the need for another instrument check. Only a sliver of yellow remained of the sunset as he eased back on the throttle. It wasn't good to burn any more fuel than necessary; never know when it might be needed. He was almost caught up. Soon they'd be putting their wheels down, shedding their metal skins, debriefing their mission, and then – hello, Sally!

"This is the last of the sugar," Ilonka said, pouring the half cup measure into the mixture.

Her mother took that information in stride. "Some days we have sugar; some days we don't." With shortages of everything because of the war, she felt lucky to ever have sugar.

Ilonka cracked an egg into the mixing bowl, then paused to push her hair back behind her ears. She thought this made her ears look big, so she usually wore it more forward on her face. Right now she was more concerned about keeping hairs out of the cookie dough than about her big ears.

"Your hair is beautiful," said her mother reaching to touch it and beginning to braid it, like she used to do when Ilonka was a little girl. Without offering any resistance to the braiding, Ilonka added a cup of flour and worked it into the dough.

"Such lovely natural curls," said Erzsi, as she finished her daughter's braid.

"Natural wrinkles," laughed Ilonka, referring to the unruly way her plain brown hair waved, not at all in the orderly fashion of evenly shaped curls.

"I think it's pretty. But if you don't like it, why don't you cut it? Maybe something cute and short, like Mariska's."

"Maybe," said Ilonka. She admired the new hairstyle on Mariska, but she had no intention of cutting her hair. Despite its wildness and its annoying tendency to get knotted in the wind, she liked her hair long.

There was a light knock on the kitchen door before it opened.

"Speaking of Mariska..." greeted Ilonka.

"We were just talking about your fashionable hair-do," said Erzsi.

"I hope László likes it," she said.

"I'm sure he will," said Ilonka, while rolling out the cookie dough. "It's gorgeous."

"Have you heard from him?" asked Erzsi.

"Not for a while. His last letter was four weeks ago." More quietly, she added, "I'm scared. The reports from the front are terrible."

Erzsi walked over and hugged her. "I know," she said. She did know. Not only had she waited for her own husband to return from the Russian front during the Great War, but she had also lost Jozsi, her oldest son, in the first year of this war. She understood how hard it was to wait with nothing more than the occasional letter to ease your mind.

"Thank you," said Mariska quietly. "Oh!" She remembered why she'd come. "I finished it." Reaching into her bag, she pulled out a blue knitted sweater.

"Lajos is going to love that!" said Ilonka admiring Mariska's fine handiwork.

"And it'll keep him nice and warm this winter," added Erzsi.

"I couldn't resist buying this wool when I saw it. The blue reminded me of his eyes," said Mariska.

"Exactly," Ilonka agreed. "It'll be perfect on him!"

"Would you like some tea?" Erzsi offered. "And the cookies will be ready soon."

Mariska accepted, "but let me make it. You two look busy." She began filling the kettle with water.

While Ilonka spooned the dough onto the cookie sheet, Erzsi stirred the pot of *gulyás* on the stove, releasing a heavy paprika smell into the kitchen. Seeing the potatoes were cooked soft, she turned the flame lower on the gas burner and began mixing the eggs and flour for the *csipetke* noodles to add to the stew.

Before pushing the baking sheet into the oven, Ilonka pressed smiling face outlines onto two of the cookies.

CHAPTER TWO

At morning mail call, the Sergeant handed Endre two letters: one from his father and one from his fiancée. He opened his father's letter first. Once a week, Ferenc Kovacs penned a letter to his son:

Kedves Fiam, My Dear Son,

I hope this letter finds you safe and healthy. I want you to know that everything is fine here at home. The harvest looks good and I bought three more cows. The apples are ripening and Mom is getting ready to make pies and jelly. We'll start picking the corn soon too.

We had some excitement last week. Wilson's sheep broke through their fence and ended up in our yard, all two hundred of them! I didn't really mind. At least I won't have to cut the grass for a while. Mom, on the other hand, was displeased because they ate some of her flowers before she was able to stop them.

We think of you all the time. I check every day for news of the war. I keep hoping to read that the war has ended and that you're on your way home, but not so far. I hope you don't think this morbid, but I must confess that I thank God for every day that I don't find your name on the lists. Your mother is afraid to look for herself. She holds her breath while I read, and only starts breathing again when she sees the relief on my face.

I know you're an excellent pilot, Son, but in the end we're all just men. When we're stretched to our limits, we find our strength in God. Your mother and I pray for you every day.

I'll keep this note brief, but I wanted to remind you once more of the family rule: come home safely! Remember when you were a little boy and you wanted to ride your bike into town to go to the store? And when you went on that river trip to the Catskills with your pals in high school? And when you went by train all by yourself to visit your friend who'd moved to Cleveland... It's still the only rule: come home safely!

With all our love,

Apu & Anyu, Dad & Mom

Endre had just finished reading his father's closing when it was time to go for breakfast. Kim's letter would have to wait. She didn't write as often as his father did, maybe once a month. Sometimes her letters were accompanied by a package filled with cookies. Endre's mouth watered at the memory of the shortbread she sent last month, but there were no sweets this time. Too bad, he thought. He would rather have had cookies for breakfast than the powdered eggs the mess was serving. He tucked both letters under his pillow and quickly made his bed, tightening the sheets to the military standard.

Later that evening, as the sun was setting and the bullets stopped flying, Endre relaxed his shoulders against the back of the cockpit seat. He counted this sortie a very lucky one, not that he was a big believer in luck. On the contrary, he liked the feeling of holding fate in his own hands. He'd told himself many times that this was the reason he had switched from bombers to fighters. In a fighter, he felt more in control and that suited him better. Still, he admitted, some days you just got lucky.

Today was one of those days. Horror surrounded him; fireballs fell out of the sky. Sometimes there was a parachute and sometimes there wasn't. Usually Endre had hope for those who had to bail, hope that they would make it to the ground uninjured and find their way home. Slim chance. More often they were killed or captured. But for those who needed to pull the ejection handle today, Endre knew there was no hope. The Germans met them north of Belgium, over the ocean. Those parachutes wouldn't save anyone. They just disappeared in the dark water below, dragging down the de-planed pilots to sleep their eternal dreams in the cold wave-grave of the North Sea.

Endre shook off the chilling images and fixed his eyes on the instrument panel. He was grateful to be, once again, heading westward. His thoughts flew farther west than England, crossing the ocean all the way back to America. Remembering this morning's letters, Endre thought, I'm like my dad. Ferenc Kovacs had never flown an airplane, but his temperament was that of a fighter. He was a risk-taker. Like his son, he was not one to allow fate a free hand in his life.

Endre remembered how his father used to talk about immigrating to America. The familiar story always started in June 1920, after WWI, when the great world powers signed the Trianon Treaty, and handed a full two-thirds of Hungary over to the surrounding nations. Suddenly, Ferenc, a proud Hungarian, found himself living in Romania. Like most Hungarians, Endre's father was enraged by this outcome. Almost immediately, the young Ferenc made up his mind to go to the USA. His older brother had gone over a few years earlier and sent back many encouraging letters. The allure of the American dream already had a firm hold on Ferenc's imagination. He wasn't afraid of the unknown; he was exhilarated by it. The first time Endre heard that story was on his first day of school, but he had heard it many times since then, probably every time he faced something new. It was his dad's favourite fatherly object lesson on taking control of your life.

After a routine instrument check, Endre recalled that sometimes the story didn't end there. He had also heard the extended version, the love story. His father used to say there was only one hitch in his plan, his fiancée. How would Eva feel about leaving her family and crossing the ocean with him? Endre smiled when he remembered how his father used to build suspense in telling this story, even though the outcome was obvious. Nervously, I waited for her answer, he used to say. He was ready to go. He was definitely going, with or without her. But, while he waited, he realized how much he loved her and how badly he wanted her to come. Soon, he wasn't so sure about going alone, but the story always ended on a triumphant note: I had nothing to fear; your mother said yes!

The next chapter of the story was always about the difficulties of life as immigrants, but that also ended triumphantly. Both Ferenc and Eva worked as farm labourers for the first two years, until they were able to save up enough money to make a down payment on their own plot of land in New York State. The day they moved into their little farmhouse, Eva was already a week past her due date. On September 15, 1922, their baby boy, Endre, was born in their own house, on their own land. Ferenc always said he had never been more proud.

When Endre was a child, they took him to New York harbour to show him Ellis Island. Like millions of other immigrants, this was their port of arrival on American soil. Endre remembered how he felt the first time he saw the Statue of Liberty, but even now he didn't have a word for that feeling. Perhaps his father said it best. He used to say that when he first set eyes on Lady Liberty, holding the freedom flame high above her head, it was as if she magically held his dreams in her hand. Everything seemed possible. This was America!

In British airspace now, Endre pulled his thoughts back across the Atlantic Ocean, and turned his attention to the air traffic controllers directing the arriving planes. The first thing he wanted to do when he landed was drink something. After hours of breathing oxygen through a mask, his mouth and throat were painfully parched. The second thing he wanted to do was head straight for his bunk and fall into an exhausted sleep, but he knew the mission had to be debriefed. Realistically, he also knew that sleep wouldn't come even if he did go to his bunk right after the debrief. He'd tried that before. It didn't work no matter how exhausted he was. The nightly witness of empty bunks was too hard to face without some fortification. He knew he'd be heading to the pub with the rest of the flyers, but right now he was just relieved to see the flare path illuminating the runway in the distance.

They were late touching down and the mission analysis went long. Even after the debrief was concluded, they weren't dismissed because a new plan was hatching that needed to be actioned. The report was that they would be moving some planes down to Italy, from where they could better reach targets in Eastern Europe. Endre and Jimmy were amongst the pilots selected to go. In the morning there would be another briefing and departure for Italy would commence immediately afterwards.

It was almost midnight by the time Endre pushed open the pub door and walked into the thick haze of cigarette smoke. The first thing he saw was Sally dancing with Marty and they looked really cozy.

"Tough break there, buddy," said Jimmy, following his gaze.

"You snooze you lose," shrugged Endre nonchalantly.

"Yeah, I heard from Nancy that Sally found a new pilot," said Jimmy.

"Uh huh," nodded Endre. "Hey, wait a minute. Marty's not a pilot!"

"I know," laughed Jimmy.

Endre laughed too, rolled his eyes, and went back to scanning the room. Jimmy gave his pal a playful punch on the shoulder, "That's my boy. Back in the game! Let me buy you a drink." With that, Jimmy was off to order a couple of pints.

Morning came too soon and brought with it that sick hangover feeling. Endre's scan of the pub had ended with eyes locking on Jenny, and Jenny kept Endre out a little too late last night. For the young captain, life was a whirlwind of flying, camaraderie, pints in pubs, and pretty girls. The serious business of war was for the politicians to sort out. For Endre and the boys, it was enough to stay alive and to live life ardently; to this they pledged themselves daily.

Endre tucked in the last corner of his bed sheet and made his way down to the mess hall. He massaged his pounding temples.

Jimmy gave him a mocking pat on the head. "Oh, poor baby. Did the pretty girl hurt you?"

Endre swatted him away. "You're just jealous."

Flying was a poor chaser for alcohol, they'd taught him in flight training. Technically, he was within the eight-hour bottle-to-throttle rule, or he would be by the time he got in the cockpit. Still, it would take a serious caffeine injection to get this day going. At least strong coffee was one thing the mess did well, thought Endre as he reached for the coffee pot and filled his cup.

After breakfast, with re-filled coffee cups in hand, the pilots made their way to the drab blue-grey meeting room and seated themselves in the hard metal chairs around the conference table for their pre-flight briefing. Endre detected a slight paint smell. In this den of men, there was nothing ornate, yet – for some reason – the walls were compulsively painted over and over again. Endre figured there must be fifty coats of paint on them, probably all the same drab blue-grey.

This morning, a colonel was here from Washington to address them and share updates on the war's progress. The colonel confirmed what they had read in Stars and Stripes: things had gone very well in France last month. Paris was liberated, along with Marseilles and Toulon. The Germans abandoned Bulgaria, but the Soviets captured Bucharest. Endre listened but he was not a student of politics. His analysis was quite simple. The Nazis were the supreme bad guys but that didn't make the Soviets good guys. It was really only a question of who to stop first.

The colonel concluded his update with the introduction of the new mission. "Our concern right now is in Eastern Europe, Hungary…"

Hungary. That sent a jolt through Endre that the caffeine couldn't match.

The colonel continued, "With the Germans advancing from the west and the Soviets breathing down their necks from the east, Hungary is between a rock and a hard place. Under Nazi occupation since March of this year, the industrial area of Miskolc has been commandeered to produce hardware in support of the German war effort. Our Italian base has been flying sorties to bomb them out of production, but they need more planes and they've asked for our support."

Escorting bombers into Hungary… Endre's thoughts repeated in his still-pounding head.

With that, the visiting colonel handed the floor back over to the squadron commander who pulled down the large map and outlined the strategy for the Italy-based mission. The meteorologist gave his briefing and assured them of clear skies. Questions were asked and answered until it was time to go, and Endre put an end to his short-lived internal conflict by concluding that the Nazi's military manufacturing must be stopped. The squadron commander closed the briefing with "God bless and good luck, boys!"

They pushed their chairs back, rose and headed for the flight line. Jimmy started the tune, "Off we go into the wild blue yonder..." Some were still singing, "we live in fame or go down in flames..." when they climbed aboard their Mustangs and began the orderly launch of the fighter squadron.

The Italy-based missions were long and exhausting, beyond the range of many fighters, but the Mustang P-51-D was made for the job. This was Endre's second mission escorting bombers to Miskolc, Hungary. His eyes scanned the instrument panel, monitoring his direction, altitude, speed, and fuel supply. All readings were good.

He lifted his eyes back up to the windshield but visibility was poor in this heavy cloud. A dark mass just in front of him, or was it? He strained to see. Maybe not. He'd find out when he reached the end of this cloud. He held his course.

As the cloud thinned around the emerging Mustang, Endre began a visual scan of the evening sky. There, unmistakable this time. A pair of Focke Wulfs had been waiting for him to come back out into the open. A series of orange flashes broke through the lingering fog. Attacked from above and port side, a line of gunfire ripped along the length of the Mustang's fuselage and engine cowling. Bullets sprayed into the cockpit. Instruments shattered. Endre felt the cold air rushing in through the bullet holes. Instinctively he took evasive action, diving left to get under his nearest attacker.

Assessing the damage, Endre turned just in time to see the engine burst into flames and engulf the port side wing. That narrowed his choices considerably. The Focke Wulf pilots were still not finished. They didn't intend to leave this job half done. They closed in on him a second time. Another stream of gunfire ripped across the starboard fuselage. The Mustang was quickly becoming one massive fireball. With no other option left, the young American pilot reached for the ejection handle and began, with a tumble, his dizzying rush to the ground.

Endre lived the longest seconds of his life. Grabbing hold of the release cord, he gave it a firm yank and was immediately rewarded with the sound of the pack deploying. Above him, the chute opened and abruptly halted his plunge.

Time stood still as he swung back and forth in his descent. In the midst of the battle it was just him and two Germans, but now he was aware of at least a hundred fighters still battling it out above him. There were other parachutes too. His eyes sought his own aircraft. He found it just in time to see the explosion on impact as it slammed into the ground.

Under his mushroomed canvas canopy, frightening images stormed Endre's mind: images of men with guns waiting for him on the ground. "No," he commanded himself, "focus." This vantage point, which would only last a few more seconds, was useful in determining his position. Endre surveyed the terrain. Judging by the last time he had plotted his position, he concluded that the larger city in the distance was Győr and the smaller one was Csorna. Looking down, he realized that he would be landing close to an even smaller village. He wasn't sure which one, but he checked its location in relation to the larger cities and noted that a small river ran through it, perhaps a tributary of the Danube to the north.

Night was falling heavy now but Endre could see the ground approaching, ever faster it seemed the closer he got to it. He strained his eyes in search of people. He saw no one and hoped that no one saw him either. He pulled his legs together and up as he prepared to land in a bush. Instinctively, he closed his eyes to protect them from the branches. By the time he finished unclipping his harness and working his way out of the branches, he knew he wasn't injured. Surviving the jump was a good start, he thought. He sat quietly for a few minutes, listening for any sound of people nearby. Hearing only crickets and the distant drone of aircraft was comforting. Looking around he realized that his parachute made a giant white target that seemed to glow brighter as the evening grew darker. He rolled it up as tightly as he could and stuffed it into the hollow at the base of a large tree.

He needed to find a hiding place to spend the night. Scanning his surroundings, he saw that he was in a rather dense concentration of trees and bushes. They would provide protective cover. He noted that the bushes sloped down towards the shore of the river he had spotted earlier. That was also good. He had an available source of fresh water to refill his canteen.

Unsnapping his flak jacket and taking off his helmet, Endre found a soft spot in the grass under a bush, and settled in. The moon was rising and the sky was still a little red. What a beautiful night, strange thought under the circumstances, shot down in enemy territory. He was relieved to note that, at least for the moment, there was no enemy to be seen. It was getting dark and nothing productive could be accomplished until daybreak. This hiding spot seemed as safe as any he could hope for. Endre allowed himself to drift in and out of a light sleep.

In the early dawn, Endre heard the birds singing and when he opened his eyes he saw them flitting about in the branches above him. His waking movements startled them into flight. He was startled himself with the realization that he had actually slept. Endre's mind sharpened as his consciousness was flooded with awareness of his circumstances. He remembered the sound of the bullets tearing apart the fuselage, the flames, the ejection, and the explosion as his unpiloted plane hit the ground. Now that night had given way to morning, he was eager to do a more thorough evaluation of his situation.

Endre's assessment began by lying perfectly still and listening. Just like last night, he heard nothing. Cautiously, he worked his way out of the bushes, pausing frequently to listen and look. He still heard nothing and saw no one. The second item on his assessment list was the persistent hunger signal coming from his stomach. He realized now that he had gone to sleep without eating. In fact, he hadn't eaten anything since breakfast at the mess in Italy yesterday morning. He reached for his survival pack and pulled out a can of beans. He ate them cold with a few crackers. He would have loved a cup of coffee. The pack did contain some instant coffee powder, but he was not sure enough about his surroundings to risk building a fire to boil water. The caffeine craving would have to wait but at least the hunger pangs were satisfied.

While he ate his crackers, he pulled the navigation kit out of the knee-pocket of his flight suit. He was alive; he hadn't been captured; maybe he could make it out of here. To plan his escape back to friendly territory, he'd first have to determine exactly where he was. He unfolded the chart and laid it out on the ground. He located and reviewed all the landmarks he had identified during his descent: the Danube, Győr, Csorna. From these he concluded that the river in front of him – the smaller one on the chart – must be the Keszegér. Following the line of the river with his finger, he surmised that the nearest town was Markota-Bödöge. Intending to plot his journey home, he noted September 12, 1944 beside the dot marking his current location. That's when Endre remembered his plans for September 15, his twenty-second birthday.

He had a three-day leave pass, effective immediately after this mission. Endre and the boys were planning to find some pretty Italian princesses to celebrate with. He smiled when he remembered that Jimmy promised this would be a birthday he would never forget. Turned out he was right about that! Endre could easily guess what the boys had planned for him. They weren't known for their creativity. Their imaginations didn't make it past girls and beer. He knew they would drink a toast to him, but he had no doubt that they would go off in search of the Italian princesses without him.

Endre's thoughts returned to the barracks. Now, his bunk would be empty. Sooner or later it would be assigned to someone new. On and on it would go, as if he had never been there. The boys who made it back would still go to the pub. They would raise their mugs to another day of cheating death. The end of the war was one day closer. A few more drinks, then the wistful dreaming would start. The city boys would start talking stock market numbers and entrepreneurial schemes, while the country boys longed for a peaceful life, on a small farm with the beautiful woman who waited back home.

Kim was the beautiful woman who waited for Endre. He tried to think of her and the life they would build when he returned, but no blissful images came to mind. Maybe he just wasn't much of a romantic. Or maybe he didn't really love her. He had allowed himself that thought once or twice before but didn't dwell on it, telling himself he'd have plenty of time to think about it later. He was only nineteen when he promised to marry her. A lot had happened since then. Once more, he pushed the thought aside telling himself, as always, that he'd figure that out when he got home.

Sitting on the shore of the Keszegér, swallowing another bite of cracker, Endre wondered if he would ever make it home. The talk around the base was that the war would end soon but, of course, no one knew for sure. Before that day came, Endre now realized, he could become a prisoner of war. He had heard the horror stories. He pushed those thoughts aside too.

Consulting his larger map of Europe, he had to admit the obvious. He was not simply going to walk out of here. England was a long way off. Germany to the west; Russia to the east. Every country in between was, like Hungary, embroiled in this war. Switzerland was all the way across the full length of Austria. Even if walking across Austria were possible, it was now mid-September. Winter would be here soon and there would be snow in the mountains. Endre didn't have the gear or the supplies for such a trek.

In northwest Hungary, Endre contemplated his options. The one advantage he had here, over any other country in the region, was that he spoke the language. For the first time, he wished he had paid more attention to the politics of the war. He guessed those details would probably be helpful to him now. He knew about the Trianon Treaty from his father. He knew that Hungary had lost a lot of land after WWI, and he knew that recovering that land was Hungary's incentive for joining this war.

From the American point of view, the Nazis needed to be stopped because of their genocidal rampage and because they were a threat to all of free Europe. From Hungary's perspective the situation was infinitely more complicated. Nazism was indeed a threat from the west, but communism posed a threat from the east.

Hungary had entered the war as a German ally in the hope of getting lost land back, but recently Hungary had entered secret negotiations with the Allied Forces. Of course, the negotiations did not remain secret and Hitler's outrage resulted in the German occupation of Hungary. Factories like the one in Miskolc – the target of this mission – were commandeered to make bombs for use by the Germans. Considering all of this, it was a risky business to bet your life on where the loyalties of any individual citizen in Nazi-occupied Hungary may lie.

CHAPTER THREE

The sun was barely up when Lajos came flying into the yard, sending the fallen leaves into a swirl with his feet as he skidded around the corner of the barn. Sanyi was there doing his morning chores.

"Did you see them last night?" asked Lajos excitedly.

"I heard them," said Sanyi as he dumped the corn into the feeder for the pigs.

"There must have been five hundred airplanes up there! Mustangs! The American P-51 Mustangs! And the Germans with their Focke Wulfs! Messerschmitts! I saw MiGs too!"

"Really?" asked Sanyi, impressed and envious. "I wanted to go out but my dad wouldn't let me."

Lajos nodded sympathetically. Lajos was free. He didn't have a dad to keep him inside when the bombs were falling. Mostly, he did whatever he wanted to. Whenever he heard the distant rumble of bombers in the sky or the roar of high-speed fighters, the only place Lajos wanted to be was in the cockpit with the daring pilots. Since that was not possible, he went for the next best thing: he climbed the highest hill and watched them fly right over him! It wasn't safe, of course, but twelve-year-old boys don't believe in death.

Lajos picked up the pitch fork and started tossing hay to the horses. Still fixated on last evening's events, he continued, "There were parachutes! Thousands of them!"

Without interrupting their excited airplane chatter, the boys headed over to Lajos' yard and repeated the same routine of feeding the animals there. Brushing their hands clean on their pant legs, the boys scooped up their notebooks and hurried off to school.

Assembled in the one-room schoolhouse, twenty-two children ranging in age from six to fifteen sang *Isten Áldd Meg a Magyart*, God Bless Hungary, the national anthem.

"Class, be seated," said Miss Barsi. After the morning's announcements, she directed the older students, "I've put some multiplication and division questions on the board. This is your assignment for today. Please get started."

Next, she turned her attention to the younger children. They were practicing printing the alphabet and learning the sound made by each letter.

Lajos sat daydreaming, restlessly looking out the window, absentmindedly sketching in his notebook, intermittently working on the math assignment for the first hour of the day, until Miss Barsi addressed the older students again. "Boys and girls, do you remember where we left off yesterday? We were talking about St. Istvan, weren't we?"

Heads nodded, and Lajos set down his pencil.

Miss Barsi had some pictures of St. Istvan's crown and she handed these to Lajos to look at and pass along. Lajos looked at the pictures, passed them over to Sanyi, picked up his pencil and resumed his drawings of men dangling from parachutes. He filled the page just as the sky was filled last night.

"Let's review," said Miss Barsi. "Sanyi, who was the first King of Hungary?"

"St. Istvan," Sanyi replied easily.

Miss Barsi was familiar with Lajos' doodling habits. Many times he handed in his assignments and the math sums were found somewhere between sketches of airplanes or men with rifles. He was a very bright boy but was often distracted. She thought he could be a successful student if only he would pay attention.

She saw that he was doodling again, so she threw the next question directly at him. "Lajos, in what year did St. Istvan take the crown?"

"Year 1000, at Esztergom, on Christmas day," answered Lajos, without looking up from his drawing he added, "He built the first church in Hungary."

Okay, so he was paying attention, she noted. After lunch, she gave the older students a writing assignment and worked with the younger children on learning their numbers. Checking on the older ones occasionally, Miss Barsi could see that Lajos was doodling again, but he seemed to have some writing on his page too. At the end of the afternoon, she called on Lajos to read his writing out loud.

"Very good," encouraged Miss Barsi. She reminded them of their homework assignments before saying, "Okay, class dismissed."

Finally! Lajos thought, almost out loud. "Let's go!" He grabbed Sanyi by the sleeve and they ran all the way home.

Uncle Vince was nowhere in sight. Lajos grabbed two apples from the bowl on the table and tossed one to Sanyi. "Let's get our chores done and get out of here." In the barn, both boys grabbed shovels, mucked out the horse stalls, and put the two horses back in. Lajos put out the feed while Sanyi filled their troughs with water. Done. Over to Sanyi's to repeat the ritual.

Getting out of Sanyi's house always took longer. First, Sanyi's mom greeted each of them with a kiss. Next, she fed them a snack of bread and pork fat, and then she asked a lot of questions about their day at school. What did they learn today? Did they have any homework? Little Aniko, who fell out of a tree and broke her leg last week, was she back at school yet? It seemed to Lajos that she wanted to know everything!

Lajos' Aunt Mariska was also in the kitchen when the boys arrived, and she always asked a lot of questions too.

When the boys were finished eating, Mariska said, "Lajos, I have something for you," and she pulled the knitted blue sweater out of her bag.

"Oh, wow!" exclaimed Lajos.

"Try it on," she urged.

Lajos pulled it over his shirt.

"Oh, it's a bit big," said Mariska.

"He'll grow into it," smiled Erzsi.

"I love it! Thank you, Aunt Mariska," said Lajos.

Mariska wrapped him in a big hug and gave him a kiss. He didn't tolerate as much of this mushy stuff as he used to when he was a little boy, but when he did, it was all the thanks she needed from her beloved nephew.

Finally, the boys were released to go and do their chores.

With the chores done quickly, they went back into the house to get their fishing poles. This time they were stopped by Ilonka, Sanyi's older sister. Very old, Lajos figured, at least twenty. To their relief, she didn't intend to detain them. She only packed them some fresh-baked cookies to take on their fishing trip. The ones with the happy faces were always for them. Lajos' mouth watered. Since his mother died, and Uncle Vince was left to look after him, no cookies were ever baked in his house.

Endre patted his pistol when he heard the voices. Just touching the cold metal gave him a sense of security. He knew how to use it. He was pretty good during target practice, but he was a pilot not an infantry soldier. He'd never shot anyone, and the idea of having to do so had always made him feel sick, but not today. Today he felt threatened and prepared to defend himself.

Endre wasn't naive about the realities of war. He didn't deny that people were killed when he fired on their planes or dropped bombs from the sky, but these kills were counted in number of airplanes shot down or strategic targets destroyed. Shooting another human being point-blank with a handgun seemed different somehow. He hoped he would never have to do that.

Endre poked his head out from his hiding spot. He saw two boys with fishing poles, and they were coming towards him. He pulled himself deeper into the cover of the bushes. The voices were louder and clearer now as they walked along the river directly in front of his hiding spot. Endre understood them. There was something strangely comforting in hearing Hungarian spoken – the sound of home so far from home.

They were talking about last night's air battle, excited about the planes and parachutes. On

Clouds Over Markota 35

their way here, they had seen three American parachutists being marched at gun-point by German soldiers. The boys figured there could be some Russians in the area too because there had also been MiGs overhead last night.

"What do you think will happen to them?" asked Sanyi.

"Who?" asked Lajos, looking for the perfect fishing hole.

"Those Americans that the Germans caught."

"Probably nothing good," said Lajos. "War is hell," he added in his best stoic adult voice.

The boys walked past Endre's cluster of bushes and stopped just a little farther downstream, still within earshot. Lajos sat down on a piece of driftwood, opened the homemade tackle box, and began preparing his fishing line.

Reaching for his own tackle, Sanyi began, "My dad says the Americans are the good guys."

"Well, not everyone agrees with him," said Lajos.

"I know. But why not?" wondered Sanyi. "They're not trying to take over our country like the Russians and the Germans."

"Yeah, but they're fighting the Germans, and the Germans are fighting the Russians, so if they kill all the Germans don't the Russians take over Hungary anyway?" rationalized Lajos.

"Maybe," agreed Sanyi tentatively, tossing his line into the river.

Lajos finished preparing his line and threw it in just downstream of Sanyi's.

Sanyi wondered, "Why can't we just be on the Hungarian side?"

Lajos explained, with the tone of an adult talking to a young child, "Because, in this world, you have to have alliances. Alliances are like friendships between countries."

"So if our friends get in a war, we have to?" asked Sanyi.

"Yup," said Lajos.

With that, he prepared to cast again. As he did so, he glanced over his right shoulder and something caught his eye, "Wow! What's that?" Forgetting all about fishing, he ran to investigate.

Sanyi had to reel in first, but then he was racing right behind Lajos.

Endre could no longer see or hear the boys and he didn't have enough brush-cover to risk getting any closer, so he waited. He knew they would return because they had dropped their poles on the shore nearby.

"What is it?" asked Sanyi.

"Some kind of bomb, I think," said Lajos inspecting the unfamiliar object.

Sanyi knew what this meant. The boys had found plenty of explosives lying around before, but this was something new. Still, if it was an explosive, there was only one thing to do: blow it up!

From farther up-river, a section of dock had broken free and landed on the shore just around the bend from where they were fishing. The boys decided that it would make the perfect floating platform for their fireworks. They covered it with as much straw as they could find and then gingerly placed their treasure on top. Satisfied that they had enough flammable straw to ignite the charge, the boys were ready for their show. Lajos struck a match and touched it to the edge of the straw. Together, they pushed the dock out into the current, ran back and threw themselves on the ground to wait for the kaboom… nothing.

Thirty seconds passed and nothing happened.

"Heck!" Lajos leapt to his feet.

"No!" shouted Sanyi, grabbing Lajos' left leg and pulling him back, "Stay down!" Having succeeded in lowering Lajos' mass a little, he added more calmly, "Wait a bit longer."

"Okay," Lajos agreed. He began to add, "but just a bit …" when his words were lost in the ear splitting detonation.

"What the …!" exclaimed Endre, raising his head suddenly from his hiding spot to see what had just blown up.

Ilonka, who had been on her way down to the river to call the boys home for supper, screamed upon seeing a man pop out of the bush. The two of them stood frozen in their startlement.

The post-explosion silence was broken by the sounds of the boys howling loudly with excitement, just out of sight around the river's bend. Hearing their voices, both Endre and Ilonka were relieved. Whatever that was, it apparently had not harmed them. This was all new to Endre, but Ilonka was used to them blowing up whatever leftover explosives they found laying around. She worried a great deal about them and desperately wished they would stop. That's why she fully intended to report this to her father and to Lajos' Uncle Vince. The boys would get lectures and probably even some wallops, but that would do nothing to deter them from the very next chance they had to blow something up. This is where Ilonka's thoughts would have been if today had been a day like any other when she had caught the boys playing with explosives. But on no other day had a stranger ever jumped out of the bushes.

They stared at each other, speechless for so long that surprise and apprehension began to give way to a sense of foolishness. Someone should say something!

Ilonka noted the lettering above the top left pocket: USAAF. Even if she could think of something to say, he wouldn't understand her. He was an American. She spoke a little German and some Russian, but no English. Was he a threat to her? Were the boys in danger?

Then Endre surprised her with, "*Jó napot kivánók, kisasszony.* Good day to you, Miss."

Ilonka blinked hard. She was completely unprepared to hear the American speak words she understood. Regaining her composure, she returned the greeting and a tiny smile appeared at the corner of her mouth, but only for a second. Suddenly, she felt conscientious about her big ears. She pulled her hair forward. "Do you speak Hungarian? Or did you learn only those few words?" she asked, trying to keep a chill in her voice.

"*Igen, beszélek magyarul.* Yes, I speak Hungarian."

Ilonka looked puzzled. He's Hungarian; why is he wearing an American pilot's uniform?

Endre saw the need to explain himself. "My parents are from Hungary. They moved to America before I was born. At home we always spoke Hungarian."

She believed him. That accounted for a Hungarian wearing an American uniform. His words were fluent, not even accented. She heard the way the Germans and the Russians who came through here mangled the language. This American wasn't doing that. His speech sounded – well, it sounded normal to her.

"My name is Endre," the pilot continued. "May I ask what yours is?"

"Ilonka," she replied. Feeling uncomfortable about having given her name to the stranger, she went back into interrogative mode, "How long have you been here?"

"I landed here last night." He thought a moment, then added, "If I'd known I was going to meet you, I would have landed here much sooner."

She rolled her eyes at that and Endre felt himself reproached. Why did he say that? This wasn't a pub, was it? Was flirting the only way he knew to talk to a pretty girl? She was a pretty girl, he observed.

"If I were you, I wouldn't be in such a hurry to become a prisoner-of-war," said Ilonka.

Those words did strike a note of fear in Endre's heart, but he said, "I'd be happy to be your prisoner."

Again, he felt chided by those serious brown eyes.

The excited chatter from the boys was drawing nearer. They were coming back to retrieve their fishing poles.

"I don't have time for you right now," said Ilonka hurriedly. "Stay here. And don't let anyone see you." She surprised herself by adding that warning. Why should she care if anyone saw him?

Endre ducked back into the bush. Ilonka walked towards the boys and called out to them that it was time to come home for dinner. They gathered their fishing gear and began to walk back with her. As they passed the bush, it took all of Ilonka's willpower to not look in Endre's direction.

The boys were talking about fishing now, determinedly avoiding the subject of the explosion. They knew Ilonka must have been near enough to hear the explosion. Surely, she wouldn't let that go. She had to raise the subject. They knew that she knew. Why wasn't she giving them the usual safety lecture? She wasn't saying anything at all. Were they in even bigger trouble than usual? But Ilonka's mind was elsewhere.

As she walked, her thoughts raced around the question of what she should do about this American pilot. What would happen to him if she reported him? What if she didn't report him? How long could he survive and stay hidden? What if they found him and took him captive? Or didn't bother to take him captive, just killed him?

There was a lot of talk on the radio lately about an international treaty, the Geneva Convention, that was supposed to ensure that prisoners of war were treated humanely, but she had her doubts about that. No, she concluded, there was probably nothing very humane about being a prisoner in a time of war. The Germans would know he was an American pilot. Even here, in this remote corner of Hungary, it was well known that the USAAF was having great success against the German war machine. She deemed it at least possible that German guards might take out their anger on their prisoners, especially the American pilots who bombed their Nazi dreams.

Immersed in her dilemma, Ilonka wasn't watching where she was stepping. Her foot rolled on a stone and she stumbled.

"You alright?" asked her little brother.

"Yes. Yes, I'm fine," said Ilonka, flipping her hair behind her ears again, and bringing herself back to the dusty country lane leading into Markota. Her foot was fine. It hadn't rolled far enough to sprain, only far enough to interrupt her thoughts.

The boys, who had initially noticed that she was strangely quiet, had forgotten all about her and lost themselves in their talk about airplanes. In very serious tones, like only pre-adolescent males can muster, they were discussing the merits of the Russian MiGs versus the American Mustangs. Ilonka was fine, so they went back to their lively discussion.

Ilonka went back to her thoughts. First, he is an American. Second, the Americans are dropping bombs on Hungary. That makes him the enemy, doesn't it? But he speaks Hungarian, so what does that make him? What should be done about this handsome American pilot?

"Oh," she nearly stumbled again. This time the boys didn't notice. Well, he is handsome, she admitted. Just as quickly, she brushed that aside. I will report him, she decided. Really, he's nothing to me. Only yesterday he would have killed me and my family with one of his bombs, without even knowing we existed! These callous soldiers don't care one bit about killing people. Why should I care about him? They kill people without even seeing them... but I saw him. I stood face-to-face with him. I saw that he had a gun. He didn't harm me or the boys, although he could have. I won't report him, she decided, aware that she had flip-flopped her decision again.

Ilonka agonized and the boys debated until they were home. She helped her mother get supper on the table, ate in silence, then started on the clean-up while her father went out to do the evening chores and tend to the animals. In contrast to last night's bombing, this evening was quiet and peaceful, like country evenings always were before the war.

Erzsi noticed her daughter's contemplative mood. "You seem to have something on your mind tonight," she said gently.

"*Igen, Anyu.* Yes, Mama," acknowledged Ilonka. "Something happened today that I want to talk with you and *Apu* about."

"Okay then, let's wait till he comes back in," said Erzsi as she hung the dish towel on the kitchen rack.

Ilonka didn't want to raise this subject in front of her little brother. Sanyi was within earshot, in the living room doing his school assignment.

"How's your homework?" she asked.

"All finished." He was just closing his notebook and announcing that he was going out to find Lajos. Ilonka sighed with relief at that bit of good timing. Tonight there were no planes thundering across the countryside, so no one raised any objection to him going out.

When Erzsi heard Janos open the yard door, she put the tea on. While it was steeping, she set out the cups and gave the table one more wipe.

"Janos, come and sit with us."

"One minute," he replied, stopping first in the bathroom to wash the barn smell off his hands before joining the women in the kitchen.

"It's nice and quiet out there tonight," said Janos taking a seat.

"Maybe the war is over," replied his wife cheerfully, as she poured the tea.

"We can hope," said Janos.

They knew it wasn't true, but there was no harm in hoping.

"Speaking of the war," began Ilonka. "Something happened this afternoon that I want to tell you about."

Her father set down his cup and looked at Ilonka with concern.

"I was down at the Keszegér today and I came across an American pilot."

"The boys," began her mother, "they were down at the river today too."

"I know," said Ilonka, "but they didn't see him."

"Oh, dear God!" continued Mom. "They shouldn't go wandering around alone anymore, not until this war is over. Who knows what kind of dangerous people are out there!"

"Erzsi," said Janos, placing his hand reassuringly over his wife's. "This war might not end for a long time. You know we can't really keep them locked up."

"I don't think this American is dangerous," said Ilonka.

That brought looks from both of her parents. "Obviously there's more to this. Why don't you just tell us what happened," said her father.

Ilonka went back to the beginning. "I was going down to call the boys for supper when I came across him." She didn't bother mentioning the explosion incident. The boys would get away with it this time. "He was hiding in the bush right beside the spot where Sanyi and Lajos like to fish."

Erzsi twirled the edge of the tablecloth nervously in her fingers.

"Well, you can imagine my surprise," she said, "when he spoke to me in Hungarian!"

"An American pilot who speaks Hungarian?" echoed her father.

"Yes," said Ilonka. "His parents moved to America. They spoke Hungarian at home and his Hungarian is very good."

Her parents nodded silently.

She continued, "He was shot down last night and he's hiding by the river."

"The Germans have been rounding up downed pilots all day," said her father.

"I know," acknowledged Ilonka. "The boys said they saw some Americans being marched at gun point, but so far they haven't found Endre."

"Endre," noted her father. "You're on a first name basis with him?"

"We talked a little," said Ilonka. "I've been trying to figure out what to do ever since. Should we report him?"

"I don't think so," said Janos. "Nobody should be turned over to those murderous Nazis."

"But the Geneva Convention...," began Ilonka.

"Forget that," interrupted Janos. "That's for civilized people. The Nazis are barbarians!"

"So, what will we do with him?" asked Ilonka.

"I don't know yet," said Janos, thinking it over.

What could they do? He wondered. What should they do? Why should they do anything at all? What concern of theirs was an American pilot? It was too dangerous to even think about. The Germans would kill them – others had been shot without hesitation – for trying to protect American pilots.

"Maybe we should just forget you saw him," suggested Janos.

"You said the boys didn't see him, right?" asked Erzsi.

"No, the boys didn't see him," confirmed Ilonka.

"Then maybe that's the safest…" Erzsi said, even though a small curiosity was beginning to rise in her about the Hungarian boy hiding in the bushes.

"No one – other than the three of us – knows about him?" asked Janos.

"As far as I know," confirmed Ilonka.

"Then we can just forget you saw him," said Janos.

Ilonka lowered her eyes to the embroidered tablecloth. Her thoughts were revving up again. Dangerous thoughts.

All three sat in silence. The conflicted feelings that churned inside them electrified the room.

Janos asked again, "An American pilot who speaks Hungarian?"

"Yes," said Ilonka, feeling a surge of hope.

"Tell me exactly where he is and I'll go have a talk with him."

"In the big bush, right in front of the spot where Sanyi and Lajos like to fish," she repeated.

Janos rose from the table and gathered a few things together on his way to the door, "His name is Endre, you said?"

"That's right."

"Please be careful, Janos," said Erzsi.

Ilonka followed him out into the yard. "There is one more thing *Apu*," she said. "I didn't want to worry *Anyu*, but I think you should know he has a gun."

"How do you know that?" asked her father with a look of alarm.

"I saw it."

"Did he threaten you?" he asked

"No. Definitely not. And the boys were playing right there and he didn't try to harm them either. I just wanted you to know."

"Alright," said Janos, "I wasn't planning to go without my gun anyway." He opened his jacket just enough to show her that he already had it with him.

Ilonka nodded and went back inside.

Quietly, Janos closed the yard gate. Discreetly scanning the windows of the neighbor's houses for any prying eyes, he reminded himself that these days a man has to be careful just leaving his house. Everybody watches. Everybody listens. It's hard to know who can be trusted.

Crossing *Fő utca*, Main St., he heard a horse whinny. He saw that the produce in the buggy was a delivery for the general store. Two bicyclists rode past, but they were engaged in their conversation and didn't pay any attention to him. Strands of gypsy music from the inn were carried on the wind. The baker pulled down his shades and closed up shop for the day.

Leaving the town behind him, Janos picked his route cautiously. He didn't dare walk directly to Endre's location, choosing instead to meet the river at a point farther upstream. All the while, his eyes scanned the countryside, checking again and again to make sure that he was alone. Maybe I shouldn't get involved in this, he told himself. I should go back home, but he went on. He walked down the shallow bank to continue his journey by the shoreline.

Along the river the frogs were singing their evening song. The sunset was vibrant. It was great weather for flying but there were no planes in the sky tonight. Thank God for that. Janos wondered how much longer this war would go on.

Coming up to the place Ilonka had described, he easily surmised which bush the pilot must be in. It was amply large enough to hide a man. Janos paused short of the spot, ostensibly to tie his shoe. While doing so, he took another thorough look around in all directions. He saw no one. He continued to follow the shoreline until he was directly in front of the bush.

Endre saw him coming from a long way off. He knew he was well concealed in the dense bush. He can't see me. He'll walk right past, he told himself.

But the man stopped.

Endre could feel his heart pounding sharply under his flight suit. Why is he stopping right here?

Janos looked up and down the river once more. A turtle snapped at swimming insects and shattered the calm surface of the water in the eddy on the river's edge.

Endre commanded himself to stay perfectly still. Even a small movement would be noticed from this close range.

"Endre," Janos spoke to the bush.

Endre tried to will his hammering pulse to slow.

"I know you're in there." Unsure of what to say next, Janos added, "I'm Ilonka's father."

Ilonka. She didn't send the police. She sent her father.

Janos saw the leaves move.

Instinctively Endre touched his pistol before stepping out from his cover.

Janos had not made up his mind. He had only committed himself to coming out to investigate. When Endre crawled out of the bush, Janos was still unsure. He waited as Endre quickly brushed himself off. His first impression was neutral, a young man in an American uniform.

"*Jó estét kivánok.* Good evening," began Janos.

"Good evening to you, too," replied Endre in Hungarian.

Immediately Janos noted that Ilonka was right about his native-sounding speech. That was good. At least they would be able to talk to each other. Walking over to the driftwood, from which the boys had fished earlier, Janos sat down and invited Endre to join him.

"You must be hungry by now." Without waiting for a response, he opened the package he had brought with him. "It's *szalona*. Do you have Hungarian *szalona* in America?" he asked as he opened his pocket-knife, cut a piece of the fatty pork-bacon chunk, placed it on a slice of bread, and offered it to Endre."

Endre accepted the bread and pork. "Yes, we used to make a fire and cook the *szalona* on it, draining the pork-fat onto the bread. It was good," said Endre, remembering the deliciously greasy smell of large bacon chunks cooking.

"I used to like it that way too," said Janos, "but we rarely build fires now because the smoke is visible for miles."

While Janos watched the young man eat, he still had reservations. He listened critically while Endre answered every question he could think to ask: the obvious ones like, how did you get here? And the difficult ones like, why is a Hungarian boy dropping bombs on Hungary?

Clouds Over Markota 52

Endre explained about Pearl Harbour, the devastating attack on an American naval base that motivated his generation to join the war effort. "When I signed up, I thought I was going to be fighting the Japanese. I didn't even think I was going to Europe, much less Hungary. Now, of course, the emphasis is on the Nazis – "

Endre stopped. He had no idea where Janos stood on this point. Hungary and Germany were allies not long ago. What did Hungarians think of the Germans now?

Janos didn't comment on the Nazis. Instead, he asked, "Where is your family from?"

"Arad" replied Endre.

"Arad! My sister married a man from Arad. They moved there after the wedding to be near his family. You know it's part of Romania now, don't you?"

"Yes," said Endre. "That's why my father left.

"Really?" asked Janos, much intrigued.

"My father is still angry about Trianon. He thought it would be better to go to the USA than to be a Hungarian living in Romania."

"And are things better in the USA?"

"I suppose they are, in some ways," said Endre.

"Are the Hungarians there ... still Hungarian?" asked Janos.

That was something Endre had never considered before. He had always thought of himself as an American. Yet here he was, a second generation immigrant, able to speak the language of a far-away land in which he'd never set foot until now.

Janos elaborated on his question, "I've always wondered about those who left. Did they forget all about their homeland? Do their children know anything about their heritage?"

"We always spoke Hungarian at home. We went to a Hungarian church where the service was said in Hungarian, and they had a program for us kids on Saturday mornings where we learned about Hungarian history." Endre didn't mention that he hated going there because none of his friends had to go to school on Saturdays.

A Hungarian washed here by the currents of war, thought Janos. *But, does that make him my responsibility?*

Looking at the young man in uniform, Janos remembered what it was like to be a soldier; he had served in the Great War. He was also the father of a soldier. His first-born son, three years older than Ilonka, was killed in action in the first year of this war. Janos hoped desperately that there would be peace before Sanyi was old enough to be drafted.

Sanyi, Ilonka, Erzsi... his children, his wife, his family; they were the reasons he should walk away.

Endre silently broke off another piece of bread.

At least I knew where my son was, Janos remembered. It nearly killed Erzsi – and me too, he admitted – to hear the horrible news of Jozsi's death, but there is one fate worse for a parent than knowing your child is dead: not knowing where your child is, not knowing whether he is dead or alive, wondering if he has been captured, fearing that he may be tortured. That is even worse than knowing your child is dead.

Janos' thoughts moved to imagining that Endre's parents would soon receive the news that their son was missing in action. They would hear that his plane went down but they would not know that small measure of peace that comes with the finality of death. Time could not even begin its slow work of healing the grief because they still had hope – the worst kind of hope – the kind that drives a parent insane, because mixed with the hope that he may be alive is sheer terror at the thought that he may be a prisoner. And a parent's imagination is relentless because thoughts of his beloved child never leave his mind.

In the silence, Endre had been wondering if Janos would help him. He's been very kind, brought me food, asked a lot of questions about my family, but the obvious question of what is to become of me hasn't been raised. I don't think he's planning to turn me in to the authorities or he wouldn't have come down here alone. Am I to go on living in this bush? How long can I keep doing this? If he decides not to help me, how am I going to get out of here?

Endre finished the last of the bread and pork. "*Köszönöm.* Thank you," he said simply.

Janos made his decision. He stood up. "This path," he pointed, "leads into town."

"Markota-Bödöge?" asked Endre, wanting to confirm his location.

Janos was surprised. He hadn't heard that name in a long time. "How did you know that?"

"It's on my chart," answered Endre simply.

"Oh," said Janos. That made sense. That's what it would be called on something official like a chart. "Yes, Markota-Bödöge, but nobody calls it that. It's too much of a mouthful. Just Markota."

Endre nodded.

Janos pointed down the path again and gave Endre explicit directions to his barn.

Endre reached for his pistol. There was nothing threatening in his movement. Butt-end first, he handed it to Janos, "Take this. I don't want to use this in Hungary."

Janos accepted the weapon and added a final warning, "but wait until long past dark and be very sure that no one sees you."

CHAPTER FOUR

Janos woke early from his restless sleep. Had Endre made it to the barn? Did anyone see him come here? Wearing an American pilot's uniform! Fear gripped him. Not for the last time, he wondered if he was doing the right thing. He needed to get to the barn before Sanyi went out to do his chores and perhaps discovered Endre.

Janos moved slowly, trying to bounce the mattress as little as possible. In the dark, his hands found the clothes he had left on the chair beside the bed.

Erzsi stirred. "Is he here?"

Janos sat back down on the bed beside his wife, "Sorry I woke you."

"I wasn't really sleeping." She asked again, "is he here?"

"I assume so. I was just going out to check." Leaning over his wife, he kissed her on the forehead and added, "don't worry."

Janos pulled the bedroom door closed behind him and crept out of the house. Cautiously, he climbed the ladder leading to the hayloft above the horse stalls. When he reached the top, he placed his lantern on the floor above him. Even with the light, he could see nothing but hay up here. "Endre," he whispered.

Nothing.

"Endre, it's me, Janos," he whispered again, a little louder.

This time the hay rustled. From behind a steep pile in the far corner Endre heard Janos' voice and lifted his head.

"Did you see anyone on the road last night?" greeted Janos.

"No one."

Janos allowed himself a deep sigh, before asking, "Did you sleep well?"

"A little," said Endre.

"Did you find the pillow and blanket alright?" asked Janos.

"I did, thank you."

Seeing that Endre had dug himself a hole in the hay, Janos said, "That was a good idea. We just harvested so there's lots up here right now," but Janos' mind had already slipped into problem solving mode. He was thinking that he'd have to try to get some more bales over the next few weeks so there would be enough to feed the horses and keep this loft full all winter. Extra hay wasn't easy to come by, especially without money. Sometimes Janos did mechanical work for other farmers and, since they didn't have much money either, maybe someone would be willing to pay him in hay bales.

"My son, Sanyi, will be out in the yard soon to feed the animals. Make sure he doesn't see you. I'll come back after he leaves for school." Hearing the rooster crow, Janos added, "I'm going to start my chores now."

Endre felt restless and useless. He would have welcomed the chance to do some chores, but that was obviously not a good idea. Instead, he sank back into his shelter. Last night, coming here seemed like the right thing to do. What choice did he really have? Today he had some doubts. How long can I live in a hay pile? How much danger am I putting this family in?

When Janos climbed back down the ladder, he saw Erzsi, still in her full-length cotton nightdress, standing in the open doorway of the house. "*Igen.* Yes," he mouthed silently to her. Quietly, she closed the door and went back into the house to begin preparing breakfast for her family – plus one. Janos stayed in the yard and set about his farm work. He knew Sanyi would feed the livestock, so he turned his attention to the plow repair he had been working on for the past few days.

As the sun came up, the little town of Markota came to life. Erzsi called out that breakfast was ready. Janos joined his family at the kitchen table. It had always been their custom to give thanks before a meal, and these days a simple meal was a lot to be thankful for. With so much tragedy unfolding all around them, nothing was taken for granted. Janos concluded with "Amen," and silently added a blessing for Endre.

Over breakfast, Janos gave an affirmative nod to Ilonka's questioning eyes.

Sanyi gulped down his breakfast and headed off to tend to the animals. Janos followed him out to the yard to resume work on the plow – and to make sure his son didn't go up to the hay loft for any reason.

"Where's Lajos?" asked Janos.

"I don't know. He's usually here by now."

"Uncle Vince must have him on a short leash this morning."

With his chores done, Sanyi picked up his books. "I'll go find him."

Sure enough, Lajos was in his yard, feeding the pigs under the watchful eye of Uncle Vince. Sanyi helped him finish up and the two boys set off for school.

Janos waited until he was sure the boys were gone before he called Endre to come down for breakfast. As Endre climbed down the ladder, he got his first look at the place by daylight. He noticed that it was much smaller than an American farm. For one thing, the barn was actually attached – just like an extension – to the back of the house. On farms back home, animals were housed in a separate building. Here, the house and barn were joined by a shared wall, although there was no connecting doorway between them. You still had to exit the house to get to the animals. Behind the house and barn, the yard opened to crop fields, cut down now that the hay had been harvested. Towards the street there was a ten-foot high solid fence with a locked gate.

He followed Janos into the house. The yard door led directly into the kitchen, where he was greeted by the smell of vinegar and spices, a familiar smell. At home, his mother was probably also doing her autumn vegetable pickling. To the right of the kitchen, he could see the living room and the front door leading to the street. To his left was the washroom. Through the washroom, and to the right, was a short hallway that led to the bedrooms. The house was small but efficient. The smell of fried eggs rose over the pickling tang to welcome him, and he thought he was in heaven when the aroma of brewing coffee reached his nose. That's exactly what he had been craving ever since he landed.

Janos introduced him to Erzsi and, of course, he'd already met Ilonka. She returned his greeting with a small smile. Erzsi was nervous, protective of her family, but her curiosity won out. Ilonka and Janos had talked with him already. It was her turn now. She began asking questions.

Meanwhile, Ilonka poured a cup of the coveted coffee and offered cream, saying, "I'm sorry there's no sugar right now. We used the last of it in the baking yesterday. It's a little hard to come by these days." As she set the cup down in front of him, she knew her hand was shaking but she hoped he wouldn't notice.

"That's okay," said Endre, accepting the coffee gratefully and answering Erzsi's questions the best he could, although she was asking the next one before he was finished answering the previous one. Where are your parents from? When did they leave? Why did they leave?"

Endre had plenty of questions of his own: Were there Germans in the area? Was there any way out of here? But his questions would have to wait.

Erzsi's questions continued, "Do your parents like it in America? Do all the Hungarians in America teach their children to speak Hungarian? What do you think of Hungary? How long have you been a pilot? Do you like to fly? Do you think the war will be over soon?

Ilonka and Janos felt a little sympathy for Endre in the hot seat but they didn't try to rescue him because they were also interested in his answers, even though they had heard some of them before. Besides, he didn't seem at all bothered by the questions. His answers were direct and polite. Like a well brought up young man, Janos thought.

Endre was still wearing his flight suit. If anyone happened to see him, even from afar, his identity would be known immediately. After breakfast, Janos offered him a change of clothes from his own closet but the fit was too large.

He's about Jozsi's size, thought Ilonka. Remembering the tucked-away box of her brother's things, she took her mother aside to ask if it would be alright to let Endre wear something from there. Erzsi's hand went instinctively to her heart in a moment of pain at remembering the son she lost to this war, but she nodded her silent consent.

Choosing a pair of pants and a shirt, Ilonka gave them each a few sharp shakes to try to remove at least some of the wrinkles.

Endre stepped out of the washroom wearing Jozsi's clothes. They fit. At the sight of him, Erzsi set aside her pain and said, "You look... Hungarian!"

"Of course he does," said Janos.

Ilonka and Endre shared an awkward laugh, and they all agreed that Endre was a true Hungarian boy.

The laughter stopped abruptly with the knock on the front door. Erzsi, who had sat back down to finish her coffee, was instantly on her feet again and taking charge. "I'll answer the door. Ilonka, wash and put away these dishes." She pointed to the table. "Start with Endre's." Turning to Janos, "Go! ... work in the yard and get him..." The men were already on their way out the back door.

Erzsi walked, with deliberately slow steps, through the living room towards the front door calling out, "I'm coming," to buy extra time.

Unhurriedly, she placed her hand on the doorknob and turned it.

Gombos started sweet-talking even before the door was fully opened. "*Jó reggelt, Farkas-né,* Good morning, Mrs. Farkas."

"Good morning, Gombos," she returned the greeting.

"How are you and your lovely family this morning?"

For one brief moment Erzsi contemplated not letting him in. Maybe she could make something up. No, she decided, it was better to behave as naturally as possible. She opened the door the rest of the way and stepped aside so the large man with slicked back hair could walk in with the packages in his arms.

She had a panicked second thought. She should give him some excuse, some reason why he could not stay, but nothing convincing came to mind.

Gombos walked straight through the living room all the way into the kitchen and set the two shopping bags on the table.

Erzsi relaxed again when she saw that Endre's plate and cup were already put away and Ilonka was at the sink washing the rest of the dishes.

"Am I too late for coffee this morning?" asked Gombos ruefully.

"We've already had coffee," said Ilonka.

"That's alright," said Erzsi. Knowing Gombos as she did, she realized that he wouldn't be leaving anytime soon even if there was no coffee. To get rid of him, she needed a good excuse, and she couldn't think of one, so she said, "We can make another pot."

"My darling Ilonka makes the best coffee in all of Markota," gushed Gombos.

Ilonka gave a thin smile and began preparing the morning's second pot of coffee.

Gombos was unpacking his delivery. "I've just received a shipment of sugar, and these textiles might be nice for making dresses. I wanted my best customers to have them first. You know how scarce things are these days," he said, blatantly seeking the approval of both mother and daughter.

"Yes, we know how skilled you are at finding things," replied the ever-practical Erzsi. It was not beneath her to compliment and ply the devil with coffee if it meant having access to the things her family needed, but her daughter was not for sale. It was no secret that the Farkas family got first dibs on all the new stock because Gombos had his eye on Ilonka. However, when he pressed too hard and made the young woman feel uncomfortable, Erzsi switched to full defense mode. Gombos had seen this. He preferred to keep the mother in an agreeable mood, so he went on in his sugary tone hoping to charm both women.

The harvest ball was coming up and Gombos had been saying for weeks how much he hoped Ilonka would go to the ball with him. Again, he started on this topic, sitting up straight and taking on the formal tone that he imagined made him sound very refined. "This year's harvest ball will be marvelous if I may have the honor of escorting you, my dear Ilonka."

Ilonka ignored the subject altogether.

Erzsi answered for her daughter, "Ilonka is too young to date."

At twenty this was sheer nonsense, but arguing with her wasn't going to be productive. He allowed himself to fantasize that the girl liked him; it was only the mother he needed to persuade.

Launching into his bragging monologue was Gombos' next tactic. Proudly, he reported last week's earnings and showed off his new watch. It was true that he did manage to earn more money than most of the people they knew, but Erzsi wondered how honestly those assets were accumulated. Not many people had a new watch these days, or all those extra pounds around their mid-section either.

Just as Gombos' monologue was coming to an end, Janos came in through the back door claiming he had been working in the yard and thought he'd heard someone arrive. He joined them for coffee, choosing to sit down on the chair directly between Gombos and his daughter.

Gombos continued to rave about Ilonka's delicious coffee, her beautiful hair, and her pretty little hands. Ilonka answered everything he directed to her with as few words as possible, careful to say absolutely nothing to encourage him.

Finally, the coffee pot was empty and Erzsi sought to settle the bill. Gombos usually tried to give her a discount but Erzsi always insisted on paying full price. She was happy enough to have access to these hard-to-find items but she was adamant about paying for them in full. At retail cost, she avoided feeling any sense of indebtedness.

Good-byes were finally said and the door was firmly closed behind Gombos. Janos, Erzsi, and Ilonka breathed a collective sigh of relief, to which Ilonka added a dramatic eye-roll.

"I know," said her mother sympathetically.

"That was a rather close call," said Janos.

"What will we do with him?" asked Erzsi, following her husband's lead back to the dilemma of the American pilot. "We can't keep him in the hayloft twenty-four hours a day, forever."

"I know," agreed Janos, "but for the moment it is the safest thing to do."

"What about Sanyi?" asked Ilonka. "Should we tell him?"

That question only led to more questions: Was he old enough to keep such a secret? Could he grasp the danger of this situation? On the other hand, what would happen if he stumbled across Endre by accident?

As they talked through the possibilities, it was decided that the more controlled option was preferable. The little boy, who had no real memory of peacetime and had already lost his older brother to war, probably could comprehend the seriousness of the situation. Yes, it was risky, but just having Endre here was already extremely risky.

When Sanyi came home from school, Lajos was with him. The boys made their noisy debut in the kitchen, where they found cookies again thanks to this morning's sugar delivery. They were eager to finish their chores quickly and head down to the river to do some fishing.

Ilonka and her mother exchanged a look that said, "what about Lajos?"

Janos was wondering the same thing. As he came in through the kitchen door, he caught the look between them. Silently, he mouthed, "It's okay." Expecting Sanyi to keep a secret was one thing; asking him to keep a secret from Lajos was quite another.

Placing one hand on each boy's shoulder, he said, "Don't rush off. I need to talk to you about something important."

Such a serious tone in Sanyi's father's voice usually preceded something to do with the war, maybe a lecture about not playing with explosives. Whatever it was, the boys dutifully sat back down to listen.

Janos chose the long way around in getting to his point, "Do you remember the bombing two nights ago?"

The boys nodded.

"A lot of airplanes were shot down," continued Janos.

"I know! I saw!" exclaimed Lajos.

"And a lot of pilots parachuted out," added Janos.

The boys nodded. It wasn't the first time they had seen parachutes in the skies above them.

"What did you think when you saw the planes?" asked Janos, probing.

"I want to fly one!" answered Lajos quickly.

"Me too," said Sanyi, earnestly but with less enthusiasm. He also felt something else. He didn't want to say he was afraid. Instead he said, "They'd better not drop their bombs on my house!"

"Do you think they want to bomb our house?" asked Janos.

"No," said Sanyi thoughtfully. "I don't think they want to bomb our house, but a pilot can't control where his burning plane will fall, can he?"

"No," agreed Janos, "he can't."

"The American planes are the fastest and the best," said Lajos with conviction. "The

Americans are going to shoot down all the Germans and the Russians and then they'll all go home."

"That would be nice," agreed Janos.

"Why do we need the Germans here?" asked Sanyi.

Janos had explained this before but, patiently, he repeated himself as many times as the boys asked the question. "Years ago, when the war first started, we thought they would help us get our Trianon lands back."

"But if Germany and Russia both want to take over and rule all of Europe, how will we get any land back? I think we'll just lose more of Hungary no matter which one wins," stated Sanyi sadly.

"Except the Americans," interjected Lajos. "They don't want to rule Europe, do they?" he asked.

"I don't think so," answered Janos.

Janos hesitated. The Nazi youth movement was gaining momentum and strong pro-Nazi feelings had led some of his neighbors to turn parachutists over to the Germans. Had the boys picked up these attitudes? No, he heard no hint of Nazi sympathy in what the boys said. He decided to trust them.

"Did you know that some Hungarians live in America?" began Janos.

The boys had never considered that before. Everyone they knew lived in Markota.

"I met someone yesterday who is a Hungarian-American," stated Janos.

"Really?" asked the boys, wide-eyed.

"Yes," Janos proceeded slowly. "I will tell you more about him, but first I need you to promise me that you will keep this top secret."

"Promise," they both said, hungry for the secret and already sensing the gravity of it.

"I will tell you first how important it is that you keep this secret and I will tell you straight, man-to-man, because this is very grown-up stuff." Without diluting the horror one bit, Janos reminded the boys of stories they had already heard about entire families being killed for harboring pilots. Even children were not spared. Just last month a young girl, Zsuzsi, a classmate of theirs, and her mother were killed when the Germans came to the house and found the pilot they were sheltering.

The boys nodded.

"So, you do understand why it is very important to keep this secret?"

Both boys had some fear in their eyes and Janos took that as a good sign.

"He's an American pilot."

Sanyi's eyes widened and Lajos' mouth dropped open, "a parachutist!"

"That's right," confirmed Janos. "He speaks Hungarian, so you can talk with him.

But – I can't emphasize this enough – you cannot tell anyone about him. There are people here, even here in Markota, who would turn him in – turn us in. They will do it because they're frightened, or for a reward, or even because they think it's the right thing to do."

Sanyi and Lajos knew that was true. They remembered Zsuzsi, how shocked and sad they felt when they heard what happened to her and her mother. How could someone from Markota have turned them in?

"Lajos!" came the booming voice of Uncle Vince from the next yard. The pigs were supposed to be fed by now. Not finding Lajos at home, Vince knew the next place to look was at Sanyi's house.

Lajos jumped to his feet. "Not a word, sir," he said quickly to Janos, then sprinted out the front door and around the other side of the house to avoid the wallop.

"Alright, now you go and do your chores too." Janos said to Sanyi.

Sanyi ran to catch up with Lajos. They hurried through the chores in his yard first then rushed back to Sanyi's to do the chores that awaited them there. Fishing was forgotten. Their thoughts were full of airplanes and American pilots now, but they were careful not to talk about any of that while they were outside, not even in their own yards. Carefully, proudly, they guarded the secret.

Janos called them into the house when the chores were finished. "Wait here," he said. Then he went back out to the yard, climbed the loft-ladder, and invited Endre to come in and meet the boys.

When Endre walked through the kitchen door, the boys were star-stuck. Even Lajos was tongue-tied. Although he was dressed like a regular Hungarian now, they knew he was an American pilot. A pilot. A real pilot. Right here in Markota. Right here in their house!

"Pleased to meet you," they gasped.

But Endre quickly put them at ease. When he spoke to them in Hungarian, he immediately felt less like a stranger, and a little less god-like.

After the introductions, Janos, Erzsi, and Ilonka stood back and watched. It was Sanyi and Lajos' turn to ask all the questions. Once again, Endre gave simple, straightforward answers. Endre also asked the boys about the things they liked to do and he told them that he enjoyed fishing too.

"I'm hungry," said Janos suddenly.

In all the excitement, they'd forgotten to eat supper.

"It's ready," laughed Erzsi, "but I didn't want to interrupt."

While Ilonka set the table and filled the water glasses, Erzsi took the *töltöt káposzta*, stuffed cabbage, out of the oven, placed it on the table, and sliced the bread. Janos folded his hands, waited for the chatter to stop, and said grace.

Over dinner, Endre asked about their lives. What was it like for them here in Markota? Had they always lived here? What kinds of animals did they have and what kinds of crops did they raise? He told them about his family's farm in New York, and the rest of the evening was spent in wide-eyed wonder as Endre regaled them all, in perfect Hungarian, with tales of America and flying machines.

The next few weeks brought a lot of bombing nearby, keeping the boys close to home in the evenings. Even Lajos could find contentment without needing to go out and chase the planes because he had his very own secret pilot right here at Sanyi's house.

Endre liked the company of the boys and he liked being useful, so he was glad for the occupation of helping them with their school assignments. He noticed Lajos chewing on his pencil. "What's the problem?"

"I don't know how to do this," answered Lajos, pointing to the math question.

"Let me see it," offered Endre.

Lajos handed him his exercise book.

Endre worked out the question, step-by-step, and showed Lajos how he arrived at the answer. "Now, you try one."

Diligently, Lajos followed Endre's steps to solve the next one.

"Did it work?"

Clouds Over Markota 74

"I got 75; is that right?"

Endre checked the math, "that's right."

Lajos had three questions left. When he finished the last one, he started to close his book.

"Wait," said Endre. "Tell me about those drawings."

Reopening his book, Lajos showed Endre the pictures in his notebook, pictures of parachutists filling the sky. "That was you," said Lajos. "You were one of them. These are American planes." Lajos turned the pages with growing eagerness to show Endre all of his drawings.

"What's this?" asked Endre, spotting a table of information that didn't look like schoolwork.

"This," said Lajos proudly, "is a list of Allied aircraft types – Hurricane, Spitfire, Kittyhawk, Lightning, Thunderbolt, Mustang – that was yours! The P-51 Mustang."

"That's right," Endre smiled.

"Mosquito, Baltimore, Mitchell, Halifax, Stirling, Fortress, Liberator," continued Lajos.

"The Fortress," interrupted Endre, "is the plane I used to fly before the Mustang."

"Oh yeah!" Lajos exclaimed, remembering that Endre had told him that. "What did you like better, the fighters or the bombers?"

"Fighters, without a doubt," replied Endre. "I was disappointed when I was first assigned to the bombers. Driving the heavy Flying Fortress is nothing like sailing the P-51 Mustang!"

"What's the difference?" asked Sanyi, who had just closed his notebook, "besides size, of course."

"The ability to defend yourself," answered Endre. "The Fortress has impressive defense capabilities – for a bomber: gunners in the top turret, ball turret, the tail, and two at mid-ship. Still, against the German airpower, they need the protection of their fighter escorts. I didn't like feeling vulnerable."

"Who would!" exclaimed Lajos.

"Actually, it's even more than that." Endre had come to believe it was a fundamental difference of temperaments.

The boys listened.

"The bomber pilot must be steadfast and patient. The outcome of the entire mission depends on his ability to remain focused. When he approaches his target, he needs to fly in unwavering obedience to his mission orders, regardless of what is happening around him. If he misses his opportunity, there's not much chance of turning around and approaching the target again. Plus," Endre added, "he's responsible for the lives of ten crew members."

The boys nodded.

"The fighter pilot, on the other hand, must be quick and aggressive. His role is to protect the bombers. He needs to find Jerry – I mean the Germans, we called them Jerry – he needs to find Jerry before Jerry finds him. Unlike the bomber pilot, who must focus on one target, the fighter pilot has to keep track of multiple, fast-moving targets – that are firing back!"

"So fighters are more fun?" asked Lajos.

"Well, at the end of all the posturing between the fighter jocks and the bomber drivers, we always knew we needed each other. We bantered with each other in the pub, but in the air we were all on the same mission. And yes," Endre added with a wink, "fighters are more fun."

"I think I'd rather be a fighter pilot," said Lajos.

"I think you would too," agreed Endre.

He told the boys the story of his first sortie in a fighter cockpit. "We met up with our bombers over the North Sea, at about twenty-one thousand feet – freezing cold and I was having some trouble with my oxygen mask – but when we flew over the B-17s, I felt like a fierce mama bear protecting her cubs." Endre bared his teeth for effect.

The boys laughed and growled back.

"We went on ahead of the Fortresses looking for the Germans, but we couldn't find any. We bombed a ball-bearing factory that day. Completely demolished it," remembered Endre with satisfaction. "The Germans did finally show up, but by then it was much too late. The bombers were already on their way home."

"The next night," Endre added more sombrely, "was a completely different story. I lost one of my best buddies that day... We were after the ball-bearing factory near Schweinfurt. We had 382 bombers on that mission, and seventy-seven of them went down."

The boys were quiet now.

Returning to the notebook, Endre asked, "What other planes have you got there?"

Lajos finished reading the list, "Mariner, Beufort, Corsair."

"That's very good," said Endre.

"But that's not all I know," said Lajos proudly. He read Endre the next two column headings: crew members and engines. For each aircraft type, Lajos had listed how many crew it carried and how many engines it had.

Endre was impressed. "How do you know all this?"

"I ask everyone," answered Lajos, innocently.

"Who's everyone," asked Endre, trying to imagine who would have this kind of aviation knowledge in Markota.

"The Germans, the Russians, everyone I see."

"What Germans and Russians?"

"Any that come through here," said Lajos.

Endre had noticed that everyone in the family, even the boys, seemed able to speak at least a little of both Russian and German.

"These days it's mostly Germans," added Sanyi.

A fearful thought gripped Endre's mind, "You must never talk to them about me!"

"Do you think I'm stupid?"

"No," Endre shook his head. This kid was definitely not stupid. "Not at all," slowing his words to sound calmer than he felt. "I just wanted to remind you of how dangerous that would be, not only for me but also for you and for Sanyi's whole family."

"I know," said Lajos, grieved that Endre could even think such a thing.

"I'm sorry Lajos. I know that you would never do that."

"That's okay," said Lajos, quickly forgiving.

Endre had liked Lajos right from the start. Now he was even more impressed with the little boy who interviewed everyone, even foreign soldiers, on his quest for information to feed his passion for flying. This kid was bright and fearless. He would make a good fighter pilot, thought Endre.

"How fast could your plane go?" asked Sanyi.

"Four hundred miles per hour. Actually, a little more."

"How fast is that?" asked Lajos, unfamiliar with miles.

"About seven hundred kilometres per hour," clarified Endre.

"Did you ever go that fast?" asked Lajos.

"Fighter pilots are speed junkies," Endre admitted.

"Will you take me flying in your plane one day?" Lajos asked.

"Of course!" said Endre.

In the weeks to come, there were many more talks about airplanes. Endre helped them with their homework and began to teach them to speak English. Janos, Erzsi, and Ilonka were also interested in the language lessons. They asked him, "how do you say…" He would tell them and they would try to remember. "How do you say house? How do you say father? How do you say mother?"

"How do you say boy?" asked Sanyi.

"How do you say girl?" asked Ilonka.

"How do you say kiss?" asked Lajos mischievously.

They all laughed and Ilonka blushed. Endre answered, while trying very hard not to look in Ilonka's direction. Janos and the boys were oblivious but Erzsi's quiet smile revealed that what transpired had not escaped her notice.

The weeks went by and the war trudged on. Endre continued to feel the burden of the danger his presence posed, but where else could he go?

Janos was also preoccupied with this question. Every day he ran through mental scenarios of how to move Endre to some other safe location. Where? Where would the Germans not look? Where could they still bring food to him without being noticed? Was there someone who might be able to help? Could he even risk asking anyone?

The family went about their lives as normally as possible, and Endre spent his days devising English games he could play with them in the evenings to make his tutoring more entertaining. The boys were especially enthusiastic. For every object in the house and the yard, they wanted to know the English word. They were like sponges, remembering everything Endre told them.

After weeks of housebound evenings, the boys were itching to go fishing. For the first time in many days, the sky was clear of airplanes.

"I wish you could come," said Lajos to Endre.

"I wish, too," replied Endre, but since the idea wasn't up for serious consideration, he said, "make sure you bring home some fish for supper. My mother had a nice paprika fish-stew recipe. If you bring home a fish, I'll ask Erzsi if she'll let me in her kitchen to give it a try."

"Sounds good!"

Under the quiet blue sky, in the crisp autumn Saturday afternoon, the boys walked through the town and followed the dusty path towards the Keszegér with poles and tackle boxes in hand.

Meanwhile, Janos and Erzsi had walked two streets over to Mariska's house. With Endre hiding in the loft, they were reluctant to leave home, but safety lay in acting naturally and going about business as usual.

"Is my nephew behaving himself?" asked Mariska.

"Oh sure," said Erzsi.

"What! Not into any trouble? I don't believe that."

Sanyi and Lajos weren't affectionately known as the Bad Boys of Markota for nothing.

"Well – not any more trouble than usual," corrected Erzsi with a smile.

All three of them laughed at that. The waif-like little boy, with dirty-blonde hair and intelligent blue eyes, had charmed them all so thoroughly that it never seemed to matter what kind of trouble he got into; they couldn't help but love him.

"He's all we have left of Katalin," said Mariska, remembering her sister. "Crazy Katalin. What could she possibly have been thinking?"

"It was 1932" said Erzsi, "and those years between the two wars were very strange."

"I know," said Mariska. "After the war, everybody seemed a little crazy, running around like they couldn't believe they were still alive. Either that, or they were so shell-shocked they might as well be dead. But Katalin was with the eat-drink-and-be-merry-for-tomorrow-we-die crowd."

"Exactly," agreed Erzsi. "She wasn't a bad girl; it was just that the war's effect on her, like on many others, was to underscore the point that life is short."

"She was the talk of the town when she became pregnant," remembered Mariska.

"It would have been alright if Jancsi had married her. We all thought they'd be married before Lajos' christening," said Erzsi.

"She really loved him," said Mariska. "It broke her heart to see him ignore his son like that."

"And then there was the cancer," said Janos, bringing back memories of how the tumor on the side of her nose ravaged and disfigured her once-pretty face. "Turned out she was right in thinking that life would be short."

"I'm amazed at how sharp Lajos' memory of her still is," said Erzsi.

"He's certainly inherited her zeal for living life dangerously," smiled Janos.

As a single woman with a child, Katalin had lived with her brother, Vince. Upon her death, Lajos was left in his custody because Katalin believed strongly that he needed a male figure in his life. By the time he came into the role of custodial uncle, Vince was a seasoned war veteran. He knew a lot about discipline but not too much about children.

"My brother does his best," said Mariska.

"And Lajos is not an easy child," Erzsi added.

Mariska set the pot of *paprikás csirke* on the floral hot-plate in the center of the table and ladled out three servings.

After lunch, Janos would fix some things around the house and the yard. There was always a job list waiting for him at Mariska's house, but he didn't mind. He believed that's what neighbors were for. Mariska and László were newlyweds when this war started, and László had been away fighting on the Russian front for most of their married life. That left Mariska home alone to look after everything by herself. These were tough times in Markota. Folks needed each other.

Erzsi noticed that Mariska was looking very tired these days, but she didn't comment on that. Instead she said, "Your hair looks really nice."

Erzsi understood the fatigue. She recognized the exhaustion that comes from carrying the weight of worry when someone you love is in harm's way, and there's not a single thing you can do to protect him. Erzsi remembered how she had worried about her son. She worried right up until the day the horrible news arrived. Her weight of worry was finally lifted, only to be replaced by the crushing loss that the intervening years had softened into a lasting sorrow.

Coincidently, over in the Farkas family yard, Endre and Ilonka's talk was also of Jozsi. Sitting at the foot of the hay-loft ladder, Endre asked about the young man whose clothes he wore.

"It's strange," she told him. "In a way, I don't really believe my brother's gone. I think it's because he died so far from home." She struggled to put words to her feelings. "I mean, when he left home I got used to him not being here, only knowing him through my memory, but always believing that he would be home someday. Well, nothing's changed. He's still not here. I still only know him through my memory, so it still feels like he will be back someday. Does that make sense?"

Endre nodded.

After another contemplative silence, she said slowly, "but I know he won't really, ever come home again."

"I'm sorry," offered Endre. "Were you and Jozsi very close?"

"Not until he discovered my talent for football," smiled Ilonka.

"Football?" asked Endre, as he did the mental translation: in Europe, football is the sport known as soccer in America. This was one of the first lessons his British pals had taught him.

"Jozsi used to play football with his friends. They had a strict 'no girls' rule, so they never let me play, until one day when they were very short on players. Turned out I was pretty good! After that, they always wanted me to play with them. That's when Jozsi and I became friends."

"Do you still play football?" Endre asked.

"No. Not since he left. No one plays much of anything anymore. The war has made us all glum."

Endre waited.

"Jozsi and I used to talk about running away to Budapest," she said. "Well not running away really, but going to school. I wanted to be a teacher or maybe a seamstress, and he wanted to be a doctor. We always said we'd go to Budapest University together. Well, it was silly, really," she said dismissively, "we never would have had the money for that kind of education anyway."

"What about scholarships?"

"Actually, now that you mention it," Ilonka remembered, "my teacher wanted to nominate me for a scholarship, but it was too late. The war had started and Jozsi was gone to the front. I didn't want to go without him. And after we heard the news about Jozsi, there was no way I could leave *Anyu*, *Apu*, and Sanyi. It was not a time for chasing dreams; it was a time for looking after your family. It still is."

"It still is," agreed Endre.

This was the spot where Endre and Ilonka sat most afternoons, hidden from street-view and close to the ladder. If anyone should approach unexpectedly, Endre could scramble up to his hiding place. Thankfully, except for the one close-call with Gombos, Endre's days in hiding had been blessedly uneventful. The danger wasn't ever completely forgotten, but despite the worries, the whole family had settled into a new routine that had evolved to include Endre, almost as if he had always been there.

Since the time of their first meeting, a month ago, Endre had successfully rehabilitated himself from the habit of speaking to Ilonka as if she were a pub-girl. She was no pub-girl. She was a *komoly kisasszony*, a serious young woman. Talking with her was nothing like talking with Sally or Jenny. Prattle at the bar seldom went beyond witty repartee; whereas, with Ilonka he found he could talk about almost anything.

Men in uniform – especially a pilot's uniform – met a lot of women, but Endre could safely say that he had never met a woman like Ilonka. Until now, he had always thought that chatting up girls was an exercise designed strictly for his amusement. It had nothing to do with companionship. That's what Jimmy was for. But Jimmy wasn't here and Endre was learning something new about women: they made good companions too! At the foot of the ladder, Endre and Ilonka talked about frivolous things, like the neon green frogs Endre found in Hungary that he'd never seen in America; about serious things, like the loss of Jozsi; about politics, religion and, of course, the war.

While the young people were talking, and the parents were helping out at Mariska's, the boys were spending a sunny afternoon on the banks of the Keszegér. They went to their usual place. It had always been a lucky fishing hole, but recently it had also been a lucky hiding place for Endre. Feeling mellow on this lazy afternoon, the boys were sitting quietly on the log with their lines in the water, watching for the slightest jiggle. An hour passed without any success but it didn't matter. Between casts, they played the cloud game.

"That one looks like a dog," offered Sanyi.

As the wind gently reshaped the puffy figure, Lajos added, "Now it looks more like a boat."

The silent skies soothed their young, war-frazzled nerves. On they went, sitting, casting, waiting for a nibble.

The giant crept up behind them, completely unnoticed, until he snorted and his powerful nostrils blew hot air on Sanyi's bare shoulder.

Sanyi gasped.

Both boys jerked around to face the intruder.

The large white gelding reared in alarm and turned away in a hasty gallop.

Hearts were racing, first with fear then with excitement. Fishing was abandoned as they tore off after the horse. When they caught sight of him in the next clearing, they slowed their pace right down. The horse had stopped running but was still throwing his head about skittishly. They wanted to catch him without spooking him, so they moved very slowly. The horse allowed the boys to approach, almost as though he had been looking for a friend. Sanyi reached out his hand, gently. The gelding allowed himself to be touched. Sanyi took the bridle in his hand, stroked the long face, and spoke soothingly, "What a beauty you are."

Lajos approached, petting the sleek white neck. This was a large animal, at least sixteen hands. He was still carrying a saddle and heavily laden saddle bags. It was obvious that there had recently been a rider with this horse, but there was no one in sight now. They led the horse back to their lucky spot. He was thirsty and lapped eagerly from the Keszegér.

"I wonder where he came from," said Sanyi.

Lajos was wondering the same thing. "Maybe there's a clue in his saddle bags."

Gently, the boys approached the horse again. He wasn't skittish now. As long as no one was screaming, he was completely tame.

Sanyi noted that his mane was well-groomed. "Somebody's been taking good care him. He's very comfortable around people. He walked right up to us."

Lajos opened the saddle bags with no objection from the white giant.

"Ooooh, what's this? Russian uniforms!" exclaimed Lajos, as he pulled the folded clothes out of the saddle bags.

"Officer's uniforms," added Sanyi, noting the insignias.

Why would someone be traveling with saddlebags stuffed full of officer's uniforms? The possible plots were endless.

"Maybe the rider killed all these officers and kept their uniforms as some kind of sick souvenir," speculated Sanyi.

"I don't know," countered Lajos, "they look new."

"Maybe some Russian officers wore a hole in their pants and sent for new ones," Sanyi joked.

"Or maybe, someone was planning to impersonate a Russian officer and mix up some orders and mess up the war somehow," Lajos spun the plot. And then suddenly, as was often the case with Lajos, his own plot began to form.

CHAPTER FIVE

Loudly, he banged on the gate. Old man Tivador was home for sure. When was he not home? Tivador wasn't really very old, only about forty. He just seemed old because he walked with crutches. On the Russian front, in the Great War, he had lost half a leg to a gangrene amputation.

Finally, Tivador appeared at the gate. "What's all the ruckus? Who's there?"

The huge head of the white horse peered over the gate at him.

"Open this gate at once!" came the command in Russian.

Tivador hated the Russians, hated the sound of the Russian language, and now he hated this Russian horse. Angrily, he threw open the gate, "What do you want?"

There stood one small Russian officer and another one mounted on a very large horse. The horse was prancing wildly but the rider's voice was booming authoritatively. "We need lodging for ourselves and for our horse," the Russian said, now switching to somewhat broken, but surprisingly good, Hungarian.

Tivador sought to make eye contact to show that he was not afraid of them but, strangely, their collars were pulled high and their hats tilted low to conceal their faces.

"Lodging," the Russian repeated insistently.

"What do you expect me to do about that?" Tivador asked defiantly – now suspecting the ruse, but deciding to play along.

"My horse needs hay and water. We need food and bedding," demanded the mounted Russian.

Tivador's dog became alert to the commotion and started barking from inside the yard.

"Shut him up or I'll shoot him," commanded the Russian.

Tivador tried to reach around to pull the gate closed but, on only one leg, he wasn't quick enough. There was nothing Tivador could do to stop the dog. The loyal mutt didn't like the tone in the exchanges and, sensing that his owner was in need of protection, the dog charged at the Russian soldiers with teeth bared.

"Yikes!" exclaimed Sanyi. Being the one standing on the ground, he was the dog's first target. In one fluid motion he jumped up, grabbed Lajos' waist and mounted himself on the back of the horse. Simultaneously, Lajos turned the gelding and kicked it into a gallop. Off they flew. And off flew Sanyi's Russian officer cap.

"Hahaha!" laughed Tivador, calling back his dog.

Gombos rushed over from next door. He felt brave now that he saw the Russians leaving. "What was that all about?"

Tivador was still laughing. "Well, those were two Russians. They wanted board for themselves and their horse."

"I see," said Gombos, not at all seeing what was so funny.

By now, Tivador had fully regained his sense of humor. The answer he gave to Gombos was how this story would forever be told in Markota. "Well," he began, "I told them I could perhaps make room for their horse in my barn, but what was I supposed to do with them? There's only one bed in my house. Should I put them in bed with my wife? Soon they'd be gone, but then there'd be this little Russian kid running around my house and I would never understand a word he said!"

The story got told around town. Tivador never revealed the true identity of the Russian officers, but everyone who noticed that Sanyi and Lajos had a new white gelding figured it out.

"Wowee," whistled Endre when the boys led the giant mount into the yard. The horse, prancing playfully, looked as mischievous and gleeful as the two boys. "I thought I told you to catch a fish, not a horse," Endre joked. "I'm not cooking him for dinner."

Janos looked up from the well-pump handle he was repairing, "Uh… why are you boys wearing Russian uniforms?"

Sanyi and Lajos were laughing so hard they could barely walk, much less talk, but they did finally manage to tell their story. Fortunately for the boys, Janos found their prank funny. He knew Tivador well enough to know that no harm was done.

"Can we keep him, *Apu*?" pleaded Sanyi.

"We can keep him for now," said Janos.

"I don't see how we could return him, even if we wanted to," said Sanyi.

"No," agreed Janos, "but the issue isn't how to return him, it's how to feed him."

"We'll take him with us when we go down to the Keszegér, there's lots of wild pasture he can feed in there. That's what he was living on when we found him."

Janos looked skeptical.

"And look how strong he is," argued Sanyi. "He could pull the plough or the wagon, easily. We need him."

"We'll see how things turn out," said Janos.

The boys beamed. The white giant had already proven himself to be a worthy co-

conspirator and an agreeable playmate. But thoughts of play immediately evaporated when Erzsi pushed open the yard door and flew to Janos in agitated haste, while motioning frantically to Endre: get up the ladder right now! Her face registered terror when she saw the uniforms the boys were dressed in. "Get those off. I don't have time to explain, just do it!"

Ilonka followed behind her mother. "I'll look after things out here," she said. "You take *Apu* inside to meet them."

Meet who? Janos wondered.

Erzsi clutched his arm, pulled him towards the house, and began talking in the most normal voice she could assemble. "Three German officers have requested room and board at our house. They are in the front room right now. I started some tea for them and told them I was coming out here to get you."

"I see," said Janos, as calmly as he could, already following Erzsi back inside so the Germans would have no reason to come out here looking for him. With a final glance over his shoulder, he took a quick look around the yard and noted that Ilonka already had Endre tucked away upstairs and was nearly finished getting the boys out of their Russian uniforms and back into their own clothes. He'd have to trust his family to get things cleaned up out here while he went in to greet his 'guests.'

There they were, seated on his living room chairs, like three German gentlemen who had already made themselves at home. Janos had no choice but to provide the hospitality. The Germans were not really asking. Stories were told about those who refused to accommodate the Nazis. Nobody in Markota had ever refused because the tales from nearby Csorna had reached them. What the Nazis didn't get by asking, they simply took. Janos knew the best way to protect his family was to play along. Of course the Germans were welcome here. Hadn't Germany and Hungary always been friends? Certainly, they would win this war together.

Ilonka was hurriedly helping the boys get dressed back into their civilian clothes. Endre was peering down from the hayloft. Stay quiet, she gestured by discreetly putting a finger to her lips, and turned her attention back to the boys. The Russian uniforms! The Germans wouldn't be happy to find these. She snatched up the bundles of clothing shed by the boys, unclipped the saddlebags, and stuffed the uniforms back in. "Sanyi, put this horse in the barn. Lajos come with me."

Just out of sight of the house, Lajos and Ilonka quickly rearranged the woodpile to make a hiding place for the stuffed saddlebags. Sanyi joined them and Ilonka walked the boys over to Lajos' house and told them to stay there for the evening. Sanyi should only come home at bedtime. She was desperately hoping the Germans would leave tomorrow.

Clouds Over Markota 97

The following morning, Sanyi was rushed out the door right after breakfast, encouraged to go to Lajos' until it was time to go to school. He wasn't to worry about his chores for the time being. Janos and Ilonka would do his work for him.

The hope of the Germans leaving today faded with their leisurely morning manner. They didn't seem to be in any rush to leave, nor did they give any indication of how long they intended to stay. They were still sipping their coffees when Ilonka went out to the yard to tend to the animals.

Pulling the kitchen door closed behind her, she took a careful look around to make sure she was alone before scurrying up the loft ladder. Quickly, she emptied her apron pocket of bread and *kolbász*. Cautiously, Endre lifted his head out of his hiding spot. Pulling two small apples from her other pocket, she whispered, "This may have to last you all day. I don't know if I'll be able to come back."

Endre nodded. Silently, he watched Ilonka climb back down the ladder and go about the business of feeding the pigs.

In the short time that Endre had been here, a new daily routine was established. Endre had breakfast with the family, helped a little with chores – as much as he could do without risking being seen – chatted with Ilonka in the afternoons, tutored the boys in their homework assignments and taught them all English in the evenings. None of them got so comfortable with this routine that they forgot how dangerous it was for Endre to be here, but the danger seemed remote. When the bombs weren't actually falling, the countryside was quiet, giving the illusion of peace and security. It felt safe inside the Farkas family home and yard. The threat seemed peripheral. Now the threat had moved inside their walls.

With painful sluggishness, the days dragged on. Endre was on edge and there was nothing he could do to expend his nervous energy. He worried about Ilonka and her family. He regretted coming here and putting them in danger. In the lonely loft, he prayed: Dear God, don't let anything happen to her, or the people she loves, because of me! He told himself that if he had his decisions to make over again, he would have tried to walk across Europe instead.

His thoughts wandered back to the farm in New York. He thought about his parents. By now, his name would have appeared on the MIA list. At first, that would be good news; at least their son wasn't dead. But it wouldn't be long before that relief turned to worry; if he wasn't dead, where was he?

Endre imagined his mother's anguish. While he lay restless in his hay-loft, he knew that his mother would be laying awake night after night; reaching for the hope that he might still be alive; trying to block out the horror stories she would surely have heard about the POW camps; fighting against the demons that sprinkled her waking and sleeping dreams with terrifying images; and praying that her son would come home.

He knew his father would try to comfort her, but he would be burdened by his own worries too. Endre was sorry for putting his parents through this. He wished he could tell them he was safe. But was he safe? He had survived his crash and he wasn't in a prisoner of war camp. He was still alive, but the war wasn't over yet. No one was safe.

Once again, his mind turned back time. If he could sit in his cockpit again…; if he hadn't broken cloud cover at precisely that moment…; if he had seen that Focke-Wulfe first…; if…, if…, if…!

He thought about Kim. It dawned on him that, since his arrival in Hungary, this was the first time he had thought about Kim. How did she take the news when she heard he was missing? Endre felt sure she would have cried but, instinctively, he knew that her grief would not have been as deep as his mother's. Did this mean his mother loved him more? Did it mean Kim didn't love him enough? Come to think of it, he asked himself, do I love her? When the pubbing with the British girls started, he made a deal with himself to not ask that question until after the war. Well, he noted, the war isn't over yet, so he pushed the question out of his mind. He wondered if she had sent any more letters before she heard the news. Were there any cookies with it? And, if so – he smiled – did Jimmy eat the cookies?

Jimmy and the boys! He missed them. The faces of his buddies paraded through his memory. Each face came with a scene – the barracks, the canteen, the briefing room. He remembered sitting with the boys in the briefing room, listening to the squadron commander describe their mission. Everything heard in this room was classified top secret. To protect confidentiality, they were effectively quarantined between here and the airfield.

Endre drifted off to sleep. He was in the briefing room now. He could hear the rustling of paper, chalk scratching on the board as the commanding officer drew diagrams resembling a football play. The briefing concluded, as it always did, with their commander wishing them good luck and a safe return. His buddies rose. With the clatter of metal chairs dragging noisily across the floor, Endre realized that everyone was gone. He sat alone in the briefing room.

He woke with a start. Someone was coming up the ladder. "Endre," he heard her whisper.

He raised his head above the straw.

As she unloaded her pockets again, she was saying, "I can't stay. I just wanted to bring you a few more things."

"Thanks," Endre whispered back. Just as quickly, she was gone.

Ilonka brought him two more apples and a book. She must have known he was going crazy with nothing but his own thoughts to occupy him.

He opened the book, but it was too dark to see the print. Carefully, quietly, he rearranged his hay-pile so he could place the page directly below one of the gaps in the roof planks. It worked. He was able to catch just enough sunshine to light the page. Reading was a welcome diversion.

A week went by and the Germans still didn't seem to be in any hurry. They never said exactly what they were doing here, but the talk around town was that they spent their days in the town office. Janos surmised that it was a tactic in the occupation, to exert control right down to the municipal level to remind folks of who was in charge.

With the Germans occupying the front room, they had taken over every aspect of the Farkas family's life. Sanyi and Lajos were still banished from the house, lest they innocently let something slip. Sanyi slept and ate breakfast at home, but after school he went to Lajos' and stayed there until bedtime. The Germans didn't know how unusual this was. Uncle Vince knew, but he didn't mind. At least, this way, the chores got done without having to chase Lajos down. He didn't ask for any explanation. The presence of the three Germans was explanation enough.

The tension ratcheted up in the evenings. The officers made it a habit to smoke their after-dinner cigars in the yard, sitting on overturned buckets, right at the foot of the steps that led up to the hayloft. Endre could hear them easily. He willed himself to stay perfectly still, that not even the slightest sound of rustling hay might draw their attention. Every effort was made to distract them. Janos poured them glasses of his home-made wine and went on about the glory days of the Austro-Hungarian Empire, ruled jointly by Germans and Hungarians for fifty years. Erzsi brought them cookies and smiled sweetly. Even Ilonka was willing to chat with them, using her limited German. Anything to keep them from looking up.

Unceasingly, the Endre-question spun around in everyone's mind.

"What are we going to do with him?" Erzsi whispered in the dark bedroom.

Janos rolled closer to his wife and wrapped his arms around her.

Pulling the covers up to muffle her whispered voice even more, she asked, "Can Vince take him?"

"I was wondering that too," admitted Janos, "but I don't think so."

"He'd understand. He's a veteran," argued Erzsi.

"I know," agreed Janos, "but he fought against the Russians."

"It's no secret that he hates the Russians," said Erzsi.

"But the Germans are not the Russians," countered Janos. "The Germans were our allies. We have a long history with the Germans. Vince worries that if the Americans defeat the Germans, the Russians will overrun us. And he may be right about that."

"But right now the Germans are not our allies. They're occupying us!" said Erzsi in hushed agitation.

"I agree, and you know he's not pleased with that any more than we are. I'm just saying that if he had to choose between the Americans and the Germans, I'm not sure he wouldn't choose the Germans. Not because he supports the German occupation, but because the Germans are on our side against the Russians, and he sees Russia as a bigger threat to Hungary. And," Janos repeated, "he may be right about that."

With no resolution, they both drifted off to fitful sleeps.

The next morning brought some unexpected relief when the German officers suddenly announced they were going away. They would be leaving in the afternoon, but only for a week. They'd be back.

Janos was relieved, but still troubled. That was too close. He needed to get Endre out of here. This was far too dangerous. If the Germans found out that they were hiding an American it would be a death sentence. He needed a solution. He asked himself again, was there any neighbor he could pass him off to? With so many Germans around town these days, who would be willing to take that risk? After all, who knew which door the Germans would be knocking on next.

That evening, Endre came down from the hayloft for the first time in eight days. He knew he was on borrowed time. They'd be back, but for the moment it felt good to stretch his legs.

After supper, the boys spent the evening at Sanyi's house doing homework. Sanyi was glad to be in his own living room again.

Over coffee, the adults gathered around the kitchen table. The Endre-question, that had been on everyone's mind for months, now needed to be answered with a renewed urgency. No one could think of anyone who could reasonably be expected to take Endre and keep him in hiding. There had to be another way.

Janos was working on an idea. "Endre speaks Hungarian. We should be able to work with that," he told them.

"But even a Hungarian can't appear out of nowhere," said Endre.

"We need to give you a new identity," said Ilonka, catching onto the direction her father was going.

"I have a sister in Arad," said Janos. "She has a son, Endre's age, whom I've never met. No one in Markota has ever met him. You could be her son, my nephew, just arrived from Arad."

"I could," said Endre.

"That's promising," agreed Erzsi and Ilonka.

Janos called for the boys to come into the kitchen. "Sanyi, Lajos, I want to introduce you to Endre, my nephew – my sister's eldest son – just arrived from Arad."

They looked at Endre, back at Janos, then at each other.

"We're making a new secret identity for Endre," said Ilonka. "Do you boys want to help?"

They didn't bother to answer the question. They jumped right in and started spinning a wild history.

Janos interrupted, "There are a few facts you need to know. Arad is about four hundred kilometers from Markota. Endre is the eldest of her six children: first three boys and then three girls. Endre's father is from Arad, that's why they moved there. That means Endre grew up close to his grandparents and aunts and uncles there."

"Okay," said the boys, "now spinning comical tales of sibling rivalry in the fictitious household of Endre and his five younger brothers and sisters."

Janos came back with a few envelopes. "She didn't write very often. This is all I have," he said, as he handed out the letters he had received from his sister.

The boys stopped their jesting and started reading. Together, they all pored over the letters in search of useable details, then mixed in some plausible fiction. By bedtime, the American pilot hiding in the hayloft had a whole new identity

When the Germans returned, they were introduced to cousin Endre. Wearing Jozsi's clothes, and speaking fluent Hungarian, he easily passed. The obvious question arose as to why he was not off fighting on the eastern front or working in one of the German factories like other young men of his age. This had been anticipated in the family's brain-storming session and Endre had conveniently developed a severe limp, a disabling war injury. And, they threw in a – harder to verify – rare heart condition, for good measure. The German's remained convinced that this family was still representative of their old Hungarian allies. For five more days they stayed, and they were none the wiser when they finally left.

With the Germans gone, Gombos began to come around again. He brought choice wares from his store and stayed for coffee.

Janos and Endre came in from the yard, greeted Gombos casually, and sat down at the kitchen table.

No introductions were required. Gombos wasn't surprised to see Endre. Along with everyone else in Markota, he had met cousin Endre last Sunday at church. Townsfolk who remembered Janos' sister were full of questions for the newly arrived nephew. How was his mother? Of course it's unsafe to travel with the war on, but when the war ends, will she come to visit them? She had not been home since her wedding, twenty-six years earlier. People just did not travel such great distances. In fact, most of those who were asking had never been outside of Markota. Some had been as far as Győr and a few had been to Budapest, but even Budapest was less than half the distance to Arad. Since the borders had been redrawn, and Arad became part of Romania, it seemed even farther than when it was still part of Hungary. It was a pretty safe bet that Janos' sister would never really return to Markota. Endre answered all their questions, satisfying their curiosity. He didn't even find it difficult to stay in character. After all, he spoke fluent Hungarian and he had been living as part of the Farkas family for two months already.

Gombos didn't remember Janos' sister very well, so he wasn't interested in any of those questions, and he was equally uninterested in her son. It wasn't curiosity about Endre that brought Gombos here this morning. His mission was Ilonka. She still had not accepted his invitation to the harvest ball. With the German officers here, there had been no opportunity to press the issue. This visit, as always, was aimed at gaining the approval of the entire Farkas family.

The talk at the table had turned to the war. Gombos was confident that it would end soon. "Their planes will win this war for them," he said, expounding on the wonders of German engineering. He loved to play the role of well-informed man. Even more, he just loved to hear himself talk. He frequently contradicted himself, but he seemed to be completely unaware, or at least unperturbed by that. Ten minutes later, or two houses over, he could say something completely different if he thought it might put money in his pocket by making a sale, or if he thought it made him sound intelligent.

Gombos had heard about the German Schwalbe with a new kind of engine that was being developed, and that was the theme he was riding today. "These are turbine engines, with no pistons or cylinders," he emphasized authoritatively. "The Americans already don't stand a chance against the Germans in their Focke-Wulfs."

Ouch. Endre felt that one right in his gut. It was a Focke-Wulf that took him out of the sky, but that didn't give credence to the rantings of this imbecile! He knew that the Messerschmitt ME-262 Schwalbe was a threat, but it was also experiencing its share of engine failures. The new technology was still unrefined. Besides, the British were also working on turbine development in their Meteor F-8, but the young man from Arad would surely know nothing about this, so Endre sat silently.

"The American Mustangs are silly little planes," continued Gombos. "Their range is only four hundred kilometers and their speed is only three hundred kilometers per hour!"

Wrong! Endre's thoughts screamed. Even the early model Mustangs were better than that, and his P-51-D, with its Rolls Royce engine, was far more advanced. Endre knew the Focke Wulf's with their BMW engines had finally met their match. With the additional fuel he could carry in the external wing tanks, the range of his Mustang was 1,700 miles or 2,700 kilometers – remembering that in Europe they used the metric measurements and expressed distance in kilometers, not the American miles he was used to – and the speed was seven hundred kilometers per hour.

"Only four hundred kilometers?" asked Janos. "How can they fly as far as Hungary then?"

Gombos skipped the question. "The point is, the German planes are superior."

"I don't know," said Janos. "Faster planes with more powerful engines will require a lot more fuel. That's in short supply. Oil wells and processing plants are getting bombed every day. Then there's the issue of transporting fuel. I think things are getting complicated for the Luftwaffe. And, I do see a lot of American planes in the sky these days."

Gombos replied with scorn, "Yeah, and a lot of American parachutes too!"

Once again, Endre managed not to flinch.

"Just two nights ago, I saw the Germans marching at least a dozen Americans towards the train station. They rounded up all the parachutists and shipped them off to POW camps. If you ask me, they should save the money and just shoot them!"

Janos broke the awkward silence that followed. "It looks to me like the American sky power is increasing."

Gombos was sensitive to the possibility of offending Ilonka's father, so he quickly offered, "you may be right." Still, he couldn't help adding, "but my money is on the Germans."

Ilonka lifted her coffee cup to take a sip. Her movement drew his attention and reminded him of why he was here. He had allowed himself to become distracted from his mission. Re-focusing his attention on Ilonka, he started gushing over her, expressing great concern that the Germans hadn't hurt her.

I don't remember him rushing over to protect me last week while the Germans were here, she thought, trying to keep the cynicism from showing on her face.

Next, he moved on to the subject that most irritated Ilonka, the harvest ball. He began pestering her again to go with him. Erzsi offered her usual defense of Ilonka being too young to date but, with the ball coming up this weekend, Gombos was growing impatient. "She's not too young to date!" he shouted.

The room fell silent. Ilonka jumped up from the table and ran out to the yard. Gombos followed her, pleading loudly, "Ilonka, go to the ball with me!"

She stopped, intending to speak, but she was cut off by his barrage of words, "Ilonka, please. I can give you a good life. I can give you anything you want."

He had her backed up against the wall and was now keeping her caged between his arms with his palms resting on the wall on either side of her. "Ilonka... Darling... when I'm with you I feel like I'm in heaven," Gombos stammered frantically.

"That sounds more like a marriage proposal than an invitation to a ball," said Endre, catching up to them.

"This has nothing to do with you!" spat Gombos. In replying to Endre, he was distracted just long enough that Ilonka was able to duck out from under his arm and move away from the wall.

Behind Endre, Gombos saw Ilonka's mother and father. He had a lot invested in staying in their good graces. "Please, Mrs. Farkas," he implored Erzsi. "You must speak to your daughter. She needs to think about her future."

"I certainly will," said Erzsi, meaning to support Ilonka's decision.

Misunderstanding that to mean he had Erzsi's support, Gombos decided that now would be a good time to take his leave. Resuming his syrupy tone, he bid them all a good day, flashed a hopeful smile towards Ilonka and said with a wink, "I'll see you at the ball on Saturday night."

The wink was too much! Ilonka opened her mouth to speak, but she choked on her own outrage. No words came out. Who did that disgusting little pig think he was?

Erzsi put her arms around her daughter, "It's okay." Comfortingly, she caressed her little girl's long brown hair. "Of course you do not have to go to the ball with him. And – obviously! – you are not going to marry him. We've tolerated him up till now but if he can't behave like a gentleman, we'll simply have to tell him not to come around anymore."

"I'm sorry," she cried as she slumped down to sit on one of the overturned buckets at the foot of the ladder, and buried her face in her hands.

These were complicated times. Speaking your mind was a luxury no one could afford. If she were to really stand her ground and firmly shut Gombos down, her family would suffer. Instead of being first on the list to get everything new that came into the store, they would suddenly find that there was nothing left when they went to buy it – no flour, no sugar, nothing. Of course there were lines that she would not cross, but her pride could suffer a little to help her family. No, she would not be his exclusive date on Saturday night, but she would give him some space on her dance card.

Endre licked his lips. He hadn't tasted *zserbó* in years. Back in America, his mother used to make the delicious pastry with apricot jam and ground walnut layers. It had always been his favorite treat. One year, she made a big sheet of it for his birthday instead of a cake. She stuck the candles directly into the chocolate layer on top. This *zserbó* was missing its chocolate topping.

Chocolate was one of many things you could not get these days. The jam layers were made from apricots that Mariska had picked fresh from her fruit trees. Likewise, the walnuts were harvested from her bountiful yard. The *zserbó* was one of her contributions to the dessert table at this year's harvest ball. "Have another one!" she shouted her encouragement to Endre over the music of the gypsy band.

"I think I will." He replied, adding, "these are fantastic!"

"Thank you," Mariska smiled at his praise, but the best compliment was the gusto with which he devoured them.

The ladies brought their kitchen specialties. The men brought their home-made wines and *pálinka* brandies. All the goodies were shared in celebration of the harvest, even in lean years, even in war years.

"Oh, I need to ask Sari for her *almás rétes*, apple struedel, recipe," remembered Mariska.

"She won't give it to anyone," said Erzsi. "That's one of her old family secrets. I've even heard her deny she has such a recipe!"

"But she brings *almás rétes* every year."

"You know how it is," shrugged Erzsi at the protective habits of some of the women with respect to their cherished recipes.

The harvest ball was the premier event on the Markota social calendar. Decorated in a harvest theme with hay-bales, pumpkins, apples, and cornucopias, the party room at the only hotel in Markota was filled to capacity. Folks came from the neighboring towns and farmers came in from the countryside. To Endre, it seemed more like a barn-dance than a ball, but the ladies were wearing their prettiest dresses and the men were using their best manners.

Cousin Endre was in his element. Even with his limp, he was a better dancer than most of the men in the room. He had some moves that no one here had ever seen before. Handsome strangers were uncommon in these parts, and the Markota girls swooned.

"They sure dance funny in Arad!" giggled a girl after her dance with Endre.

Then came the *csárdás*. Every man, woman, and child in the room knew exactly what to do – except Endre. He announced that his leg was really bothering him and he had better sit this one out.

Gombos fancied himself a master of the *csárdás* and imagined he was really impressing Ilonka with his high jumps and vigorous slapping of boots.

With the young men away fighting the war, the young women were short a few dance partners, so even Sanyi and Lajos were in high demand. They weren't quite old enough yet to see this as a good thing. After each dance, they left the floor with the intention of escaping, but the farthest they had gotten so far was the dessert table. Trapped there by the lure of the fresh pastries, the young ladies with feet itching to dance were usually able to persuade them back onto the floor for just one more song!

When the *csárdás* was over and the waltzes resumed, Endre was back on the floor. Anika caught Ilonka between dances at the punch table and said, "Your cousin is dreamy." Ilonka just smiled and went on to dance with Béla who had been waiting patiently for his turn. Two dances later, when Rozsi and Kati said almost the same thing to her, she began to wonder if cousin Endre wasn't becoming too popular. Just then, Endre came up beside her, took her by the arm and led her to the dance floor, "I believe it's my turn to dance with you."

Ilonka turned to mush. Never had she felt so helpless in all her life. She closed her eyes and allowed herself to fall into his arms. She hadn't realized until this moment, how much she craved to be touched by him. In his arms, time stood still. There was nothing else in the world, just Ilonka, Endre, and the rhythm of the gypsy band. She let her head fall against his chest and felt his heart beating. For blissful seconds, she floated along, under the warmth of his palm gently resting on her back. Endre lowered his head to her ear and whispered, "we're supposed to be cousins."

Ilonka's head shot up and they both laughed. Most of the eyes in the room were on them. The girls jealously eyeing Ilonka. Gombos jealous of Endre. Everyone confused... until the couple broke into laughter. But Gombos' proprietary feelings towards Ilonka didn't leave any room for humor. The moment the last note sounded, he had Ilonka's elbow. "The next dance is mine."

Ilonka conceded, even feigning a little pleasure. This was her fourth dance with Gombos tonight. Endre released her. The first girl he saw was Rozsi. With a bow he invited her for the next dance, and she curtseyed back her acceptance.

As far as anyone else knew, Ilonka danced with her cousin only once that night, but for Endre and Ilonka every dance was their own. They twirled around the dance floor with a succession of partners, yet their eyes sought only each other. A peek here, a glimpse there, then a long glance over their unsuspecting dance partners' shoulders, until they were torn apart again with the next twirl.

The boys were finally stuffed full of goodies, to the point where the pastries lost their luring power. Now they were able to get past the dessert table and escape their would-be dance partners, out into the still autumn night.

Noticing the quiet sky, Lajos said, "It's decent of them to stop bombing and let us have our harvest ball."

"Darn right!" rejoined Sanyi, with emphasis added by too much *pálinka*.

As they rounded the corner of the inn, they startled a wild turkey. In defense, the turkey spread his flightless wings wide to make himself appear huge and threatening.

The inebriated Sanyi started giggling. "Look!" he said, "it's the Árpád bird!"

Every school-aged Hungarian child was familiar with the popular myth. Pre-Christian legend has it that the turul, a giant mythical falcon, impregnated Árpád's grandmother, resulting in the Árpád dynasty and royal lineage. The outspread wings of the great bird remain the symbol of the House of Árpád.

"No, it's a turkey, you turkey," said Lajos.

"No! It's Endre," said Sanyi with conviction.

"Endre? Now what are you talking about?"

"Endre is from Árpád and he's a bird, right?"

Lajos laughed at his friend's folly. "Endre is from Arad and he's a pilot!" Oops. As soon as the word was out, he slapped his hand over his mouth and took an anxious look around. No one heard.

Sanyi asked again, "Are you sure Endre is not from Árpád?"

"Yes, I'm sure." Changing the subject he said, "I think Gabi likes you."

"You're crazy," retorted Sanyi.

Around the corner of the inn's stone wall, the door opened again. Gombos came out and joined the men who were gathered there enjoying their cigars.

"She thinks you're cute," teased Lajos.

"Well," mused Sanyi, "at least she's pretty."

"Hah! You like her too!" exclaimed Lajos, as the boys started walking towards home.

"She's pretty," said Sanyi again, this time in English. These words were part of the essential vocabulary the boys had been taught by Endre in their language lessons.

Over the din of the party and the band, Gombos caught the elevated voices of the boys. He didn't understand what he heard but it wasn't Hungarian, or German, or Russian. Maybe it was the *pálinka*, or maybe it was English.

CHAPTER SIX

The chill of winter was settling on Eastern Europe this November morning. Erzsi was the first in her household to see the soft white blanket of the first snowfall and, with her family still sleeping snugly, it gave her a cozy feeling. She shivered, and the warm feeling was chased away by the cold draft that blew in from under the front door. As she stuffed a tattered rag into the gap to stop the draft, she wondered if she should build a fire to warm up the house. There was still a good supply of wood in the wood-pile, but the deepest cold of winter was yet to come. Instead she put on an extra pair of socks and another sweater and set to work in the kitchen. One by one, the rest of the clan awoke to the smell of brewing coffee.

"Saaaaanyi," Lajos cajoled from the yard.

Sanyi knew Lajos was up to something, but he went out the door anyway. Plop! The wet snowball landed on the top of Sanyi's head. Naturally, this meant war. Sanyi formed a snowball and fired back achieving a direct hit to Lajos' left shoulder, which splattered up into his face. Snow-fire was exchanged until Endre descended his ladder. Now the boys had a common target. Endre was assaulted with snow-grenades. When he reached the ground he, too, started forming snowballs and firing back. He caught Lajos and gave him a face washing in the cold white stuff. When Sanyi piled on, they all collapsed in a heap of soaking wet laughter.

"Breakfast is ready!" called Erzsi from the safety of the doorway.

Discreetly scooping up two more handfuls of snow, Endre rubbed both boys on the tops of their heads and made a run for the door quickly before they could retaliate.

Erzsi made them all change into dry clothes before she would allow them to come to the table. "You'll catch your deaths running around wet in this cold!"

After a meager breakfast, the boys got ready to go to school. Erzsi tore up the newspaper. "It's always only bad news anyway," she said, "but it is good for keeping your feet warm."

The boys stuffed their boots full of the newspaper shreds. Sanyi gave his scarf an extra wrap around his neck and Lajos pulled his favorite blue sweater over his head.

Endre followed the boys out. Since his transformation to the cousin from Arad, he could move about more freely and was able to be of more use in helping with the family chores, so he had taken over the job of tending the animals.

Janos and Erzsi were headed over to Mariska's this morning to help her with the preparations for her husband's homecoming. László was recently promoted to the rank of major and transferred to Budapest. Mariska was delighted as this transfer brought him closer to home and farther from the dangers at the Russian front. She was hoping that he would have a few days – maybe even a week – of leave and be able to come home for Christmas.

"Tell Mariska I'll be over to help too," said Ilonka as she saw her parents out the door, and resumed cleaning up the kitchen and the breakfast dishes.

Humming to herself softly, she wiped the last plate dry. She was reaching up to put it in the cupboard when she heard the howling whistle sound and was suddenly flung backwards. The blast lifted her off her feet and threw her clear across the room. Missing the table by a fraction of an inch, she landed hard against the wall. The shattered window glass mixed with the broken plate shards and covered the floor in sharp fragments.

The kitchen door was hanging on only one hinge. Endre ripped it off and threw the door aside. "Ilonka!" he called.

No response.

Stepping into the room, he saw her slumped against the wall. "Ilonka!" he called again as he raced to her side. Dropping to his knees beside her, he took her in his arms, "Ilonka," he said gently. "Talk to me."

"Endre." She managed a whisper.

"Oh, thank God." He could see the blood, but she was talking and that was a good sign. "You're going to be alright," he added reassuringly.

Ilonka was still holding the tea towel with which she had been drying the dishes. Tenderly, Endre took it out of her hand and began wiping the blood from her cuts. He was relieved to see that none of the cuts looked very deep. She shifted herself to sit more upright and put a hand up to her head. She was increasingly alert and able to move, so Endre was confident that the glass cuts were the extent of her injury. "You're going to be alright," he said again. "We just need to clean you up a little."

While cradling her in one arm, he wiped her wounds with the other. She let her head fall against his chest. He leaned down and kissed her hair lightly. Turning her face up to his, she kissed him back.

Suddenly there was a mighty thunder and another detonation. The walls shook violently. The dishes rattled in the kitchen cupboards. Everything that had been on the living room shelves was on the floor now. Bombs were falling nearby. Endre cleared a short path through the glass on the floor and pulled himself and Ilonka under the heavy dining table. It would provide some protection against falling objects. Directly above the house, they heard a bomber pass at low altitude. The uneven rumble of the distressed engine shook the house one more time. After that, things grew quieter.

Safely in their shelter, under the table, Endre resumed the wiping of Ilonka's wounds. Hearing nothing but distant planes for a long while, Ilonka began to relax and let herself melt into the comfort of Endre's arms once again.

Endre and Ilonka were still under the table when they heard Janos and Erzsi coming in through the front door. That door, unlike the kitchen door, was still on its hinges.

"Ilonka!" cried Erzsi anxiously. "Endre!"

"We're in here," they answered in unison, breaking their embrace and crawling out from under the table.

"Oh, dear God!" Erzsi had come through the living room and had seen everything on the floor, but here in the kitchen things were even worse. There was glass everywhere. "Oh, dear God!" she exclaimed again on seeing her daughter and the blood-soaked tea towel. "Are you alright?"

Ilonka looked a little faint, so Endre answered for both of them. "We're fine. Ilonka's a little cut up, but nothing serious."

Janos nodded and began surveying the damage. Erzsi went immediately to get fresh bandaging for the wounds.

While Endre and Erzsi bandaged Ilonka's cuts, Janos began cleaning up the glass. It had been the same at Mariska's house and all over town. On their way home, they had seen several windows blown out from the explosion, but as far as they knew no one had been seriously injured.

"Oh!" exclaimed Sanyi as he came into the kitchen through the frame where the door used to be. He was relieved that he could see everyone – his mother, his father, his sister, and Endre – registering instantly that no one was hurt.

Lajos was right behind him. "You should see the hole that made!" Once everything quieted down, the children had been dismissed from school with explicit instructions to go directly home. Of course, the Bad Boys of Markota went straight to the bomb crater. "It's gigantic! You could put a house in it!"

He looked around at his family again, as if to make sure everybody really was safe. That's when he noticed that Ilonka was bleeding. Switching to an affectionate brotherly tone he asked her what had happened.

Ilonka told them she was putting the dishes away when the bomb went off, shattered the window, and threw her across the room. She told them about Endre coming to her aid and dragging her under the table when they heard the second explosion. Naturally, she kept the morning's secrets between herself and Endre.

"Thank God we're all safe," said Erzsi. "We have a mess to clean up, but at least we're all safe."

Janos asked the boys to give him a hand cleaning up the glass. With Ilonka safely bandaged, she and Erzsi started picking up everything in the living room that had been flung off the shelves by the second explosion. Janos left the boys to finish the glass clean up, while he and Endre set about the task of repairing the frame and re-hanging the door. Except for the cuts on Ilonka and the missing window glass, which would have to be replaced quickly to protect them from the dropping temperatures, by supper-time, the house was almost the same as it had been before the explosion. Of course, nothing would ever be the same between Ilonka and Endre.

By mid-November, the kitchen window was repaired. Gombos had succeeded in finding the needed glass pane. Anything for his Ilonka, he said. He always bragged about his connections, which really did seem capable of supplying him with items that were otherwise in short supply for the rest of the country. Except for the bandage still on Ilonka's left forearm, covering the deepest cut she received that day, life had more or less resumed the same rhythm it had before the bombing.

"Can I help carry something?" offered Ilonka, as she pulled the door closed behind them.

"No, you're recuperating," answered Erzsi, carrying a loaf of fresh-baked *almás rétes* to share with Mariska and László.

Endre put on his best limp and hobbled alongside of Janos, each of the men carrying a bottle of home-made wine.

"The garlic is strong this year," Ilonka commented on the strands of garlic and paprika hanging to dry on the sides of the houses.

"And the paprika is sweet, the way I like it," added Erzsi.

Rounding the corner, they saw Lazslo in the yard pulling some dead weeds that Mariska hadn't made it to yet.

"Stop working," called Janos. "You're only home for a week with your wife. You must have something better to do than work."

László smiled and greeted his guests with hugs and kisses. "Come in. Come in! Mariska is just setting the table."

Endre, Janos, and the ladies filed into the kitchen with their baking and their bottles.

Mariska accepted their gifts and poured everyone a glass of deep red wine.

"Egri Bikavér!" Janos noticed the label. "You rich people don't need my home-made bottles then! Where did you get this?"

László laughed. "In the city. It was an early Christmas present from one of the Germans. He told me to keep it for a special occasion."

"We're honored." Janos gave an exaggerated bow.

"Delicious," said Erzsi, taking a sip.

"Is it true what we hear on the radio," began Ilonka, "that Horthy's been trying to break out of our alliance with the Germans?"

"I think so," said László, closing the door behind them. "People are divided on this issue. You know, of course, that we've lost Debrecen to the Soviets."

Ilonka nodded.

"Some people think Russian rule will be better than German rule."

"That doesn't sound like much of a choice, really," said Ilonka.

"I know. We began as German military allies so I have my doubts about changing horses at this point, except for the fact that the Arrow Cross Nazis really must be stopped. They're corralling the Jews into ghettos in the city and their brutality knows no limits."

"But the Russians are savages," said Janos.

"Oh, stop," said Erzsi. "Can't we forget all of this just for one afternoon? László is only home for a week. I'm sure he doesn't want to talk about this."

"Well, actually, I don't even have a week. I have only until tomorrow. All hell is breaking lose in Budapest. We've all been called back."

"Well, that's it then. We're leaving you two alone," said Janos. "Come on, let's go." "Don't be silly," said Mariska. "Dinner is already on the table. Come, sit, eat."

"No, no," protested Janos.

"Yes," said Erzsi, "but we won't stay long."

"So, Endre…" began László, "tell us about your family in Arad."

Endre was prepared for questions like this. He rattled through the catalogue of parents and siblings before he realized he was sounding rehearsed. He tried to lighten it up by throwing in a humorous story about his pretend-sister, but it fell flat.

Erzsi tried to save him, "Oh, she sounds just like her mother when she was young! I remember Janos' sister always clowning around in school, usually ending up in trouble with the teacher."

They tried to avoid the subjects of war and politics but it was the only thing on everyone's mind so every attempt at small talk dried up quickly. Dessert was a welcome distraction. Mariska cut up and served the *rétes*. Eager comments about the sweetness of the pastry with the tanginess of this year's apples tried to keep the topic away from the war, but failed.

"Which alliance do you think is best for Hungary?" Ilonka asked, addressing the question to the major.

"A sovereign, independent Hungary should stand with the Allies – no Communists; no Nazis," he said without hesitation. "That would be the best."

"Can we do that?" she continued.

"Horthy tried to do it. That's what resulted in our occupation by Germany."

"So now Germany is 'defending' us while Russia is trying to 'liberate' us," added Janos.

"That's right," agreed László, "and to make matters worse, the population is divided on this – even my men. There have been some desertions."

"Going over to fight for the Russians?" asked Janos.

"Some have," László admitted.

Quietly, everyone took another bite of *rétes*.

It occurred to László that Endre hadn't said much. He began to have some doubts that he couldn't put his finger on. Was the accent not quite right for the Arad-region? Was his injury really severe enough to exempt him completely from duty? As a career officer, he had no respect for malingerers. "And where was it you served?" the major asked Endre.

It was Janos' turn to jump in. Pretending he hadn't heard the question, "That was delicious. Thank you, both."

Ilonka caught on to her father's maneuver and shoved the last of her *rétes* into her mouth as she rose from the table.

Erzsi chimed in too, "Yes, it's really time for us to leave the two of you to have some time to yourselves."

"Thanks so much. It was delicious," added Endre.

With quick hugs and best wishes for László's safety as he headed back to Budapest, they were out the door.

"That was strange," remarked László to his wife as he helped her clear the table.

"It was," agreed Mariska. "I've never seen them like that before." She added a little soap to the dishwater. "I guess they felt awkward about imposing on the little time we have together."

"How well do you know Endre?"

"Well enough. He's always there with the family. The boys adore him."

László was silent.

"Why?"

"I'm not sure," said László, "they all seem very protective of him for some reason."

"Well, why not? He's family, right?"

"Yes…" He was thinking it was strange that Janos, who had fought on the front against the Russians and had lost his own son in the war, would protect a young man who should be – should he be? – serving his country right now. But maybe he was wrong.

He took the dishcloth from Mariska's hand, threw it back into the kitchen sink, and pulled her close to him. "The dishes can wait."

Gombos set down the grocery bag and Erzsi looked for some money to pay him with, but his refusal was firm. "This is my Christmas present to my darling Ilonka and the entire Farkas family, but I'd love a cup of coffee."

Without waiting for a reply, he seated himself at the kitchen table to make his big announcement: he had a new job. "Well, the Soviets recognize talent when they see it," he gloated.

"What is the job exactly?" asked Janos.

"A promotion to police chief. I will be given a staff of constables to bring order to the country after the last of the Germans are driven out," said Gombos triumphantly.

"I thought you favored the Germans," said Ilonka, pushing her hair behind her ears, to keep it out of her face while she drank her coffee.

"My dear, you don't understand politics," he replied patronizingly. "Women usually don't," he winked at Janos and Endre. "We must form alliances with strength," he explained. "The Soviet Union is the new rising power. You know, they're throwing the Germans out of Budapest right now."

"Yes, we heard on the radio this morning that the city is under siege," said Erzsi.

"Not for long," said Gombos confidently. "They'll send the Germans packing and everything will be fine."

"We'll get rid of the Germans and be occupied by the Soviets!" retorted Janos.

"Then we'll finally have an equitable and just system of government," said Gombos. "That's why it's called communism. It's all about community and sharing everything equally."

Janos raised an eyebrow. Could anyone – even Gombos – really believe that? Or was he just taking advantage of his latest opportunity?

"What about the brave Hungarians who fought against the Communists on the Russian front? What will become of them?" asked Erzsi, thinking of Jozsi, her son who gave his life to protect his country from communism. And also, Janos, László, Vince, and so many others for whom this could be dangerous.

"If they're smart, they'll get on board with the new Soviet order. There's no sense fighting it. Communism is here to stay." Turning to Endre, he said, "There will be tremendous opportunities for young men like you. Even though you fought in the war against the Russians, I'm sure I could help you. You wouldn't have to worry about your bad leg. I could find you a desk job at the police station, working for me."

"Hmm," said Endre noncommittally.

"How did you get the job of police chief?" asked Janos.

Puffed up and leaning back in his chair, he answered, "As I said before, they know talent when they see it."

"Okay," said Janos, "but how did they happen to see it?"

"Oh, I was just doing my civic duty a few weeks ago. Actually, it was right after the bombing that knocked out your window."

Everyone nodded and automatically looked at Ilonka, remembering her injuries from that day. For a moment, Gombos forgot about himself and remembered to be attentive to Ilonka. "How are you feeling, my dear?" he gushed as he tenderly put his hand on her shoulder in a gesture of concern.

"I'm fine," she said quietly, instinctively moving her entire body away from him.

"That's good." Resuming his self-centred talk, Gombos said, "A few days after that I noticed two Americans hiding in the forest on the other side of town. I assume they were shot down in the bombing or the air-battle that followed. They got hungry, caught a rabbit, and their cooking fire gave them away. I went straight to police headquarters in Győr to report them."

"You reported them?" echoed Ilonka.

"Of course, dear. Why wouldn't I? They are the enemy," he said casting Endre and Janos a glance that said, Sheesh! Women. They just don't get it, do they?

Neither Endre nor Janos said anything.

"Well anyway," continued Gombos, "it was total chaos at the station, but eventually the Russian captain noticed me and asked why I was there. I told him about the Americans. Well, he was pleased. He told everyone to stop what they were doing immediately. Then, he told them that I was exactly the kind of loyal patriot that this country needed and immediately appointed me to the post of police chief."

The stunned silence was finally broken by Janos, "What did the current police chief think of that?"

"He wasn't there." Gombos hesitated. "I think they shot him."

"Shot him!" exclaimed Ilonka.

"Yes dear, but you needn't worry," imagining her exclamation to be an expression of her concern for his safety should he take that post. "They shot him because he had previously fought on the Russian front and wasn't now willing to work for Russian bosses. He wasn't smart enough to form an alliance with their strength."

Form an alliance with their strength. There was that phrase again. Is that what we call being a traitor these days, Janos wondered.

"But really, dear, you needn't worry," continued Gombos. "I won't make that mistake."

Ilonka was worried, but not about Gombos. Like her mother, she worried about the loyal Hungarians who had fought against the Russians. If the Russians took control of the country things would not go well for them. Her own brother had died on the Russian front. Plus, of course, she worried about Endre.

"My dear," Gombos continued, turning his attention completely to Ilonka now, "don't you see how good this is for us?"

"For us?" asked Ilonka.

"Why yes! Once we're married, you'll be the wife of an important man!"

"Oh," said Ilonka, hardly able to believe he had actually spoken those words.

Another long awkward silence followed, while everyone searched for some way to rescue Ilonka. Eventually Erzsi said, "Congratulations, Gombos! You must be very proud of yourself to have landed such an important position." Playing on Gombos' pride was usually a safe bet for turning the conversion.

"Thank you," said Gombos, as if it was about time somebody congratulated him.

"Yes, congratulations!" echoed Janos, Endre, and Ilonka, all following Erzsi's lead.

"Thank you," Gombos said again, rising from his seat to take an exaggerated bow. When he sat back down, he stopped harassing Ilonka and went back to the subject of his promotion. After that, he expounded at length on the merits of communism and what a wonderful future this would bring to Hungary.

When he finally left, Janos went out to the Horvath farm. Occasionally, he earned some extra money by repairing equipment for other farmers, and Horvath had a wagon that needed rebuilding. He didn't have much money to pay for the work, but he did have an abundant harvest this fall, so they were able to negotiate a deal.

Erzsi walked over to Mariska's to check on her friend. She knew Mariska was terribly upset. She had been eagerly anticipating that László would be home for Christmas, but now that fighting had broken out in Budapest, all leave passes were cancelled. Worse, it meant that László, was engaged in fighting again. She had hoped he would be safe in the city – behind the battle lines – but suddenly, Budapest had become the frontline, the central battleground between the Russians and the Germans. Erzsi struggled to compose some reassuring words in her head while she walked, but they all sounded hollow. In the end, she just hoped that her presence might bring some comfort.

For Ilonka, it was laundry day. She set up the wash board and collected everyone's soiled clothes. When she finished scrubbing the dirt out of everything, she hauled the dripping pile out to the yard. Endre was cleaning out the stalls, but he stopped to help her clip the wet clothes onto the drying line.

With everyone gone for the day, Ilonka and Endre looked forward to their afternoon together. The drop in the temperature made it too cold most days to sit at the foot of the ladder anymore. To solve that problem, Endre arranged some hay bales to form furniture at the back of the horse barn. With the added body heat from the animals, it was almost warm enough in the afternoons.

Since the first kiss, the loving had continued with growing intensity, but Ilonka knew where to draw the line. One afternoon, when they were home alone, she felt herself getting swept away in Endre's passion. Stop! She panicked. Oh yes she did love Endre's kisses, but she reminded herself that he was a stranger. He was not from here. One day the war would be over and Endre – the American – would go home. She dreaded the thought of having a fatherless child. She remembered Katalin and the terrible scandal surrounding the birth of Lajos. This would be even worse! At least Lajos' father was from Markota. Katalin could be excused for believing his promises of marriage, even though those promises were never fulfilled. If Endre left her and their child behind, she would be thought a complete fool. Why would any decent, self-respecting, country girl believe the promises of a foreign soldier? The thought of being the center of a scandal unnerved her. No! She was unyielding. Nothing would happen between them that could result in a war-baby.

Endre knew Ilonka's limits well although he still occasionally tried to push them, especially

Clouds Over Markota 138

when her parents were not home. Today he was being a complete gentleman, wrapping her up in a blanket to keep her warm and drawing her in to lean against him on their make-shift hay-sofa. "So, I hear you're going to be the wife of a very important man," he joked.

"Yes! And you will be in the employ of my very important husband," she teased back.

"Seriously, is he telling the truth?" asked Endre, adding, "I mean about him being police chief, not about you becoming his wife."

"I'm afraid so," answered Ilonka. "I don't know what to think anymore. The world changes so fast from one day to the next. I remember when this war was about Trianon. That made sense because it was for Hungary. The Germans were helping us. These days we hear the horrible stories about what the Germans are doing to the Jews. That's why you and the Allies are here, right? To stop the Nazis? On the other hand, are the Russians any better? Why do some people think it's good for our country to be ruled by Russian Communists? Why shouldn't Hungary be ruled by Hungarians?"

"I hope Hungary will be free one day," said Endre, talking like an optimistic American. More realistically, he added, "but in the meantime, if what Gombos said is true, I'm afraid communist rule may be next."

"It's already started," stated Ilonka flatly. "I heard on Magyar Radio, while I was doing the wash, that Budapest is in ruins and the Germans are in retreat. The Russians have moved their command from Debrecen to Budapest, and they've brought Rakosi back from Moscow to run the Hungarian Communist Party."

Endre added. "And, they're installing goons like Gombos into positions of authority because they are easy to control. The goons, in turn, keep the rest of the citizens under control." Endre knew this meant through the use of terror but he refrained from saying so.

"Then who will help us?" asked Ilonka. "Will the Americans?"

"I don't know," answered Endre honestly.

CHAPTER SEVEN

László woke early. On the briefing board he noticed the date, February 15, 1945. Three months had passed since he was last home. Christmas had come and gone without any sign of peace on earth or goodwill towards men, only bombs falling and bullets flying through the city streets. The Germans had been driven out of Budapest. Maybe now he'd be allowed a few days leave to go home to Mariska. That was his one hopeful thought. All the rest were gloomy.

Dressed in civilian clothes, he stepped out onto Ulloi St. and turned towards Kalvin Square. From there he walked down to the Danube. The bridges. Budapest's beautiful bridges demolished. The sight threw his thoughts into a rage. Damn the Germans! Why did they have to be so arrogant? Blowing up our bridges! Taking over Buda Castle to set up their high command! It was that damned German superiority that drove our men to desertion. They didn't want to be subservient to the Germans. Who could blame them?

Calmed a little by the rhythm of his own steps, he had to admit that it wasn't that simple. Nothing ever was. Sure, German attitudes drove some Hungarian soldiers to defect to the Soviet side, but there were other soldiers and civilians who became even more German – more Nazi, he corrected himself – became even more Nazi than the worst of the Germans. The Danube quay he walked on at this moment was still blood-stained. The Arrow Cross – the Hungarian Nazis – had rounded up Jewish citizens, marched them down here, shot them, and dumped their dead and nearly-dead bodies into the icy river below. For the Arrow Cross, the Siege of Budapest was just another opportunity to spill Jewish blood. As the Soviet troops moved in, they frantically ramped up their executions of Jews, as if this were somehow serving the country.

Budapest. The jewel of the Danube. It was. Not anymore. Buildings reduced to heaps of rubble, shattered glass, tangled wires. Bloody, broken bodies.

We should have evacuated the city. Why didn't we evacuate the city?

Civilian bodies. Body parts. Women. Children. Babies.

The bombs stopped falling. A ceasefire. People emerged from crowded bomb shelters crazed by hunger and cold. A mother called her son's name, "Misike!" He left the shelter two days ago, she told everyone she passed. He was on his way to the Gellert Springs for drinking water to bring back to his family. He must have gone this way. Did you see him? She asked no one, and everyone. He might still be here somewhere. Maybe he's hiding. "Misike," she called again.

The building was blown open. He could see into the room. A wounded man lay on a kitchen table, screaming. Was that someone trying to remove a bullet? Was he even a doctor? More screaming.

The shops were all closed. The people were hungry. A dead horse lay in the street. Swarms of people descended and hacked off whatever pieces of flesh they could before they were pushed aside by someone with a bigger knife. Injurious battles were fought over a single potato. There were bread rations, but the rations were small and the line-ups were long.

More wounded. More screaming. László became aware that, as he walked, there was an almost constant moaning sound, punctuated occasionally by screaming. It had become the sound of the city. Suffering. Crying. Sometimes a burst of gunfire.

A gas line was broken. Flames were shooting up into the sky. Hell. László looked at the rubble, smelled the death, rubbed his eyes to ease the sting. This has to be hell.

László kept walking. He could hear the mother, in the distance, still calling her son's name.

A pile of blankets. No, people huddled in blankets, in doorways, or under other precariously hanging bits of broken buildings. The electricity was off. There was no heat. February. Freezing cold.

The Chain Bridge, used to be the Chain Bridge. László didn't want to see another demolished bridge. He turned away from the Danube and walked towards Voros Marty Square. The elegant square was a favorite hangout of the fashionable Budapesters and their international visitors. Today, Voros Marty Square was just another scene of restaurants and stores smashed and looted. And bodies. Everywhere bodies.

Bodies in German uniforms; bodies in Russian uniforms; bodies in Hungarian uniforms; and civilians.

The German army received organized food drops. Many hungry civilians were shot trying to snatch these. The Red Army lived off the land, plundering and looting. They had no supply chain, so they helped themselves to whatever they wanted, shooting anyone who tried to stop them.

The Russians took no prisoners. For the Germans, there was no chance of surrendering. The Russians just slaughtered everyone.

The Germans were arrogant but the Red Army was hungry and mean. Soviet soldiers had forced unarmed civilians to walk ahead of them as living shields. They might as well be animals, thought László, for all they know or care about civilized rules of engagement or the Geneva Convention. Women were being hidden everywhere. Soviet gangs went on raping rampages. Dirty and diseased.

László felt sick and angry at the thought. It was his duty to protect the women of Hungary. His Mariska. He wanted nothing more than to go home to her. What was happening in Markota? Not this, he hoped.

Another poster. László tore it down. The Arrow Cross militia had plastered the city with posters, advising the population that anyone found to be hiding a Jew would be executed. László ripped it up and watched the pieces flutter to the ground.

A passbook caught his eye. He picked it up. Someone's identification papers, probably falsified. Student groups tried to help the Jews by forging identification papers. Raoul Wallenberg, a Swedish diplomat, the Vatican, plus the governments of Sweden, Spain, and Portugal, declared Jews living in their safe-houses to be under their protection, but the street gangs had little respect for any government authority.

The Germans were gone, replaced by the Russians. Nowhere did László see signs of celebration. Where were those who defected to the Russian side and those who hoped for deliverance by the Soviets?

László had no sympathy for the Nazis, but he really could not get his head around the idea of the Soviets as their savior, their liberator. Hungarians had a sense of familiarity with the Germans. They had co-ruled an empire; they had, at times, been allies. Most Hungarians spoke at least some German and viewed Germany as part of civilized Europe. Russia, on the other hand, was perceived as backward and barbaric, culturally foreign. Hungarians wanted a neutral and independent Hungary but, despite Horthy's efforts, there was no deal with the Allies. The only choice left was between the Germans and the Soviets.

Churches in ruins. Restaurants, stores, shot full of holes. Cemeteries vandalized. László heard sporadic gunfire as he walked.

A Russian soldier passed by, pushing a baby carriage full of loot – the loot of the bourgeois. László and his men had laughed at that. To these savage brutes, anyone who owned two pairs of pants was bourgeois.

At least half the buildings are destroyed, thought László. Probably all were damaged, but at least half were completely destroyed. Hitler had promised to defend Budapest – every street, every building – but it was the Luftwaffe that finally bombed the bridges. The beautiful bridges. Damn the Germans! And damn the Russians too!

A troop of Russian soldiers marched nearby, carrying submachine guns. László turned down the next street, instinctively avoiding their attention.

He turned again at Karoly Kert, a right turn back towards the barracks. There were other people walking the streets that morning, but mostly men. The women were hiding from the marauding Russians. Men scavenged through garbage piles. Vacant eyes. These were the survivors.

CHAPTER EIGHT

The overnight snowfall gave a fresh, clean look to the first day of March 1945. The town of Markota was still asleep at three o'clock in the morning, but Janos was sitting quietly in the dark kitchen.

The question of what to do with Endre was troubling him. It was obvious that Endre and Ilonka had grown very close. Under different circumstances, Janos would have been nothing but delighted with that. He liked Endre. It was almost uncanny how well he fit into the family. In quiet moments like this, it would be easy to forget how dangerous it was to have him here. Of course, he never really forgot. Ever since Endre arrived, five and a half months earlier, Janos had been searching for a way to move him along safely. In his mind he had run through endless scenarios, but each one was judged too dangerous and had to be discarded.

The fast-changing political landscape only intensified Janos' worries. With the Communists increasing their stronghold, and men like Gombos being put into positions of power, there was a fresh sense of apprehension rising. If communism enclosed Hungary within its iron curtain, the options would soon become even more limited.

There was nothing he could do on his own, he realized. He would have to risk trusting someone.

Who could be trusted these days? Who could help? Perhaps László. Every time he went through his mental check-list, he came back to László.

Ever since Mariska first mentioned that László might be coming home for the holidays, Janos had been wondering if László was the man. His recent promotion to the rank of major in the Hungarian army certainly could be helpful. At one time, Janos would have said he knew László well, but war changes people. Had László changed?

They were all hoping – especially Mariska – that László would make it home for Christmas but, as the fight over Budapest intensified, it became obvious that no soldier would be allowed to leave. Finally, László was home, but only for three days. And for that, he said, he had to cash in a lot of favors. The city was a disaster zone. The army was needed to restore order and help with the clean up.

Decision time. If he was going to ask for László's help, it would have to be today. Janos walked over to the window, so he could read his watch in the moonlight, 3:35. He couldn't talk to anyone yet. He still had a few more hours to spend in torturous rumination. Reminding himself again and again, I have to trust someone.

Sitting in the dark, his mind wandered over the events of the last few months. They had heard the horrifying reports on Magyar Radio and yesterday they heard László's first hand account of what had happened in Budapest. The Soviets closed in, but the occupying Germans didn't let go without a fight. The Hungarian army, once again, fought alongside its old ally, Germany. By Christmas day, the city was surrounded by Soviet troops, and the combined Hungarian-German forces were vastly outnumbered. Buildings crumbled in the mass bombings. Together, the Hungarian and Germany armies lost forty thousand soldiers in the bloody siege plus, László estimated, the Red Army lost double that, and at least another forty thousand civilians also died in the city, in just the last two months. "But the thing I'll never forgive," László had said, "was that the Luftwaffe – hadn't Hitler declared that he'd defend Budapest street by street? – bombed the bridges of Budapest, the beautiful bridges that spanned the Danube, even the magnificent Szechenyi Chain Bridge, bombed by the Germans as they retreated. Gratuitous destruction." He shook his head.

Janos checked the time again, 4:15. He heard Sanyi tossing restlessly in his bed, and remembered the youth of Budapest. Even while the Soviets and the Germans were fighting over Hungary, angry kids not much older than Sanyi and Lajos, organized into the para-Nazi Arrow Cross organization, went on a killing spree. They were killing Jews, primarily, but any citizen – if the rebels believed he had more wealth than they had – could become a target. Complete anarchy, thought Janos.

Ever since the Soviets gained control of the country, the radio had been broadcasting promises of communist bliss. Did anyone believe this drivel? Janos wondered.

His thoughts returned to the problem of Endre. Yes, he reaffirmed his decision. Talking to László today might be his last chance. If the borders weren't actually closed yet, they soon would be.

Janos wanted to go and talk to László first thing this morning, but he couldn't bring himself to intrude on Mariska's precious time with her husband. He forced himself to be patient. Erzsi had invited them over for lunch, so Janos knew he would have his opportunity in a few hours. In the meantime, he noticed that the sun was starting to come up, so he could distract himself with chores.

Janos picked his way through the morning, his hands milking the cow, pouring feed into the trough for the pigs, and pitching hay to the horses, while his mind swirled around in search of the right words.

The hours dragged on, but eventually, his guests arrived. Janos was anxious all through lunch. He was paying very close attention to everything László said, trying to read meaning behind words and innuendo between lines that would tell him how he might feel about the American sitting at the table with them. Finally, lunch was eaten and while Erzsi began clearing the table, Janos invited László to walk with him down by the river.

Along the banks of the Keszegér, the small talk turned serious. Janos began tentatively, "I have a situation…. I need your advice…"

László waited. He had noticed during lunch that his friend was on edge.

"It's about Endre…"

"Your nephew? Is something wrong?"

"Endre's not really my nephew…" There was no way to say this except to get straight to the point. "He's an American pilot."

László was silent for so long that the momentary relief Janos felt was beginning to freeze back into fear.

"An American pilot?" echoed László.

"Yes," said Janos weakly.

"Who else knows?"

"No one," said Janos. If this went badly, he'd take the blame for the whole thing. He'd say he lied to everyone about Endre's identity, even to his family.

"That's good," said László.

Janos wiped his sweaty palms on his pant legs.

"We need to get him out of here quickly," said László.

"Then you will help?" asked Janos, relieved.

"I'll do what I can," said the major, but he looked puzzled. "I've met some Americans in Budapest, but never one that spoke Hungarian like Endre does."

"His parents are Hungarian. They moved to America and Endre was born there."

László nodded. That explained it. "Actually," he admitted, "I have quite a few American contacts. We've done some operations in support of the Allies."

"Hitler's a madman. He must be stopped," said Janos.

"He will be," said László.

Returning to the subject of Endre, Janos said, "I've been trying to figure out a way to get him out of here ever since he arrived."

"We need to act quickly. The Communists are already closing the borders," said László.

Janos agreed. "So, what can we do?"

László knew of an underground network that worked to return Allied airmen to the west. "If he were in Budapest, I could probably make arrangements to get him back to England."

Janos nodded. That sounded promising.

"However," cautioned László, "Time is running out. Now that the Russians have control of the country, that window will close."

"Then we need to get him to Budapest," ventured Janos.

"That may be difficult because the entire countryside is crawling with Russians," said László.

"What if he were a Russian?" asked Janos.

"What do you mean?"

Janos was remembering the Russian uniforms the boys found. László had already been entertained with the tale of the boys' antics. He considered the plan. "Does he speak Russian?"

"No, only Hungarian and English," answered Janos.

"Then it would be dangerous to put him in a Russian uniform. If he's confronted by Russian soldiers and can't reply in Russian… that will end badly."

"You're right, of course," acknowledged Janos. "Can he travel to Budapest as a Hungarian civilian?"

"I think so, especially as a wounded ex-soldier, the role he's already playing." László contemplated that for a few more minutes before giving his final verdict, "Yes, I think that will work."

Janos felt fifty pounds lighter. He was so relieved, not only to share the burden of this secret with a trusted friend, but also to be presented with a solution to the problem that had been weighing so heavily on his mind.

Gombos had been making himself comfortable at his new post and additional constables were being assigned to his staff daily. None of them had any investigative experience or training in law, but no one seemed concerned about that. They were all good party men, committed to the cause. No experience; no training; but lots of enthusiasm; together they would build a bright new Hungary.

To Gombos, the future looked wonderful. Only one piece was missing from his perfect world: Ilonka. Why did she sometimes seem cold towards him? Was there someone else? Nonsense, he told himself. Who could offer her more? He was sure she merely needed a little coaxing. She was probably just shy or playing hard to get. Girls are like that sometimes, he told himself. He had been patient long enough. Today he would have his answer.

The Police Chief decided to make good use of the power at his disposal. He dispatched one of his minions to watch the Farkas house and report to him when the parents went out. By noon he had word back that Erzsi and Janos were not at home. They left the house with a young man. Oh yeah, that would be Endre, Gombos realized. He had forgotten about the cousin living there. No matter, he wasn't there now, so Ilonka was alone. He set off for the Farkas house.

This afternoon Ilonka was scrubbing clothes when Gombos appeared at the front door.

He was wearing his new police uniform. On another man it might have looked handsome. On Gombos, it looked ridiculous. With inane charm, Gombos handed her a sparse bouquet of flowers. She accepted it only out of the instinctive impulse to put your hand out when something is being thrust at you.

"Ilonka, will you accompany me for a walk?" asked Gombos.

She stumbled for an answer, "I can't. I have to get all this laundry done for mother."

"Oh, my dear," he said patronizingly, "the laundry can wait. Walk with me."

Quietly, Ilonka repeated her refusal.

Letting a little irritation show, he said, "Alright then. Make me a coffee and we'll talk here."

Reluctantly, Ilonka agreed to that. He followed her into the kitchen, prattling on about how communism had made their lives better. "Take the Jews, for example," he said. "As the Soviets drove the Nazis out of Budapest, they freed seventy thousand Hungarian Jews awaiting deportation. They owe their lives to the benevolence of communism."

Ilonka switched off the gas burner and brought the coffee to the table.

"Of course, some people think the country would be better off without the Jews after all," concluded Gombos, seating himself at the kitchen table.

Ilonka poured the coffee and sat down.

Gombos began again, "Ilonka, you know I've been waiting a long time to ask you this."

Ilonka panicked, fearing what was coming.

"You know how much I've always adored you."

She looked away, hoping he would stop.

Noticing her averted eyes, he tried to regain her interest by making her jealous, "You may not know this," he said, "but I've had girls throwing themselves at me. I've even had mothers come to me and ask me to marry their daughters to secure their futures, but you're the only one for me Ilonka. Everything I have will be yours."

The only thing Ilonka could hope to do was change the subject, "Oh Gombos, what will happen to your store now that you're the chief of police?"

Taking the bait, Gombos answered, "it will have to close. There is no private business in communism. We all work together for the good of everyone. Private enterprise is for selfish capitalists. All the farmers will work in collectives and everyone will share in the bounty equally."

Mistaking her question to be motivated by concern for herself and how she would get the rare consumer goods he used to bring her, he added, "but you have nothing to worry about. With my senior position there are some nice perks, a good house, and maybe even a car some day."

"But I thought everyone was supposed to be equal," queried Ilonka with feigned innocence.

"Sure," Gombos added patronizingly, "but good work is rewarded."

"I see," said Ilonka, rising to clear the table and hoping that he would take that as his cue to leave.

Instead, he stood also, caught her hands in his and asked, "Ilonka, will you be my wife?" There it was, spoken at last.

Ilonka gasped, taken aback at actually hearing the question. "No!" she said firmly. "I will not." Softening her answer, she added, "I am simply not ready to consider marriage." She tried to pull her hands from his.

Rising to his feet and tightening his grip, he argued foolishly, "Ilonka, darling, you're not getting any younger you know."

"My age isn't the issue, Gombos," she said, hoping she could leave it at that. She tried again to break his grasp on her wrists.

This time when he tightened his grip he hurt her and she let out a cry.

"Please go," she said. "The boys will be home from school soon. I need to start their dinner, and mother and father will be hungry too… and Endre," she added quickly realizing that she had omitted his name from the list.

The mere mention of Endre's name was enough to upset Gombos. Even in his ego-enhancing uniform, there was something about Endre that intimidated Gombos so much that he immediately released his grip on Ilonka. He left without a word, but he was fuming.

All the way back to the police station, his thoughts churned, growing increasingly menacing. Who did this country girl think she was, declining an offer of marriage from a man of his rank and importance? Then jealously he thought, maybe there is someone else. Who is this cousin from Arad? Suppose he's not a cousin. He remembered the way they danced at the ball. And the English he thought he heard the boys speak. If he isn't a cousin, why would he be pretending to be a cousin?

Self-righteously, his venomous thoughts continued. Could it be that this family that I have been so generous with has been harboring a fugitive right under my nose? He remembered Janos' response – non-response really – when he told him about the Americans he turned in, and how shocked Ilonka was. Maybe.

"Oh! No! They shot me! Eject! Eject! Eject!" shouted Lajos before he jumped from the roof of the schoolhouse, holding an open umbrella as if it were a parachute.

The girls gasped and the boys laughed. Even Miss Barsi smiled before reprimanding him and lecturing him on the dangers of jumping from rooftops.

Lajos was in full swing now. He had an audience. With both feet firmly planted on the ground, he went on entertaining: "Did you hear about the robbery last night?" He paused for effect... "Two clothes pins held up a pair of pants!"

Lajos liked to leave them laughing, so this was an opportune moment to quit. He found Sanyi in the crowd, and the two boys headed home to do their chores.

When they burst through the kitchen door, they found Ilonka crying. "What's wrong?" Lajos asked.

On their way home they had seen Gombos in his new police chief uniform. "Was he here? Did he upset you?" Sanyi asked perceptively.

"No," Ilonka answered honestly. "It's not him," but she would say no more. She wiped her eyes and went back to cooking supper.

The boys exchanged a look and a shrug, and then went out to the yard to look for Endre. Not finding him anywhere, they came back in. "Where's Endre?" they asked Ilonka.

"He went to Mariska's with *Apu* and *Anyu*," she replied, trying hard to sound casual.

The boys knew that something unusual was going on, but Ilonka wasn't saying anything more.

Resignedly, they went outside to do their chores, expecting that everyone would be home soon for supper and then they'd learn what the big mystery was.

Janos and Erzsi came home for supper, as expected, but Endre was not with them.

"Where is he?" they queried insistently.

Again the casual tone seemed forced, "He's staying over at Mariska's to help her and László with some work around the house. He'll be home tomorrow," said Janos.

"Has something happened to Endre?" Lajos demanded, unable to contain his fear.

"No." Janos wanted to trust the boys with the plan, but the stakes were too high tonight, not only for Endre but also for László. "He's safe," was all he said.

The two officers liked each other immediately. László was intrigued by Endre when he thought he was Janos' nephew, and he liked him even better now that he knew he was a military pilot. The fact that their two countries were at war should have made them enemies, but time and circumstance reduced that to a technicality. From László's point of view, he was fighting for Hungary. The German alliance was a matter of survival. Being geographically in the middle-space, between Germany and Russia, precluded neutrality.

As the two political monsters stormed towards each other, in their efforts to conquer Europe, Hungary would eventually be over run by one or the other. Allying with Germany seemed like the best bet for Hungary's primary goal in this war, to regain territory lost after WWI. From Endre's point of view, he was sent to Europe to stop the Nazis. The reason his plane was in Hungarian airspace was that Hungary had fallen to Nazi occupation and the Nazis had commandeered Hungarian factories. But the Hungarian blood that coursed through the veins of both men transcended all politics. On the journey to Budapest they were not enemies. They were two officers with a trunk-full of war stories to share.

The major was an infantry soldier. He had lived in the trenches for months on end. He knew what it was like to be freezing cold, soaking wet, hungry, and dysentery-sick with bullets flying over his head. He told Endre things that he would never have told Mariska.

He told the tale of his friend, a young lieutenant, who longed to be a pilot. "He wanted nothing to do with the infantry," recalled László. "He dismissed the land-forces as a bunch of brainless grunts. Unfortunately for him, his vision was too poor to be a pilot, but he was very bright and a natural leader so, ironically, he was put into infantry officer training. He hated it, at first," recalled László. "But over time, you could see the change in him. I remember one night when he came back mud-covered and exhausted from a successful, strategically-complicated attack. He was so proud of the mission's accomplishment and the safe return of all of his men, but the exact moment when I knew he had really become an infantry officer was when I heard him wonder out loud if pilots ever had to sweat this hard!"

Endre smiled. He'd heard that kind of talk before.

The train station was six kilometers away. They walked under cover of darkness, hoping no one would notice that Endre was gone until at least the next day, and much later would be even better. Crossing the highway, they were delayed by the passing of a long Russian military convoy. Cargo trucks and tanks clattered past them while they waited. When there was a short break in the procession, the two officers made a dash for the other side.

They arrived at the station just as the sun was rising. Before long, they saw the locomotive lumbering towards them, chugging itself out of the morning fog. "We'll be in Budapest by noon," László said.

The major's story about his lieutenant friend reminded Endre of an army general he knew in England, who also didn't believe that pilots were real soldiers. He used to say their lives are cushy. They live on luxurious bases. All they do is a few hours of flying a day, only when it's their turn, and only when the weather happens to be nice. A real soldier is at his post twenty-four hours a day, seven days a week, in constant danger, regardless of weather conditions. He holds his ground.

"Eventually, my commanding officer got fed up with listening to this and invited the general to fly with our squadron on a night mission. He was assigned to my bomber," said Endre. "When he saw my crew, smoking cigarettes and bantering lightly before boarding the Flying Fortress, he looked smug. He said it was more like a Sunday afternoon picnic than a war.

"The flight began normally. The engines were running at a low rumble and I ran through my pre-flight instrument and equipment checks: charts, radio, altimeter, oxygen masks, intercom... check. Each man took up his position. Stations confirmed their readiness: bombardier, navigator, top turret, ball turret, tail gunner... check. The general made himself comfortable – well as comfortable as he could on a bench seat just behind the cockpit.

"Before us, a parade of planes rolled towards the runway. With the first dozen already in the air, the controllers directed our take-offs in thirty second intervals." Endre recalled the feel of the large aircraft beginning to roll – slowly at first – as he eased off the brake, then the power of the four engines under his command roared to life as he pushed the throttle to the wall. The bomber increased speed and the runway lights blurred into one shiny line, until the heavily loaded airplane lifted into the sky.

"Within a few minutes, we lost all visibility. We were enveloped by fog and completely dependent on our instruments. This worried the general," smiled Endre. "He asked me if we were going to collide with another plane. 'I hope not,' I told him. I wanted to leave it at that. It would have been so much fun to leave him sweating in the dark, but I decided to be kind and explain that, provided each plane held steady its compass heading, altitude, and speed, the separation at launch would get us safely through the fog.

"Ten minutes later, our bomber broke through the cloud ceiling and the general was treated to a glorious view of the stars that even seasoned airmen were awed by. There was no chatter amongst the crew now." Endre remembered the sensation of soaring between the glittering stars above and the dark ocean waves below as the Flying Fortress pressed on, carrying its deadly cargo towards its target.

"Once out of the clouds, we tightened our formations. It's unnerving to fly with wingtips only inches apart, but it's a good defensive strategy for the Fortress because a tight formation can put out a protective wall of bullets.

"Our engines droned on. As we approached enemy airspace, I warned my crew that we might expect to see some action soon, and sure enough, the Germans appeared almost on cue. Up ahead, one flaming fighter was already going down. We were too far away to tell if that was one of ours or a German."

Endre recalled, "At this point in the mission, there is a palpable tension that permeates the aircraft, but I glanced back and saw that the general was still feeling safe. After all, he was a seasoned fighter. He had seen men die face to face; he wasn't much moved by a distant fireball falling from the sky.

"Then the agitated voice of one of my gunners broke the silence, 'bandit two o'clock high!' he called. The bullets pattered against our fuselage like hail stones, but friendly fighters rushed to our aid. They appeared from above, below, and between the enemy fighters with lightning speed, and we were spared. The general was impressed. 'Nice!' I remember hearing him say over the headset.

"Directly ahead of us, though, a different story was unfolding. A pack of Focke Wulfs had succeeded in isolating a bomber and they were furiously pumping it full of bullets. There was nothing I could do. Helplessly, I held my own heading. The general was quiet now. The targetted Fortress was damaged and fell out of formation. We saw the disabled bomber drop its artillery to lighten its load and begin to limp towards home, but the Germans didn't let it go. They continued their attack. The Fortress began to spiral and the black smoke streamed out behind it. I counted four parachutes before the explosion that signaled the end of the doomed bomber's flight."

László nodded.

"Two minutes to target,' I heard my navigator say. Around, above, below – everywhere – exploding shells from anti-aircraft guns. I held our course, telling myself that I hadn't come all this way to miss my mark.

"On the starboard side, one of our fighters burst into flames before the pilot could eject. It turned into yet another fireball falling from the sky. All around us, shells exploded ceaselessly, punching holes in planes.

"The general looked a little pale now. I could see that he was ready to go home, but it was three more eternal seconds before we were in position to release our cargo. Finally, I heard, 'Bombs away!'... And that was the same moment when we were hit."

"Oh," said László, following the story.

"Yeah," continued Endre, "One of my gunners died instantly at his post. He was badly torn apart, actually. I was struck by some flying debris. I wasn't injured, but I did lose control and we took a downward plunge. By the time I regained control of the aircraft, we had lost significant altitude.

"One engine was hit and quit. A second engine was catching, but sputtering. The other two weren't putting out maximum thrust either. I considered our options. We could bail now while we were still over land – but behind enemy lines – or we could attempt to limp home over the vast sea. I chose the sea.

"My navigator took quite a bump in the attack, but he was able to re-establish our heading. Once we were back on course, I took stock of the situation onboard: one man was dead; two men were dying, with two others engaged in the frantic attempt to stem the flow of blood. The general, to his credit, promptly undid his lap belt and joined in the first aid effort. Everyone else was knocked around somewhat, but not injured.

"Our course led us back out over the water. When we were well out to sea, the second engine quit. That left two engines, the outer engine on each wing, neither performing to full capacity. We were still airborne, but I didn't know if that would last all the way to England or if we'd have to ditch. To avoid detection, we were already flying low, just above the crest of the waves. We weren't home yet, but at least no one was shooting at us.

"As we approached land, we faced a new challenge, the towering cliffs on the English shoreline. I didn't know if we had enough power to make the ascent.

"I asked for a status report on the two injured men. The news was bad. Our tally was upgraded to three dead. The status report on the lifeboats was not good either. They were damaged, unusable. Our best option seemed to be to keep flying and try to reach the shore. To lighten our load as much as possible, we tossed everything expendable, the machine guns, the ammunition, the radio that wasn't working anyway. Still, with the diminished strength of the engines, it was doubtful that we'd get enough altitude to clear the cliff. Again, I considered ditching.

"Over my headset, I heard, 'what if we put our three dead overboard?' I caught the general's head snap as he looked at me to see what I was going to say about that. I didn't know what I was going to say. My crewman's voice continued haltingly, 'I know it's not... but maybe under the circumstances... I don't mean to be...' I really didn't have much time to consider the ethics of the dilemma. I only knew I didn't want to do it. I calculated around five hundred pounds. That could make a difference, so I instructed my crew to check all three again for signs of life. They did. 'Negative,' they reported." Endre paused. "The general nodded his silent approval."

So did László.

"I hesitated. I had to try one more thing: I tested the throttle. The fragile response was discouraging. I gave the order. I've second guessed it a hundred times, but – who knows – it may have saved the rest of my crew. The cliffs on the shoreline were growing more distinct. It was time to pull for all the lift I could get. The general picked this moment to ask if we were going to make it. I remember telling him, we'd know in a minute.

"We made it. We cleared the craggy ridge but, by then, I knew that my ailing aircraft had given all it had. I dumped the remaining fuel, let down the landing gear, and advised the crew that we were touching down. I've never heard such creaking and cracking as when that Flying Fortress ploughed across the rugged terrain until the starboard wing caught a tree, spun us around, and finally brought us to a halt.

"I ordered everyone off the plane. Even though I had dumped the fuel, I was still concerned about the possibility of an explosion. The general was the first one off."

Aboard the train to Budapest, the two officers chuckled at each other's stories. Each acknowledging that war is hell, whether it is fought on the ground or in the air.

CHAPTER NINE

The boys had finished their chores and gone off to school, leaving Ilonka and her parents to finish their morning coffees. Their sad faces said it all. Life was just not the same without Endre. Ilonka hadn't said much, but the redness in her eyes revealed that she had been crying. Wordlessly, she rose to begin cleaning the kitchen when suddenly there was a loud banging on the front door.

Janos frowned, "I'll get that."

It was an authoritative knock, like when the soldiers came to demand lodging or other supplies. Opening the door he saw two of Gombos' officers, although the Police Chief himself was nowhere in sight.

"Yes?" asked Janos stiffly.

"We have a report that you are harboring an American fugitive," said the constable.

"A what!" said Janos with forced astonishment.

"We'll need to search the premises," he said, pushing his way into the house. Now Janos could see that the two constables were backed up by six Russian soldiers. The army of eight stormed the house and yard.

Ilonka let out a scream when one of the Russians pushed her aside brusquely and started throwing things around the kitchen.

Erzsi wrapped her arms around her daughter, pulled her into a corner on the floor and held tightly to her, trying to appear small – or even invisible – but she couldn't keep herself from trembling.

They ransacked the entire property, the house, the barn, the hay-loft, but came up empty handed.

"Where is he?" demanded the lead constable.

"Where is who?" replied Janos, standing his ground.

"The American named Endre," he boomed.

"Endre!" exclaimed Janos in convincing disbelief. "Who's ever heard of an American named Endre? Endre is as Hungarian as St. Istvan. He is my nephew. He was staying here with us until two days ago when he went back to his family in Arad. Where is the crime in that?" demanded Janos, going on the offensive.

"We'll need to conduct an investigation," said the constable.

"You just did! You tore my whole place apart. You can see with your own eyes that there is nobody here," argued Janos.

Even so, there was an investigation. The Police Chief insisted on it. The constables went door-to-door and asked everyone for information about Endre. All of the neighbors confirmed that Endre was the son of Janos' sister. Some people remembered her well and that seemed proof enough to them. Nobody could give any reason to suspect Endre of being an American. In fact, most people thought the suggestion quite ludicrous.

To Gombos' great embarrassment, the investigation concluded that Endre was Hungarian. To his communist bosses he protested, "A Hungarian that speaks English!" But it fell on deaf ears because the investigation found no evidence that Endre had ever spoken English. Nevertheless, his zeal was commended. Men who were that passionate about defending the country against capitalist Americans were highly valued by the new regime.

The communist stronghold on Hungary was becoming more powerful each day. Since the fall of Budapest, the Russian presence was growing. Their tank convoys rattled through the nights. Their bad-mannered, poorly-supplied, and vodka-soaked troops swept a new wave of terror across the countryside.

Store shelves were bare all across the country. Communism promised bounty to the workers, but already there was less of everything.

Rising poverty touched every household. Ultimately, it didn't even matter that people had no money because there was nothing to buy.

Under Gombos' command, the population was squeezed out of even the little they had. Corrupt police officers charged the poor farmers protection money. People were executed for allegedly harboring capitalist spies because they could not or would not pay the extortionists.

Occasionally, Gombos still made gestures towards Ilonka, promising her rare luxuries if she were his wife. Increasingly, his overtures became tinged with a threatening tone. Not only would she have to forego the comforts he could give her, but life might get even more difficult for her and her family. She began to grow fearful, but she also grew to hate Gombos almost beyond the point where she could even maintain cordiality. It appalled her that such a despicable man should be given so much power and be allowed to abuse it so blatantly. She frightened her parents when she declared, "I'd rather kill myself than become his wife." The only thing there was no shortage of was fear.

It was a very somber Easter weekend in Markota. Maybe religion wasn't exactly against the law yet, but who could know? Laws were made up daily at the whim of thugs with guns. People were certainly beginning to understand that communism was opposed to religion. The opium of the people, Karl Marx called it. There was no God. The State would answer all your prayers, create a benevolent society, and meet all your needs. If the State can do all that, who needs God?

The Farkas family had been in church every Sunday for longer than anyone could remember. Their babies were baptized, their young men and women were married, and their dead were buried at the Mindenszentek Church in the center of Markota. Generations of family concerns were offered up to God from the pews within. No one quite knew if it was safe to go to church, so the pews were not as full at this year's Good Friday service as they had been in other years.

Ilonka went. She had to. Who, but God, was big enough to deal with these troubles, she wondered, as she knelt with her face buried in her hands. Crying softly, she unloaded her burdened heart.

After the service people talked quietly, fearful of the communist ears that might be in their midst. Was it now illegal to go to church? Nobody knew for sure, but the dark tension cast a long shadow over the Easter season. Even the children were tense. Sanyi was louder than usual. Lajos was more quiet.

On Saturday night, Erzsi reminded the boys to go to church for confession so they could receive communion on Easter Sunday. Sanyi went first. While Lajos awaited his turn, he searched his conscience in earnest to find the things he knew he had done wrong. After all, he reasoned, there was no sense in trying to hide anything from God. He remembered the scuffle he got into last week. No, he shouldn't have punched György, but he asked for it. György was a hooligan, always looking for a brawl. On those grounds, Lajos was not thoroughly convinced of his own guilt. Still, he thought, God was probably not happy about people getting punched. He decided he would confess it, but in the confessional he also admitted that – because György started it – he wasn't sorry all the way down to the bottom of his heart. Father Kiraly smiled at the boyish reasoning.

The boys started towards home along the dusty road. The politics were ugly, but at least the weather was beautiful. On this warm spring night, crickets chirped and the nearly-full moon shone in the sky, bathing the trees in a silvery light. Occasionally, a gentle evening breeze blew between the branches, and the branches responded in the quiet whisper of new leaves. The calm was broken when the peaceful whispering of the trees was swallowed by the droning. Somewhere on high, beneath the sparkling stars, war planes were fighting in Hungarian airspace. Not only the full moon and the stars were shining in the sky, but also the fire from anti-aircraft guns in the distance. The explosions lit the nightscape. The boys knew they should hurry home but they couldn't quite manage to tear themselves away. Soon the countryside was quiet again. Clouds moved in and covered the twinkling sky and, slowly, a gentle rain began to sprinkle the ground, tears for those for whom the sun would not rise tomorrow.

Hitler shot himself. Rumors swirled that perhaps he wasn't really dead; perhaps he had only gone into hiding somewhere. Nevertheless, Germany surrendered one week later on May 7, 1945, and on May 8 the war was officially over.

The end of the war was wonderful news, but the icing on the cake for the Farkas family – especially for Ilonka – was that Gombos was being promoted and transferred to Debrecen, far away, on the eastern side of the country. Most folks wondered how such a man could possibly get promoted, but Ilonka and her family were so relieved to see him gone, they didn't bother to question that. While everyone else celebrated the end of the war, they also celebrated the end of Gombos.

Under the summer stars, Erzsi was breathing a sigh of relief. "It's nice to be out here on such a beautiful night and not have to worry about bombs falling," she said, holding lightly to Janos' arm as they walked through the schoolyard on their way home from Mariska's.

Janos agreed.

"And Gombos is gone," said Erzsi, "that's one less worry in our lives."

"Sure, but he's just a pawn," said Janos, "The whole evil system won't go away because he's gone. It's much bigger than him."

Erzsi heard the rustling in the trees at the edge of the yard. Probably a rabbit, she thought.

"I know," said Erzsi. "I was only thinking about Ilonka."

Erzsi could see their outlines now.

"Stop!" came the command in Russian, as the first Soviet soldier stepped out from the trees.

Janos moved in front of Erzsi protectively.

"Your papers!" demanded the soldier.

She squeezed his arm tightly.

More soldiers spilled out from the forest and ten or twelve of them formed a circle around the couple.

"Your papers!" he shouted again. This time Erzsi could smell the vodka on his breath.

Janos tried to explain that they had only gone to a neighbor's house. They had no papers with them.

The Russian glared angrily.

He doesn't understand what I'm saying, thought Janos. I don't know how to explain all of that in Russian.

"The curfew! It's dark. It's past the curfew!" screamed the Russian.

Janos understood that well enough, but this was the first he'd heard of a curfew in the town of Markota. It sounded like another one of those rules that just got made up today, he thought.

"Answer me!" screamed the Russian.

Janos searched for an answer, but he didn't remember hearing a question, at least not one that he understood. The Russian kicked him in the stomach. He doubled over and Erzsi fell on him, protectively.

"Your cards!" snapped the Russian impatiently.

They weren't party members. They had no cards, but Janos certainly didn't want to say that.

The Russian grabbed Erzsi's hair and pulled her off of Janos. A second kick caught Janos square in the face with the heavy combat boot.

Erzsi screamed and tried to pull herself back to Janos.

"Your cards… your cards…" the slurred echo was repeated menacingly around the circle as more and more Russians came out of the trees.

The Russian grabbed Erzsi and dragged her off Janos again. Another one came at her and ripped her blouse off.

Janos surged and threw himself into the fray to protect his wife, but the mob pulled them apart again.

Blood poured out of Janos' nose and he fell to the ground. He writhed under the thud of each kick. "Erzsi," he called out, extending his arm helplessly in response to her screams.

She struggled against the force of the Russian men, but it was hopeless. She could hardly breathe. The stench of vodka mixed with unbathed body odor was nauseating.

Janos tasted his blood as it streamed past his lips. His ears were filled with the sounds of Erzsi's terrified cries. He couldn't get up. He couldn't get to her. He couldn't see what was happening to her, but he knew. "Don't hurt her," he pleaded, hopelessly, as his world faded into the darkness of the night.

Ilonka woke up and knew right away that something was wrong. The house didn't sound right. There was no sound at all. It didn't smell right. *Anyu* always had the coffee brewing by now. Her feet touched the floor.

Did they get home so late that they slept in? She couldn't ever remember them sleeping in. She didn't hear them come in, but she was asleep, maybe she just didn't hear them. Stepping out of her room, she could see immediately that their bedroom door was wide open. Their bed had not been slept in.

"*Anyu*," she called. "*Apu!*"

She threw on some clothes and stepped into a pair of shoes. Mariska. They went to Mariska's last night. Maybe it got late and they decided to stay there. But it was only two streets away. That doesn't make sense, she told herself, even as she flew out the door and ran all the way to Mariska's.

She knocked on the door, commanding herself to calm down. *I don't need to rouse the whole neighborhood. They're probably here. They're probably fine. They're probably asleep.* She knocked again, a little louder this time.

"Ilonka!" said Mariska, pulling open the door to let her in.

"*Anyu, Apu!* Are they here?"

"No…"

"When did they leave?"

"Last night, a little after ten," said Mariska, seeing Ilonka's panic, lacing up her shoes and throwing on a sweater. She hurried to catch up with Ilonka, who was already walking, although she had no idea where she was going.

"Where can they be? Your house. My house. They wouldn't have stopped anywhere else, not after ten o'clock at night."

Ilonka kept walking, up one street and down another.

"Wait," said Mariska. Seeing Old Man Tivador, she stopped to ask him if he had seen Erzsi and Janos last night. He hadn't.

When they walked past the school, Mariska spotted something that looked like the blouse Erzsi was wearing last night. A chill ran through her. Ilonka caught the look on her face and followed her eyes. She saw it too.

Ilonka ran to it, picked it up, torn and bloody. She pressed it to her heart. Then she heard the crying, a quiet sobbing.

"*Anyu!*" She ran to the small crouched figure in the tall grass and saw her mother bent over her father's blood-soaked, lifeless body.

Mariska took off her sweater and gently wrapped it around to cover Erzsi, and Erzsi fell into her daughter's arms.

"Wait here," said Mariska, but she doubted that Ilonka heard her. It didn't matter. It didn't need to be said. Of course she would wait here.

Only minutes later, Mariska came running back with her brother.

Erzsi refused to leave her husband until Vince assured her that he would look after Janos. Then, Erzsi allowed Mariska and Ilonka to take her home.

Vince went to find the priest. There was no sense calling the police, and it would do no good to call the doctor. Janos was gone. He had succumbed to his injuries in the night.

Sitting alone at the foot of the loft ladder, Ilonka sat watching the chickens pecking the ground and the horse grazing lazily. She thought about her father. One of the last things she remembered him saying was that Hungary's dark days were only beginning. His gloomy prophecy. She wondered if he knew how true he spoke.

The end of the war had brought many changes. Endre was gone; her father was dead; her mother was frail.

Ilonka looked up and saw Erzsi pushing open the kitchen window.

She did that every day, but it didn't help. The nauseating smell that tormented her mind stayed so sharp in her nostrils that it still caused her to vomit sometimes, so she kept pushing the windows open trying to get more fresh air. But most of the time, she just sat quietly at the bottom of the dark pit of depression she had tumbled into.

The big white horse moved closer. Ilonka pulled a tuft of hay out of the bale she was sitting on. Laying her fingers flat, she let him eat it out of her hand. He seemed to miss the boys too.

"It's much quieter around here with them gone, isn't it?" she said to the horse.

After Janos died, they quit school and went to work at the factory in Győr. Each week they commuted the thirty kilometers together on bicycles and brought their paychecks home on the weekends. The time for childish games was over. Ilonka and Uncle Vince did what they could to keep both farms going, but after the Communists seized their share, there wasn't much left.

She took a sober tally of the situation. Russian soldiers were all over the place. Women everywhere tried to look old and unattractive, dressing in baggy clothes to avoid drawing the unwanted sexual attention of the Russians. Gangs of drunken soldiers raped mothers in front of their children and daughters in front of their fathers.

Ilonka shuddered at the thought of the nightmare her own parents had experienced. As if all the raping wasn't awful enough, venereal diseases ran rampant and no medications were available to treat the afflicted.

The Iron Curtain was drawn and there was no escape. All of life was reorganized to conform to the communist model of a productive society. The Communists boasted of their zero percent unemployment rate, but even two income families could scarcely afford life's bare necessities. School children were taught Russian. Adults who wanted to keep their jobs had to learn Russian. Farmers were forced to join collectives, through which they were robbed of their produce. To add insult to injury, farms were raided because the "wealthy" peasants were accused of secretly hoarding harvests. Factory workers were pressured to study Marxism and become card-carrying Communist Party members.

True, the war was over. But after so many lives had been lost, what had been gained? They got into the war for one reason, Trianon. Part of Transylvania was briefly recaptured, but in the end not one acre was restored. During the war, there were friendly moments with the Germans but it led to occupation by the Nazis and Budapest was bombed into rubble. Now, the Nazis were gone, only to be replaced by the Communists.

On the radio, in the newspaper, in the schools and workplaces, they were told continuously how grateful they should be that peace had finally come and that the Russians had liberated them. Ilonka noticed that everybody seemed to understand very clearly that such nonsense must never be mocked in public, and they all grew very skillful at saying one thing while meaning another.

On the weekends, when the boys were home, they all gathered around the Farkas kitchen table and vented an entire week's worth of frustrations. It was the only place where it was safe to speak freely. They were sure others felt the same way – in private – although, no contrary talk was ever heard in public. The mechanisms for control by terror were fully operational.

That's when I miss him the most, she thought, remembering her father and the many, many talks they used to have around the kitchen table.

"Ilonka," Mariska called from the window. "Come inside. I've put the coffee on." Mariska knew her way around the Farkas kitchen. She came over a few times a week to lend a hand with the household chores and to help look after Erzsi.

Ilonka got up to go, pausing just long enough to give the horse one more rub on his sleek white neck. In the kitchen, she picked up the bowl of vegetables she had left on the counter and started washing the carrots.

Mariska poured the coffee and told Ilonka how much she missed her husband. "I thought he would be home so much more often now that the war is over, but he hasn't been home much at all."

The Russians kept the Hungarian army intact, but increasingly they were transforming it into just another arm of their own military. Mariska said that László was not reconciled to serving as a major in the de facto Soviet army but, for the time being, he had no choice.

"Nothing is simple these days," Ilonka acknowledged. "Have you heard from him?"

"No, not since he was home, three weeks ago."

"Oh, that's right. He doesn't know, does he?"

"No," said Mariska sadly. László didn't know that Mariska had miscarried her pregnancy eight days ago. "He still thinks he's going to be a father."

Ilonka wanted to say something encouraging – he will be, just not this time – but since this was Mariska's third miscarriage it would have sounded hollow. Instead, she said, "sit down. You should be resting, not cooking."

"I'm okay," said Mariska, but took a seat anyway.

Loss, thought Ilonka, life is all about losses now.

"The last time he was home, before that, was March. Your dad was still here," said Mariska.

"And Endre was still here. That's when Endre left with him," remembered Ilonka. She paused to take a sip of her coffee. "I'll never forget the day I found him hiding in that bush down by the river. What a shock! There he was. At first, I was terribly worried about taking him in. All I could think of was what would happen if someone found out. Things got a lot easier after he became cousin Endre," she smiled.

"It sure helped that he spoke Hungarian," said Mariska.

"Right," agreed Ilonka. "I don't know how that would have turned out if we had not been able to talk with him. And talk we did! *Anyu, Apu,* and I had so many talks with him right here in this kitchen. And the boys," remembered Ilonka, "they loved him. He taught them English."

"He became part of the family, didn't he?"

Ilonka nodded while she fiddled with the embroidery on the tablecloth. Her fingers traced and re-traced the little red flowers. "One thing we never talked about ..." Ilonka began again, "One thing we never talked about was what would happen when the war ended. I think – maybe, in some way – I didn't want it to end because I knew it meant that he would leave. Maybe that's why we never talked about it."

"It's hard to make plans when the world is blowing up around you."

"That's it exactly," said Ilonka. "Everything just felt so uncertain." Pausing, she added, "Now things are certain – certainly awful."

"I know," said Mariska, "but we need to stay hopeful. It's true that a lot has changed for the worse, but things can change for the better too. Take Gombos, for example, he's gone."

"That's definitely a change for the better," agreed Ilonka.

"He sure made a lot of trouble for you."

"Oh yes! He was always an ugly nuisance, but when he got some power he became really scary. I can't believe he actually reported Endre. It's all thanks to your wonderful László that, by then, Endre was gone." Ilonka was silent for a moment before continuing, "On that day, I was glad he was gone, because that meant he was safe. I can't bear to think what might have happened to him if they had found him here. In the four months since he's been gone, that was the only day I was glad he wasn't here."

"Ilonka," Erzsi called from the next room.

Ilonka rose and went to her side, "Yes, *Anyu?*"

Erzsi was on the couch in the living room. Except for the deep sadness in her eyes, she was a picture of domesticity sitting there in her flowered house-smock, quietly peeling potatoes. "I'd like a glass of water, please," she said.

"Are you sure you wouldn't like to join us in the kitchen for some coffee instead?" encouraged Ilonka.

"No, I'll stay here," said Erzsi.

"Alright," smiled Ilonka. "I'll get you some water."

When Ilonka returned from the kitchen with the water, Erzsi showed her the peeled potatoes. "These are ready for the *gulyás*."

"Yes they are," said Ilonka taking the two bowls, one full of peels and the other full of potatoes. "Thank you, *Anyu.*" She brought the potatoes back into the kitchen and set them on the counter.

"It's good that you find little jobs like that for her to do," said Mariska.

"I have to. Otherwise she just sits there all day looking sad."

"I'll go in and talk with her for a while," suggested Mariska, "since she doesn't want to sit in the kitchen.

"That's a good idea," agreed Ilonka, adding water to the tub to start washing the dishes. She turned up the radio that had been playing softly.

Gloomy Sunday. The original, Hungarian title was "*Vége a Világnak,* End of the World." Ilonka had heard that the song had been picked up and made popular by the American Jazz singer, Billie Holiday, and that it had been banned by the BBC because it was rumored to have inspired hundreds of suicides.

She sang along:

*"Sunday is Gloomy;
My hours are slumberless.*

... She put another plate in the drying rack...

*Dearest, the shadows
I live with are numberless.*

... She picked up the drying rag and began to wipe the mixing bowl...

*Angels have no thought
of ever returning you.
Would they be angry
if I thought of joining you?
Gloomy Sunday."*

Ilonka reached across the kitchen sink to close the window, and noticed that the sky had darkened and a cold wind was picking up.

CHAPTER TEN

In the cozy New York State farmhouse, Eva set the pot of *paprikás csirke* on the dinner table. Taking another long look at her son, she said again, "I can't believe you're really home."

After a lengthy, covert journey across Europe, from Budapest to London, followed by a series of debriefing sessions in England with interviewers wanting to learn every detail about his time in hiding, the war was finally over. By the time Endre made it back to his family it was mid-July.

He wrapped his mother in another big hug, sending the tears rolling down her cheeks once more.

"Alright. Enough you two," said Ferenc good naturedly, as he took his seat at the table.

Eva and Endre let go of each other and sat down. Ferenc said grace with heartfelt gratitude for the answered prayer of seeing his son safely home. Choking back his own tears, Ferenc silently made the sign of the cross, and added a quiet, "Amen."

"Amen," echoed Eva and Endre.

Eva rose to ladle the *paprikás csirke* onto her son's plate.

"My favorite!" beamed Endre.

Eva smiled, and walked around the table to fill Ferenc's plate. "Did the Hungarian ladies in Markota make *paprikás csirke?*"

"Of course," said Endre, "but no one made it as good as you, Mom!"

"Oh, I don't think I believe you," she said, brushing off the compliment. "I know it's best with freshly ground, Hungarian-grown paprikas."

"I like yours the best," Endre assured her.

Eva wasn't able to eat. She couldn't stop looking at her son. The last few months had been full of emotional extremes for her: terrible days, like the one last September when Endre's name was found on the MIA list; emotionally exhausting days of struggling to maintain hope while they waited for news; wonderful days, like April 15, when she learned that Endre had returned safely to England; exhilarating days, trying to contain her excitement while she waited to see him again. Now – finally – he was here. He was home. It was almost too wonderful to be true. Eva kept asking herself if she was only dreaming. Just to make sure he was real, she got up and hugged him again.

Endre was glad to be home. He had never before thought of himself or his family as rich, but from the moment he set foot on American soil he began to notice all sorts of things he had never paid attention to before. Cars. Every family had one. Even some young boys had their own car. Televisions, radios, telephones, were all commonplace. Clothes. Women had lots of pretty dresses. Even a man who owned only one suit had enough slacks and shirts to wear a different one every day of the week. On laundry day, women used machines to wash the clothes, not scrubboards. Some even had machines to dry their clothes. Food. Fresh food, canned food, frozen food! Junk food, potato chips, chocolate bars. Fast food, hamburgers, fries, milkshakes, sodas. The grocery stores were always stocked. Endre never walked into a store –any kind of store – and saw empty shelves. He wondered what Ilonka would think of this. He wished he could show her.

While his mother and father fussed over him, he looked around his own home, much larger than any house in Markota. In Endre's house there was one television plus three radios. He noticed the bookshelf in the living room and guessed that three or four average American households had as many books as the entire collection of the library in Markota.

Many of the titles in Endre's house were Hungarian. He'd lived with these books since his childhood, but he never actually noticed them before. Suddenly, titles like *Magyar Történelem*, Hungarian History, seemed irresistibly interesting to him.

Eva and Ferenc were full of questions about his time in Hungary. They had not been back to their homeland since they left in 1920. When Endre described the paprika and garlic strands hanging to dry on the side of the houses, the image conjured up in their memories was so real they could smell it.

"Hopefully," said Eva, "there will soon be peace and we can all go home together to see our family again."

"That would be wonderful," agreed Ferenc.

"I haven't even had a letter from my sister in over a year," said Eva. "Maybe now that the war is over, the mail will move freely."

"Depends on the Russians, I suppose," said Ferenc, less optimistically.

"Tell us more about Markota and the people who looked after you," urged Eva.

In the three days since he'd been home, Endre had already told them about the Farkas family, Uncle Vince and Lajos, Mariska and her brave husband László, who was ultimately responsible for his safe escape. Now, he told them about the Keszegér, the small school house, the old church, and the harvest ball. Their favorite stories were the ones about Lajos and Sanyi, so Endre entertained his parents with tales of mischievous conduct by the Bad Boys of Markota. Whenever he talked about Ilonka, his parents noticed the light in his eyes grew a little brighter.

They fretted when he told them the story of the three German officers who lived at the house for a few weeks. Eva panicked, even now, just to think what might have happened!

"But I was transformed into Janos' nephew from Arad," he told them.

"Arad! Of all places," exclaimed Ferenc. "Your lie was almost true. One generation back, you really are from Arad."

Endre had always vaguely known that, but he never really had a clear understanding of the geography. Like most children of immigrants, he had only a hazy concept of the land that was home to his parents.

Eva made *zserbó* for dessert, of course, Endre's favorite. Unlike the *zserbó* in Markota, this pastry had the chocolate layer on top that Endre had missed so much.

After dinner, Endre thanked his mother for the *paprikás csirke* and the *zserbó*, and he thanked his father for the car keys. There was one other person he must see. Kim was expecting him to pick her up at seven.

Endre loved the feel of the solid American Ford engine. He cranked up the radio, rolled down the windows, and let the warm evening wind whistle through as he sped down the country road heading into town. Two years ago, Kim had moved into her own apartment in Manhattan, but she was home this weekend at her parents' house. He had no idea what to expect when he saw Kim. It had been ten months since he'd read a letter from her and more than three years since he'd seen her. Has she changed? Have I changed? Has she forgotten me?

He pulled into the long driveway that divided the meticulously groomed yard. Shutting down the radio and the engine, he walked up to the front door of the American Colonial style home and rang the doorbell. Kim's father was the first to greet him with a handshake, and her mother was right behind with hugs and kisses.

"Can I pour you a drink?" asked Kim's father, walking over to the liquor cabinet and reaching for the whiskey decanter.

His wife added, "Kim's not quite ready yet. I'm sure she'll be down in a moment. Please, come sit down."

"Thank you," said Endre, accepting both the drink and the seat in the parlor.

They were delighted to see Endre and they asked a lot of polite questions about the time he spent in Europe.

"What do you plan to do now that you're home?" asked Kim's father.

"I don't know yet," answered Endre honestly.

Right on cue, Kim appeared at the top of the stairs, saving Endre from any further questioning.

She was stunning. She wore a red polka dot dress with a matching bright red scarf tied daintily on her neck, and in her crimson pumps she floated down the grand staircase. The scent of Mademoiselle Chanel No. 1 drifted seductively down the steps ahead of her, and Endre was charmed. She smelled wonderful and she looked like a movie star. When she arrived at the bottom of the stairs, Endre took her hand and kissed it.

They smiled at each other, quickly bid the parents good-bye and flew away in Endre's father's car, with Kim's scarf and her beautiful perfume dancing in the breeze. Endre took his eyes off the road to look at her. Wow! She was beautiful. It was great to be back in America!

They hadn't made any specific plans for the evening, but Kim had a suggestion, "What do you say we go into the city? There are lots of fine cafes there," adding sweetly, "afterwards I can show you my apartment."

Endre smiled. New York City was a two-hour drive. "Will anything still be open by the time we get there?" he asked naively.

"The city never sleeps," laughed Kim.

"Nice!" exclaimed Endre, accelerating the Ford loudly.

Over cocktails they talked about the lost years, but foremost on both of their minds was getting back to Kim's apartment. This was a girl Endre hadn't met before. Up to the moment when he left for the war, Kim had only allowed him to kiss her, a little. Obviously, the years and the city had changed Kim too. Endre floated blissfully under the spell cast by the new Kim.

In the morning, Kim suggested they go down to the bagel place for breakfast and coffee, as she did not cook. That sounded fine to Endre. The pulse of the city carried him along and he was glad to be back in America.

Over bagels, Kim explained that she had a really good job in her brother's brokerage firm so she could afford her own apartment, a cleaning lady, and eating most of her meals out. Endre was impressed with the new, independent Kim. This morning again, she looked as fresh as if she'd stepped right off a page from a fashion magazine. Endre noticed that other men glanced her way too, and he felt proud that this beautiful girl was his.

"Have you seen the Statue of Liberty since you've been back?" asked Kim.

"Not yet," said Endre.

"Let's go down to Battery Park then," suggested Kim.

Endre agreed.

"I'll hail us a cab," said Kim.

"A cab!" balked Endre. "It's not far from here. It would be a nice walk."

"Endre," she said reproachfully.

Well, I have my dad's car," said Endre. "Do we still need to take a cab?"

"No," said Kim. "Your dad's car will do just fine."

"I'd still rather walk," said Endre.

"Seriously?" she said, looking down at her high-heeled shoes.

Endre's eyes followed hers and he noted the problem with the footwear. They were only a block away from her apartment, surely she could select a more sensible pair of shoes, but this thought was interrupted when he became distracted by the lovely pair of bare legs that were so acutely accented by those impractical heels.

"Alright," Endre agreed. "We'll take the car."

In Battery Park, they found a picnic table with a view of the harbor and Lady Liberty. Endre wanted to tell her all about Europe, but Kim didn't seem interested. "You're home now. That's what counts," she said.

"Yes," said Endre, "but it was amazing to be in Hungary…"

"But you're an American," she interrupted. "Thank God you came home safely from enemy territory."

Endre's thoughts got stuck in trying to reconcile enemy territory with the Hungary he had experienced.

Kim continued, "I was so worried about you while you were missing, so afraid you would never come home." She snuggled close to him. "I'm so glad you're home with me now."

Endre forgave her for not understanding the things he was trying to tell her. After all, she wasn't there. She had been sheltered here in America and, looking down at the pretty face resting on his chest, he decided he didn't want it any other way. She should be sheltered from the horrors of war. There was no reason why she should understand. He was lucky to have such a pretty fiancée to come home to. Fiancée? Were they still engaged? He hadn't given her a ring before he left, only a promise. He had to ask, "Are we still engaged?"

"Of course!" she answered in astonishment, raising her head from his chest to look him in the eyes. "I love you Endre. I have always loved only you. I can't wait to marry you!"

They kissed a long kiss and that settled it.

"Endre," she started again, excitedly. "I can't wait for us to be married and for you to move to New York and live here with me."

"New York! What would I do here?"

"You're brilliant," she smiled. "There are plenty of opportunities for bright young men like you on Wall St. To begin with, you could get a job with John's company. If you like it, you can stay. If not, it will be a good start for you to get a job somewhere else."

Endre wasn't sure Wall St. was the right place for him, but they could talk about this later.

Kim wasn't letting it go. "You'll see John at your welcome home party next Saturday night and you boys can talk things over."

Endre agreed to talk to Kim's brother about a job, letting pass without comment the fact that this was the first he'd heard about the welcome home party that Kim was planning for him.

"Did you hear that Tom and Angie are getting married next month?" Kim asked.

"No," Endre had not heard.

"Yes, he just got back. Like you, he was missing in action, but I think he was in a camp or something," she said. "Anyway, he's back now and they're getting married. Seems everyone's getting married as soon as they get back."

When Endre said nothing, Kim added, "maybe we should do the same…"

Endre nodded.

"I was thinking a September wedding would be nice," said Kim. "It gives me a little bit of time to get things organized. I'm not like those small town girls who have nothing else to do. I have a very busy job, but I'm sure I could get it all together by September."

"September is only two months away, said Endre. "Don't you think that's a little soon?"

"We've waited almost four years!" exclaimed Kim. "What's soon about that?"

"I know," said Endre, "but still, I think…" What did he think? Did he want to marry her or not? Yes, he thought, but not in two months. "I think next summer would be nice. That way, you'd have lots of time to plan."

"Next summer?" repeated Kim, disappointed.

"Yes," said Endre, with more conviction this time. "I need the time to get myself established in a job."

"But my brother will give you a job. I already told you that," she protested.

"Kim," said Endre, with increasing firmness, "a man needs to be able to do certain things for himself. I will talk to your brother about a job, but I will also consider other jobs. I need time to think that through. By next summer, I think I'll be settled enough."

"Alright," agreed Kim reluctantly. It was a beautiful sunny afternoon in New York City. Endre was home. What did it matter that the wedding wouldn't be until next summer, they could still share weekends at her apartment or even weeknights once Endre started his job in the city. Kim put her head back on Endre's chest and sighed contentedly.

Two days later, Endre returned with his father's car. Sheepishly, he handed the keys to his dad, "Sorry, I was gone a little longer than I thought. We went to the city and ran into some friends..."

"That's alright," said Ferenc. He hadn't needed the car. His work was right here on the farm. Both his mother and his father suspected correctly that it was Kim alone who detained him not any other friends.

"What's that you've got there?" Endre asked his mother, noticing a box on the table.

"This –" she went to the table and sat down, "I wanted to give to you."

Endre took a closer look.

"This is what the Air Force brought us after they told us you were missing," said Eva.

Endre could see now that it was the contents of his barrack box. Thinking back to the day of the crash, he realized that when the boys returned from that fateful Italy-based mission someone had to go and clean up his stuff. On a few occasions, Endre had done that duty for other flyers who had gone down. He was a little nervous when he saw the box. He hoped that whoever cleared it for him had done a good job of sanitizing the contents. There were some things in there that his mother should not see!

"I've been looking at these things for months," said Eva, "hoping they would bring you home." She smiled softly as she lifted out the packet of letters. "These are the letters your dad wrote to you." She handed him the packet. "There were letters from Kim too. I didn't read those. I gave them back to Kim."

Endre nodded.

There were ribbons that had been used to wrap goodies sent by Kim or by his mom. There were two cigars. "When did you start smoking!" exclaimed Eva as she set those on the table. "Well, I suppose all the boys do now."

"I suppose," said Endre. Showing them to his dad he said, "After supper, we can smoke these together. They'll be our victory cigars."

"Absolutely," agreed Ferenc.

Inside the box there were also two chocolate bars, the pocket Bible his dad sent him, and a photo of Kim. "Oh, I probably should have given this to Kim too," said Eva when she pulled that out.

"That's alright," said Endre. Phew, he thought, when he could see there were no more photos of girls. He knew there had been another picture of Kim that he would not have wanted his mother to see. He also knew there had been some photos of Sally, Nancy, Diana and some other girls whose names he could no longer recall. Whoever sorted his barrack box contents had wisely edited these out. He remembered clearing barrack boxes for other guys and being careful to remove things like pictures and letters from other girls, girly-magazines – things you don't send to a mother, or a wife, or a fiancée.

"And then there are these pictures of you with your buddies," referring to an assortment of group shots in uniform. "There was also this one," she walked over to the fireplace mantle. "I liked it best so I framed it and put it here." It was a photo of Endre on the tarmac with his P-51 Mustang. "You can have it back now if you want it."

"No," said Endre, "I think that's a fine place for it."

"Oh Endre!" said Eva, hugging him again. "For all these months, I was afraid this picture was all I had left of you." The tears started again.

"No, Mom," comforted Endre, "I'm home now."

"Yes, you are," she said. "Thank God! And thanks to the Farkas family. I wrote them a letter today. You can read it before we mail it. Endre, you should write them also to let them know you're safe."

"I don't know, Mom," hesitated Endre. "We don't want to do anything that will put them in danger."

"Of course not!" said Eva. "Would my letter put them in danger?"

"It might," replied Endre. "If you came right out and thanked them for protecting your American son, that would be dangerous. In the wrong hands, that would be incriminating."

"Yes, I see," said Eva, "but how do I thank them then?"

Endre wasn't sure. He said, "I think we have to wait a little while until the political situation changes, or at least settles down."

"Alright," agreed Eva.

The last thing she wanted to do was endanger the very people who had risked their lives to keep her son safe, but the idea of waiting was not entirely to Eva's satisfaction. She continued to ponder the problem of safely getting mail through until she struck upon an idea. "Endre! We could send the letter to my sister. It is not unusual for her to receive mail from America. Then, she could forward it on to the Farkas family and it would appear to come from Arad. They are known to have family in Arad, right? So that shouldn't raise any suspicion either."

Endre thought about that and it seemed reasonable. "You're right, Mom. I think that would work. Just be careful. I mean, choose your words carefully."

"I will," she said. "You can read it before I send it. I'm going to re-write it – carefully – right now."

Endre knew that he should write too, but the truth was that he had been caught up in such a whirlwind of activity since he got home that he really hadn't thought much about Hungary lately. Nevertheless, to the bottom of his mother's revised letter, he added his own lines of personal greeting before it was sent off.

Endre accepted the job on Wall St. in John's office. He was determined to save up some money, so he rented a room instead of a whole apartment. He spent most of his time at Kim's apartment anyway. Summer turned to fall. On the weekends, Endre rode the train to Philadelphia, Chicago, Boston, and other cities where his Air Force buddies were building new lives for themselves. Sometimes, his travels took him to visit the families of flyers he'd known in Europe, who did not make it back after the war. Other weekends, he went out to the country to visit his parents. Usually, Kim came with him and they spent time with her family also.

He liked his job well enough. It was certainly more money than he was likely to make anywhere else, but the cost of living in New York City was also high. After he received his second paycheck, Kim mentioned that he could now afford to buy her a diamond engagement ring. Every time they walked past the Tiffany & Co. window, she stopped to point out the particular style she liked, a modern multi-stone arrangement. He noted that Kim had very fine taste. Her appetite for shoes was insatiable. Her closet was stuffed full of dresses, yet she still spent her Saturday afternoons shopping on Fifth Ave.

When Endre returned to the city on Sunday nights, she wore her new purchases. She met him at the train station in her new dress, shoes, and magical scents. From there they went out for dinner and back to Kim's apartment. Kim began to complain that her apartment was too small. "Once we're married," she said, "we can buy our own apartment, a bigger one."

"Yes," said Endre sarcastically. "We'll certainly need a bigger closet!"

"Oh Endre," she smiled. "I mean, when we have children, we'll need a lot more space."

"Children!"

"Don't you like children?" she asked.

"Of course I like children. I just hadn't thought about having any yet."

"You know," said Kim condescendingly, "people get married and then they have children."

"Yeah, sure – eventually," acknowledged Endre.

"Well not now," agreed Kim, "after we're married of course."

"Of course," repeated Endre. "But won't we want a country house to raise them in? The city is really no place for children."

"Endre!" said Kim, again as if she were speaking to a child, "Look around you. There are plenty of children here. Central Park is full of children. There are schools here in the city, probably much better schools than in the country. No, I see no need to leave the city just because we have children."

Endre was unconvinced. "We'll see," he said noncommittally.

Endre wondered if this was what their life would be like. They would buy a large New York apartment. Kim would work until they had children. Endre would need a promotion to compensate for Kim's lost income. Maybe, Endre speculated, when she has children, she'll be too busy to shop so much and we won't need as much money. No, that's wrong, of course. She'll shop for herself and the children, and we'll need more money.

Mail traveling to a remote corner of Hungary, via a remote corner of Romania, and back along the same route, was a very slow way to communicate. It was late November before Ilonka's letter made its way back to Endre, in Eva's mailbox. The following weekend, when Endre and Kim came out to visit, Eva passed on the unopened letter, discreetly, to Endre.

Endre and Kim always spent Sunday night at Kim's apartment, so it was Monday after work before Endre had a moment to himself. On several occasions he had tried talking to Kim about his time in Hungary and the people he had met there, but she was never interested in any of that. He was certain she wouldn't be interested in this letter either.

Endre loved to walk in Central Park. Within the shelter of its large trees he could tune out the city completely. Even though it was only four weeks till Christmas, winter was slow coming and the evening was mild. He sat down on a park bench and pulled the envelope out from his breast pocket.

Holding it in his hands, he remembered Janos, Erzsi, Ilonka, Sanyi, Lajos... life had changed so much. While he was there, they were like family to him. Now, half a world away, it was hard to believe they really existed. The distance between Markota and New York was much more than miles. Endre was astonished to realize how much life could change, and how quickly.

Carefully, he broke the seal on the envelope. The letter was written by Ilonka. He recognized her handwriting. She began in a formal tone, replying to Endre's mother, acknowledging her thanks and wishing her and her family well in return, all without ever directly mentioning the circumstances that brought Endre to Hungary.

The second paragraph began "I have some sad news to share," and went on tell that her father had died. Endre thought his heart actually stopped when he read that. His first reaction was sympathy, followed immediately by a dreadful fear... because he hid me?!

He read on. She must have anticipated that he would worry about that because she wrote, "This was not a war injury." Endre understood that she meant his death had nothing to do with the war, nothing to do with him. However, his sense of relief was short lived because it was immediately clouded by a new feeling of dread. He read for further clues. There was nothing else, only:

> *I'm sorry that I have some sad news to share. Apu passed away in July. This was not a war injury.*

That was all she said about it. How did he die? Why didn't she say? If it was some kind of illness or a farming accident, Endre felt sure she would have written that. No, Janos' death may have had nothing to do with the war, but it was not likely from a natural cause or an accident either. He feared for the Farkas family in Markota.

His eyes fell back on the letter. Next, Ilonka wrote that Sanyi and Lajos had quit school and gone to work at a factory in Győr to make some money. She said that she would go to work there too, except for the fact that Erzsi has completely collapsed and is unable to care for herself, so she stays home to look after her.

"Oh, Ilonka!" he heard himself say, "The end of the war has brought you nothing good."

After that, she wrote an apology for having to share such sad news and tried to go on to the ordinary details of everyday life. She didn't quite achieve the lighter pitch she was striving for. She did, however, attain a tone that was familiar to Endre, the casual tone of the endless afternoon chats at the foot of his ladder. Endre folded the letter into his pocket and began the stroll back through the park, towards his rented-room, walking slowly, feeling the loss of Janos, thinking what a dark Christmas it would be in Markota this year.

Kim slammed the door loudly behind her as she stormed into the small apartment.

"Please, just calm down," pleaded Endre.

"Calm down? You've ruined Christmas! I waited all these years for you to come home and you've ruined everything!" she raged.

"We can't talk if you just keep screaming at me."

"Talk! What's to talk about? I thought you wanted to marry me! You don't seem to want to marry me at all!"

The diamond ring she was expecting was not amongst the packages under the tree, even though she was sure she had dropped enough hints to ensure its appearance.

"Kim, I really think we need to talk," Endre tried again.

"There's nothing to talk about!" she cried as she ran into the bedroom and slammed that door too.

Endre didn't know what to do. Should he go after her? He knew he had hurt her by not buying the ring she was waiting for, but he was also beginning to pay attention to his own feelings. Since he'd been back Kim had arranged everything: where he would live, where he would work. He wasn't sure he didn't want this... but he wasn't sure that he did either.

He needed time to think. The New York pace was too quick, with no time for simple contemplation. He just wanted to get away, maybe go visit Jimmy out in California. California seemed like a nice place to think things over. He hadn't mentioned this to Kim. He knew she would be against it.

He also really longed to talk with his father. Whenever he went out to visit his parents Kim came with him, and then they had to visit her parents too. There was never time to just talk. That's what I need to do, he told himself. He called his parents and told them he was coming home for a few days, and that he would be coming alone. He wasn't due back in the office until after New Year's anyway. Endre spent the rest of his vacation days going for long walks around the farm, but a week later he still had no clear idea of what he really wanted.

"Maybe you should go out to the west coast for a while," encouraged his father. "It seems like you need a little more time to think."

Endre went back to the city knowing only one thing for sure: he was going to California. His first stop was at John's house, where he thanked his boss for the opportunity and handed in his resignation. John said he understood that the war had messed up his head; he hoped some time in the California sunshine would be helpful; and there would be a job waiting for him when he came back.

Next, Endre braced himself for his encounter with Kim. He knocked on her apartment door instead of letting himself in with the key she had given him. When she opened the door, he could see she had been crying. Instinctively, he hugged her. "I'm sorry," she sobbed. "I'm sorry I was such a baby about the ring. There's still plenty of time before the wedding next summer."

"I'm sorry too," said Endre. "Sorry that I made you cry. We really need to talk. Please, will you just listen – please – while I say some things that I need to say?"

"Yes," said Kim tearfully, leading him over to the sofa.

"Since I've been back," Endre began, "I haven't had any time to think. Everything just happened so fast."

Already Kim didn't like where this was going, but she stayed quiet.

Endre chose his words carefully, "I just need some time to myself. I need to get away for a while, and I've decided to go to California to visit my buddy, Jimmy."

Kim was stunned, "you're leaving me?" she stammered.

"No…," protested Endre.

"Well, what then?" demanded Kim.

"I don't know."

"You don't know!" Kim's voice was escalating again. "You don't know if you're leaving me!"

Endre tried again, "Kim, I need time to think. I just don't know if New York is the place for me, if Wall St. is the job for me."

"Me?" Kim asked, more subdued. "Am I the girl for you?"

"I don't know that either," answered Endre honestly.

Kim was angry again. "So, you're going off to California to be a beach bum with your old army buddy! Do you miss the times you had together over there, seducing naive little girls?"

"Kim…"

Mockingly, she continued, "How many girls fell for your lame lines: please just let me hold you tonight because I might die tomorrow and never see the stars again, or listen to sweet music, or ever see a face as pretty as yours?"

Pausing only to catch her breath, she went on, "How many girls consoled you and your buddies while you laughed at them?"

"Kim, please…"

"Well I have no intention of marrying a surf-bum!" exclaimed Kim.

Endre rose to leave. He had no intention of becoming a surf-bum. He only knew that he needed to get away and think.

When Endre closed the door behind him, he heard Kim's anger turn to sobbing. He felt helpless. He didn't even know how to help himself right now, much less another distraught person.

Clouds Over Markota 214

The next day, Endre cleaned out his room, moved his few belongings back to his parents' house, and boarded a plane bound for Los Angeles.

Jimmy was there to meet Endre at Burbank's Lockheed Air Terminal when his TWA flight landed.

"What a welcome sight you are!" exclaimed Jimmy greeting his friend with a manly hug.

"You too, old pal," said Endre returning the hug.

Glancing back at the impressive DC-3 on the tarmac, Jimmy whistled, "Aren't you the big man, jetting around the country?"

Endre shrugged, "New York pays well."

"I can see that! How was your flight?"

"A little turbulence at about twenty thousand feet," said Endre with a smile.

"Still, a bit more comfortable than the old P-51 Mustang, I'd guess."

"But not nearly as much fun," replied Endre.

"You don't know how worried I was about you while you were missing," said Jimmy. "I just knew you weren't dead. And you know – over there – sometimes it was better to be dead," referring to the POW camps.

Endre nodded.

"I saw your plane, on the Miskolc mission, you know?"

Endre didn't know.

"I saw the flames and I knew you had hit the silk. I just kept hoping Jerry didn't find you. When we got back to Italy, we heard they'd rounded up a lot of jumpers."

"That's true," confirmed Endre. "I saw them being marched at gunpoint by the Germans."

"But you dodged them?"

"I had a guardian angel."

"I can't believe you're here!" said Jimmy, grabbing Endre's travel bag and hailing a cab.

The cab took them to Jimmy's apartment on Venice Beach. "No way!" exclaimed Endre. "You didn't tell me you live right on the beach. This is amazing!"

"Yeah," said Jimmy. "My parents are paying for this apartment until I get on my feet."

"What are you doing for work?" asked Endre.

"Selling junk to tourists," said Jimmy, followed by the sheepish admission, "mostly, I surf."

Endre smiled. Maybe Kim was right. Maybe he had come to California to become a surf-bum. Well, he mused, at this point I'm not ruling anything out.

January and February ambled by in a lazy California haze. While Jimmy was working at his Santa Monica pier beach stand, Endre strolled along the shore, watching the waves roll in and contemplating life. Occasionally, he took one of Jimmy's shifts, to give him some extra surfing time.

Jimmy told him, "surfing is just like flying on water. You need to try it!"

That sounded good to Endre, so he bought himself a board and Jimmy taught him how to surf. The days were spent in the warm sunshine, and when the sun went down, they practiced their pub lines on the California girls.

Endre liked beach life. It was so much slower and less complicated than the pace of New York City, but he knew it couldn't last. New York wasn't for him, but neither was he really a surfer-boy.

With the waves crashing at his knees, he reviewed his options. Following the shoreline south, and making his way around the Playa del Rey estuary, Endre arrived at Dockweiler Beach, just in time for an aviator's treat. Right over his head roared a Lockheed P-80 Shooting Star on its descent into Los Angeles Airport. Probably a test flight out of Burbank, thought Endre. The P-80 was still in the testing stages and off to a rough start. He remembered reading in the New York Times about a test flight last summer that ended with a crash in a field somewhere near here. Still, the Allison turbo-jet powered P-80 was considered a very promising combat aircraft.

I do miss flying, thought Endre. He wondered if he could get a job as a pilot with an airline, or maybe as an engineer. The world was changing so fast – new technology everyday – and it was engineers who made it happen. Maybe he'd like to be part of that. Every time he met someone new he asked two questions: "What do you do? And do you enjoy doing it?" He considered and eliminated school teacher, bank teller, gas station manager, film maker, bus driver, chef, zoo keeper, and accountant, but he met a lot of interesting people that way.

In the first week of March, a letter arrived from his mother. Inside the envelope was also an unopened letter from Hungary. Endre remembered the last time he held a letter with a Romanian postmark in his hands. Sitting on the park-bench in New York, Hungary had seemed a world away. Now, New York seemed a world away too.

Since receiving the first letter from Ilonka, Endre had replied with a letter back to her. Writing to her was a bit awkward. What part of his life could he tell her about? He certainly didn't want to describe to her the prosperous America he had come back to, or his fancy new job. Even less did he want to tell her about Kim. Instead, he told her candidly about the confusion he was feeling about what to do with his life now. She had closed her first letter with, *I wish you were still here.* When he wrote back, he closed his letter with, *wish <u>you</u> were here!*

Thinking about Ilonka, Endre had the feeling that if she were here he would know what to do with his life. He could send the fare to bring her here, but getting out of a communist country was not as simple as buying a ticket. Still, Endre thought, people do it. Refugees arrive in America everyday. It must be possible.

Endre sat down on the sea-wall to read the letter. When he tore open the envelope it released a pleasant scent. Not an expensive New York bottled fragrance, something different; something like the smell of Ilonka's hair when he kissed her; something that brought back images of floral-printed house smocks and finely embroidered table runners. He looked out at the Pacific. If I could walk straight across this vast ocean, he thought, I'd only be in Japan. After that, it's still a long way to Hungary.

Ilonka's letter was cryptic. Endre read it and re-read it, searching for the meaning he felt sure was concealed somewhere on the page. He could tell she was choosing her words very carefully, like when she wrote about her father's death. Part of that meaning he had understood, but this time, he could discern no secret message. This time, her fear was the only thing he understood.

Endre tucked the page into the envelope, feeling like he'd only read half a letter.

He walked back along the beach just in time to find Jimmy getting ready to close up the souvenir stand.

"These waves are too good to waste sitting in the sand," said Jimmy when he saw his buddy.

Together they grabbed their surfing gear and locked up shop.

"Did you decide yet what you want to be when you grow up?" asked Jimmy as they walked down the beach towards the surf that was building nicely in the gathering afternoon wind.

"I was thinking about circus clown or maybe chimney sweep," said Endre.

"You're crazy," said Jimmy.

"More seriously, I was thinking about re-enlisting in the Air Force."

"That's even more crazy," said Jimmy.

Endre didn't agree, but he did admit that it probably wasn't the right thing for him.

"Well, I haven't made a career decision yet, but I have made another decision..." He told Jimmy about Ilonka's cryptic letter. "I want to bring her to America."

Jimmy was very enthusiastic. "Yeah! That's what you should do!"

"Really?" asked Endre.

"Yeah."

"Why?"

"Well," considered Jimmy, "since you've been here, you've mentioned her far more often than your New York girl."

"I have?" asked Endre with genuine surprise. "I didn't realize I talked so much about her."

"I don't mean constantly, but the subject of Hungary does come up quite often."

"Yeah, I suppose that's true," admitted Endre, realizing that Ilonka and Markota were frequently on his mind.

"Maybe that means something..." suggested Jimmy.

"Maybe it does," agreed Endre, "but there's still a problem. I could send her the fare right now, but the Communists aren't allowing people to leave the country."

"That's true," acknowledged Jimmy.

"Still," said Endre, "that's the only thing I know for sure that I want to do."

"Well, that's progress!" shouted Jimmy, hitting the surf.

March came and went, and Endre was still walking endless miles in the southern California surf. But on one important point, his mind was made up: he was determined to bring Ilonka to America.

He realized it was time for a frank conversation with Kim. He was beginning to feel a little guilty about not calling her. Was she still making wedding plans for this summer?

He had called his mother last week and she told him that Kim telephoned every few days wondering if she had any news of Endre. He knew he should call. Finally, he mustered up the resolve to face the inevitable confrontation.

"Endre?... Endre? Is that really you?" Kim's whole plan to sound cool and composed evaporated at the sound of his voice.

"It's me, Kim. How are you?" Endre asked, awkwardly.

"I'm fine. Fine. Really good, now. Are you coming home? When are you coming home?"

"I don't know yet."

"... still, don't know..." She willed herself to calm down. "Listen, Endre, I'm sorry. I understand that you had a lot of things to work through, the war and everything. I understand that you needed time to think about your life, and I'm sorry I pushed you into the job with John. You know, if that's not the job you want, that's okay with me. Just come home, Endre. You can work anywhere you want to. I just want us to be together again." She paused. When he didn't answer, she jumped right into the subject he'd been dreading.

"Endre, I've found the perfect dress, and I've been working on the invitations. I haven't ordered them yet, of course, because we don't know the exact date yet, but we can set the date when you get back. When are you coming back?"

Again, he said, "I don't know, Kim."

"You must know, Endre"

Silence.

"… Are you coming back?"

"Well…"

"Endre!"

"No, Kim. I'm not. I'm sorry."

He wanted to say so much more. He felt he owed her an explanation, but she was upset again, "I knew it! Having too much fun in California with your army buddy? Is that it?"

Endre said nothing.

"That's it; isn't it? Well, I'm tired – damn tired! I'm through with waiting for a surf-bum!" With that, she slammed the phone down.

"Okay, Kim," said Endre, into the now dead telephone line.

Endre set the phone back in its cradle and headed out for another walk in the surf. He took a deep breath of the salty air and let out a long sigh of relief. She said it was over. He hadn't needed to say a word about Ilonka.

That evening, over a couple of beers, he told Jimmy about the phone call.

"She sounds like a spoiled brat," said Jimmy.

"She's not that bad," replied Endre charitably.

"Well, how do you feel now that it's over?" asked Jimmy.

"Relieved," admitted Endre. "Truth is, Ilonka's been on my mind a lot lately."

"I hadn't noticed," teased Jimmy.

Brushing that remark aside, Endre said, "Ilonka's a girl who took risks for me."

"She's the reason Jerry didn't find you."

"Yeah, she hid me, brought me food, blankets, even when the Germans were right there! She protected me. I always knew I could trust her."

"That's some girl," Jimmy agreed.

"And she's someone I can talk to. I'm sure I've never talked with anyone as much as I talked with Ilonka."

"I've seen you chat up plenty of girls!"

"But Ilonka was different. When we talked, we really talked."

"Did you talk with Kim?" asked Jimmy.

"We talked about silly things, like the new shoes she bought or the latest film she wanted to see. With Ilonka, we talked about everything."

"Sounds like you're stuck on her," observed Jimmy.

"I am," acknowledged Endre. "I miss her terribly. I want her here with me."

"Have you figured out how you're going to do that?" asked Jimmy.

Endre shook his head, "The borders are closed. Even if I could get the money to her, she can't simply board an outbound plane."

"Are there other ways out of the country?" asked Jimmy.

"I assume there are, but they're probably dangerous," said Endre.

"Can you go in and get her?" asked Jimmy.

"That's just what I was thinking."

Jimmy raised his mug and took a drink. "What exactly were you thinking?"

"Well, it relates to my career search," explained Endre. "I've been thinking that I'd like to be an engineer. Of course, the first thing I'll need is a degree in engineering. I could apply to the Budapest University of Technology and Economics. If I can get into the country on a student visa, maybe I can find a way to get both of us back out."

"That's clever. Sounds like a good plan."

The sound of high pitched laughter burst into the room, carried by three tall sun-bleached blondes. "Oh look, our evening entertainment is here," said Jimmy. "One for you, one for me, and one more for good luck."

"You can have all three," said Endre.

"You've got it bad," he said, placing his hand on Endre's forehead, as if to take his temperature. "Okay." Rising from the table, "I'll take all three. Don't wait up."

Endre laughed. He finished his beer, paid the waitress, winked at Jimmy on his way out the door, and walked back to the beach-front apartment.

First thing the next morning, Endre drafted his letter to the Budapest University and requested an application package. Time seemed to speed up now that he had a plan. By the end of June he had an offer of admission and his student visa papers were all in order. The Communists had no problem with an American coming to their university to study. After all, it was proof of their superiority over the capitalists.

Now that it was official, he sent a letter to Ilonka telling her that he was coming to Budapest to study engineering. He thanked Jimmy for six months of therapeutic California sunshine and boarded a plane back to New York.

The only thing left to do was tell his parents. Ferenc met him at the airport. On the drive home, he told him all about the beautiful beaches in California, but put off mentioning his decision because he wanted to tell his mother at the same time. As they made their way through the New

York City streets and out to the countryside, Ferenc was filling Endre in on all that had happened while he was gone. The cows broke out of the pasture last week. What an adventure it was to round them back up again. Old man Wilson, next door, died about a month ago. He was alone on the farm since Tricia died, so now the kids would probably sell the land. He wondered who their new neighbors would be.

While Endre listened, he was also looking around, and noticing all things American again, just as he had on his first return to New York. He tried to see them with fresh eyes, tried to imagine how they would look through Ilonka's eyes. Paved roads, cars – lots of cars. He thought of Ilonka. In Markota, cars were rare. Mostly, they were still getting around by bicycle or horse and wagon. Diners – so many diners; there was food everywhere. In Markota, food was scarce. A family had to carefully budget their harvest, use what was fresh, pickle what could be preserved, and share with their neighbors. Consumer goods – everything – clothes, radios, household appliances. He couldn't wait to show Ilonka.

Eva ran to meet the car in the driveway. Of course, she had *paprikás csirke* waiting for dinner and *zserbó* for desert, her little boy's favorites. After dinner, Endre told them he was going back to Hungary, disguised as an engineering student, to get Ilonka and bring her to America. As he expected, they had mixed feelings about the grand plan. Certainly, they were relieved that he had cancelled his wedding plans with Kim. They would never have told him not to marry her, but both Eva and Ferenc agreed that she just didn't seem to be the right girl for their son.

On the other hand, the Hungarian girl they had never met, but had heard so much about, seemed perfect. From the first time they heard him speak her name, they noticed that he had a spark for her. They liked the idea of Endre marrying her and they liked the idea of her coming to America. They didn't like the idea of Endre going back into a communist country. They were just getting used to having their son safely home, and now he would be in danger again.

"Hopefully not for long," said Ferenc, attempting to console Eva. "He'll just go in, find the quickest way out, and before you know it they'll both be back here with us."

"Alright," agreed Eva, knowing she didn't really have a choice.

"He's not our little boy anymore," reasoned Ferenc.

"I know," she said. Bravely adding, "He's his own man now and he has to make his own decisions."

"That's right," said Ferenc. And from that moment, both of them resumed their quiet vigil of hope and prayer for the safe return of Endre with Ilonka.

CHAPTER ELEVEN

That's how they've achieved maximum employment, thought Endre, by creating minimum efficiency. Hungarians were generally not permitted to leave the country, nor could they afford to travel, so the Budapest border services office was not very busy when Endre's train arrived. Nevertheless, it took three hours to get through customs.

Endre was exhausted. He'd been travelling for three weeks already. Through his former commanding officer, he was able to arrange a transatlantic sail aboard Cunard's Queen Mary. During the war, the ship had been used for troop transport but now it was bringing the European wives and children of American servicemen to the USA. Endre boarded the ship in New York harbor, after the Queen dropped off her passengers, and headed back across the sea to Southampton, England. From there, he caught a boat to Calais, then a train to Paris. He changed trains three more times, in Zurich, Innsbruck, and Vienna, before finally arriving in Budapest. Exhausted and hungry, he wasn't feeling very patient with the long delay in the customs office, but he continued to behave with forced civility, reminding himself that these bureaucrats were unlikely to make the process any smoother for him if he blasted them.

In this masterful design of communist disorganization, one officer asked the arriving passenger the purpose of his visit and if he had anything to declare; a second officer stamped his passport; and a third officer reviewed all the documents again to determine whether or not his bags should be inspected. If so, the passenger, along with his bags, was turned over to an entire team of search agents.

The arrival of an American citizen was enough to warrant automatic bag inspection. Endre expected this and took it into consideration when he packed. There was nothing in his bag that was unusual for a travelling student to be carrying. He allowed himself a small sigh of relief when he finally cleared the inspection and was permitted to continue on his way.

Endre's plan was to be out of the country – with Ilonka – before the first day of class, before anyone had time to notice that he hadn't reported to the university. His visa allowed him entry fifteen days before school started. Effectively, this gave him two weeks of scrutiny-free travel, provided he didn't draw any attention to himself. That wasn't difficult. He was well rehearsed in the role of average Hungarian young man.

Endre checked the map and schedules for the local trains. He could get as far as Kony by rail, but from there he would have to walk the last six kilometers to Markota. He remembered walking that route with László on his way out of the country. Maybe László could help him get Ilonka out. He would have to wait and see. At this point, he didn't have an exit plan. In fact, at this point, he didn't even know if Ilonka was aware that he was coming. He had sent a letter to her as soon as his admission to the university was confirmed, but he had no way of knowing whether or not she had received it.

Inconspicuous in the crowd at the Budapest station, Endre boarded the last train of the day, intending to reach Markota after nightfall in the hope that his arrival would go unnoticed. As the train rolled out of the city, it seemed to Endre that he was travelling back through time. Cars and trucks gave way to horse-drawn wagons. Tall apartment buildings flattened into small country homes. Grey city streets turned into rolling hills, farm fields, and green countryside.

Sitting on the train, Endre thought about Ilonka, the girl who drew him out of the safety and affluence of America into the danger and uncertainty behind the Iron Curtain. It was almost two years since Endre arrived in Hungary by parachute. On that day, he only wanted to be safely out of here. He never would have guessed that he would someday sneak back in. It seemed like only yesterday he was a debonair young fighter pilot, prowling the pubs with Jimmy, in pursuit of passionate love affairs. We had fun, he admitted, but I never would have crossed an ocean and a continent to be with any of those girls again. Ilonka is different.

Ilonka was never merely a target for his passion. Long before their first kiss, they were friends. Endre remembered the afternoons they spent together. How pleasant it was to talk with her, because it seemed there wasn't anything they could not talk about. His thoughts were safe with her. She was his trusted friend. Not many friends would risk as much as Ilonka had risked to protect him, or be as faithful as she had been in making sure that he had everything he needed when he was completely dependent on the kindness of strangers.

The train arrived in Kony and Endre gathered his belongings to disembark. It was dark by the time he made his way out of the station and began his trek along the dusty road to Markota. Approaching town, Endre slowed his steps. He heard voices. He jumped into the ditch, crouched low and waited until the three horse-back Russian soldiers passed by.

It was close to midnight by the time Endre arrived at the Farkas house. All the lights were out. A knock on the door in the middle of the night was the most feared sound in the country, and the last thing Endre wanted to do was frighten Ilonka. Instead, he made his way up to his hayloft. He fell asleep easily in the familiar bed of hay.

At the first light of dawn, Endre heard movement in the barn below him. He peered down and saw Ilonka getting the feed for the pigs. "Ilonka," he spoke softly.

Startled, but not afraid, she looked up and saw him. A smile broke across her face. Endre jumped down and scooped her into his arms. Time turned back as he held her for a long, speechless embrace.

"What are you doing here?" she finally asked, pulling her hair forward from behind her ears.

"You didn't get my letter?" he answered with a question.

She looked puzzled.

"I wrote to say I was coming," he said. "I'll tell you everything, but first, tell me how things are here."

"Oh!" exclaimed Ilonka, "I don't know where to start." She slumped down to sit on a hay bale, but the clucking of the chickens and the snorting of the hungry pigs was hard to ignore.

"I'll help you with the chores," said Endre, pulling her back up onto her feet.

While they fed the pigs, collected eggs from the chickens, and pitched hay to the horses, Ilonka told Endre about some of the things that had been happening. Endre already knew about the boys going off to work at the factory in Győr and about Janos' death.

Ilonka stopped working and, haltingly, told him the whole awful truth of that terrifying night in the schoolyard.

Endre felt sick. It was one thing to know that such things happened, somewhere far away, behind some abstract iron curtain, but quite another to know that this had happened to Janos and Erzsi, people he knew, people he cared about.

"These are just some of the ways that communism has made our lives better," she said sarcastically. As soon as she said it, she clasped her hand over her mouth. It was exactly that sort of talk that got people killed.

Before they went into the house, Ilonka warned Endre that Erzsi was not the same as he remembered her. Ilonka stopped at the door, "I think you should stay here. I don't want her to be shocked when she sees you."

Endre waited while Ilonka went inside to talk to her mother.

"Of course Endre is here," said Erzsi, as if she'd forgotten everything that had happened in the meantime.

When Endre came in, Erzsi accepted his presence as if it were the most natural thing in her home.

That afternoon, Ilonka and Endre talked at the foot of the ladder, just as they always used to. Endre told her that he had entered the country on a student visa, and that he was here to get her and take her back to America with him. In his letters, he had avoided giving her a detailed description of American prosperity, but this seemed like the right moment to tell her about all the affluence and abundance that America had to offer. After all, he was asking her to leave the only home she had ever known.

"It sounds like heaven," she admitted.

"Ilonka," he said, dropping to one knee. "I came back here to ask you to marry me. Please come home with me."

Ilonka was speechless. She had no doubt about her love for Endre. She missed him desperately, but she had spent months convincing herself that it was over. It was wonderful while it lasted, but now it was over. His life was in America and hers was here in Hungary. Even when the letters started arriving, she didn't dare to hope they would actually see each other again. She thought they would write back-and-forth for a while, and life would move on. Yes, she loved him, but the realities of her life demanded that she be practical. Yet, here he was, asking her to come to America.

"Ilonka, I love you and I want you to be my wife."

"Oh Endre," she breathed, "I love you, too." She knelt down beside him and leaned her head against his shoulder. "I never imagined that I would see you again. I missed you terribly."

"Please say you'll marry me," urged Endre.

"I want to Endre. I want to marry you.

Endre exhaled. *She wants to marry me! She wants to be my wife!*

"I know there is no one else in the whole world for me, but..."

But! –

"I can't go to America," said Ilonka.

"Yes you can," said Endre, mistaking her concern to be related to the government allowing her to leave. "You can," encouraged Endre. "We can do it together."

"No," stated Ilonka more firmly. "I can't leave mother. I can't leave Sanyi or Lajos. They need me here."

Endre hadn't considered all of that. He was really only hoping that she wanted to marry him as much as he wanted to marry her. After that, he was sure the rest would all work out. He was right about her love for him, but her life was more complicated than he had understood. Her strong sense of loyalty would not allow her to abandon the people who needed her just so she could run off to America with her prince and enjoy the finer things in life. Endre told himself he should have known better. After all, wasn't her strong sense of loyalty one of the things he loved about her?

Then she threw him a curve ball. "Endre, why don't you stay here? You speak Hungarian. You can find work here with the boys." She hesitated. "I know you won't have a car or any of the other fine things you would have in America, but we'd be together…" her words trailed off. She realized that was asking a lot. Why would he give up a good life in America to live here, where every day the AVO secret police grew more powerful and the people grew more terrified? Who in his right mind would choose to live in a communist prison when he could be free?

Endre didn't answer. He didn't like that idea at all. He knew first hand how much more America had to offer. She didn't know. Her world did not extend beyond the borders of Markota, a tiny town that no one in the West had ever heard of. He was sure that, because of his broader worldview, he knew what was best for both of them.

On Friday afternoon, Endre helped Ilonka prepare an extra large pot of *gulyás* and some fresh baked bread for Lajos and Sanyi, who were expected home for the weekend. Between peeling the carrots and chopping the peppers, Endre continued his efforts to convince Ilonka, but she would not be persuaded.

When the boys came home they were ecstatic to see Endre. They showed him how much English they still remembered and taught him some of the Russian they were learning. They told Endre – honestly and quietly – how much they hated their jobs and the new regime. Endre and Ilonka were evasive about exactly why Endre had returned. It was obvious that it was his love for Ilonka that brought him back, but Endre's escape plan was kept between the two of them.

All that week, Endre tried to convince Ilonka to come with him. He painted ever-rosier pictures for her of life in America.

"I believe you," she said. "I'm sure there is much wealth and plenty of everything, but my life is here. I'm sorry. I can't go."

After seven days, Endre finally admitted to himself that he was making no progress. She would not be leaving with him. He had only one week left of his grace period. Soon the authorities would be informed that an American student had entered the country but had not reported for classes at the university. Endre needed a new plan.

Under the ladder, the next afternoon, Ilonka said again, "Why don't you just stay here?"

Was that the new plan, Endre wondered. Could he just stay here in Markota and work at the factory in Győr with the boys? No, he did not think he could do that. He knew he wanted more. What more did he want? He reminded himself that he had gone to California to answer that question, and he had found his answer. He wanted to marry Ilonka and he wanted to be an engineer. Well, he realized, she said yes. He could marry Ilonka. Also, he was registered to begin classes next week at the Budapest University leading to an engineering degree. He could actually attend the classes and earn his degree. Right here, he could marry Ilonka and become an engineer. It wasn't exactly as he had imagined it, but it was all that he said he wanted.

"I have a new plan," he told Ilonka his thoughts.

She smiled and kissed him. "I like your new plan. And I love you!"

Clouds Over Markota 238

Endre's letter arrived the next day from Romania, but it was old news now. Ilonka opened it and read that he was coming to Hungary. He was already here.

Before dawn, while the town was still quiet, Endre and Ilonka pushed open the heavy door of Mindenszentek Church. Their footsteps echoed in the lonely sanctuary. Father Kiraly heard them come in and rose from his morning prayers to welcome them. Endre explained that they had come to arrange for a speedy wedding, before he had to go away to Budapest to begin his studies.

Father Kiraly was agreeable, "but it has to be very quiet," he cautioned. "Attending church, even for a wedding, is increasingly viewed as an anti-government activity."

They set the date for Saturday so Sanyi and Lajos could attend. Besides the boys, Erzsi, Mariska, and Uncle Vince were the only guests.

Ilonka looked radiant, even though the only clues that she was a bride were the small bouquet of wildflowers she carried and the few blooms that Mariska had arranged in her hair.

Sanyi stood in his father's place of honor and walked his sister down the aisle. No music played to accompany their solitary procession, only the sounds of their shoes tapping lightly with each step. Erzsi beamed with pride, even as the tears streamed quietly down her face.

Lajos read the marriage verse from 1 Corinthians:

> "Love is patient, love is kind. It does not envy, it does not boast. It is not proud. It is not rude, it is not self-seeking, it is not easily angered, it keeps no record of wrongs. Love does not delight in evil but rejoices with the truth. It always protects, always trusts, always hopes, always perseveres. Love never fails."

Father Kiraly gave a brief sermon on the sanctity of marriage and prayed a blessing on the new couple.

Endre and Ilonka repeated their vows, pledging to each other: to have and to hold, for better or for worse, for richer or for poorer, in sickness and in health, to love and to cherish from this day forward.

Sanyi stood up and presented the rings he'd been entrusted with, while Ilonka handed her bouquet to Mariska to hold.

As Endre slipped the simple band onto Ilonka's finger, he thought about the dazzling rings in the Tiffany's window and hoped someday he'd be able to buy her one of those.

After the ceremony, the bride and groom set off with the horse and wagon that Uncle Vince lent them. Mariska had discreetly added a few flowers to the wagon to dress it up just a little for the special occasion. They made the short trip to Győr, where Endre used some money from his savings to buy a nice dinner and one night in the honeymoon suite.

After dinner, Ilonka enjoyed a leisurely soak in the luxurious bath tub before slipping into the alluring negligee that Mariska had helped her sew only two days earlier. Together they rummaged through their collective fabric supplies, finding enough lace for the bodice and even bits of ribbon for adding pretty accents. They giggled their way through the project while Mariska offered advice to the blushing bride.

Endre waited patiently, enjoying a cigar and the brandy he had ordered up from room service. His patience was rewarded when his bride emerged from the bathroom looking more beautiful than he had ever seen her. For one marvellous night, the universe compacted into only him and her. Just for tonight there was no tyranny; there never had been a war; there was nothing outside the walls of this hotel room.

In the morning, the sun shone a little more brightly; the sky was a bit bluer, and the muskatli blooms in the flower box outside the window were just a shade deeper red. Endre ordered breakfast to be brought by room-service. They lingered over every bite, trying to make it last forever. But check-out time came, and the honeymoon was over.

Endre brought Ilonka back to Markota and, with a long kiss, he promised her he'd be back soon. Ilonka packed him a couple of pork-fat and paprika sandwiches along with a few jars of pickled vegetables for the trip – a far cry from the elegant dinner they'd enjoyed last night. Uncle

Vince took Endre to Kony by wagon. From there, he caught a train and began his journey back to Budapest. He was due to report at the university first thing Monday morning and he was there, as if that had been the plan all along.

Endre took an instant liking to university life. He enjoyed his studies in civil engineering. The campus was beautiful. Located in the Gellert Hills on the Buda-side of the Danube, it was serene and conducive to academic thought. He liked his professors and he looked forward to his studies. He was intrigued by the ancient architecture nearby, reminding him that history was much longer here than in America. His previous trip to Budapest had not afforded him any opportunity to see the city. Now he had plenty of time to roam the medieval streets of Castle Hill and explore famous sites like Matthias Templom, where King Matthias Corvinus married Beatrice in 1474. He even had time to just sit and drink in the magnificent view of the mighty Danube winding through the city, dividing Buda from Pest. Surveying the view from the Fisherman's Bastion, Endre felt like he was part of something much larger than himself. The seven white turrets of the Bastion represented the original Magyar tribes that arrived in the Carpathian Basin one thousand years ago. Endre had always known that Hungary was his ancestry by birth, but now he was beginning to know it with his heart. He felt the current of the Danube in his veins.

Endre went back to his dorm room and sat down to write his parents a note. He knew this was a good news / bad news letter. They would be happy to read that Ilonka had become his wife, but disappointed that they weren't on their way back to America. They'd be pleased that he was studying towards his engineering degree, but concerned about his decision to stay in a communist country.

When Eva read the letter, she was just as worried as Endre knew she would be. The horror stories from Eastern Europe were reaching the West with regularity. Ferenc did his best to reassure her that this time was different. This time, he was in the country officially, not hiding from enemies. That should provide him some measure of safety. In fact, Endre even had a few points in his favor in the new Russian-Communist Hungary. First, as an American, he had fought against the Germans, as had the Russians. Second, he came to Hungary voluntarily to study. If anything, that made him less of a threat and more of a valuable propaganda piece. Eva still worried.

When word got around to Endre's friends that he had returned to Budapest to study engineering, and that he had married a Hungarian girl, the reaction was mixed. Some, like Jimmy, were happy for him, knowing how thoroughly he had searched his heart in making that decision. Others, like John, thought going to a communist country was a bad career move. Kim said he was crazy. Going to a communist university and marrying a peasant girl! Obviously the war had messed up his head.

Eva allowed herself to cling to the hope that the happy couple would be home within a few years, as soon as Endre finished his degree. In her more optimistic moments, she even dared to dream that Hungary would be free by then. Ferenc was right, she admitted, it was different this time. It was still hard to have Endre so far away but knowing he was safe, and being able to communicate with him, made it bearable. In the meantime, she decided to make it her mission to spoil her new daughter-in-law with packages containing chocolate treats, cosmetics, and trinkets, plus blue jeans and other goodies for the boys. She could send the packages directly to Endre at the university. Now that he was in the country legally, there was no reason to route the mail through Romania anymore.

In Budapest, Endre reconnected with László. They didn't have much free time during the weeks, each busy with their own responsibilities, but on those rare weekends when they were both going home, they travelled together. László confided to Endre that he was increasingly uncomfortable with his role in the army, now that it was under Russian command, but he believed it was his duty to stay. Although no one dared to speak of it openly, László believed there were others like him, men who stayed in uniform as career officers because they were waiting for the opportunity to fight for the freedom of Hungary. He was sure the time would come, eventually. He spoke these thoughts to no one but Endre. He felt sure that Endre, being an American, would understand Hungary's yearning for freedom.

Endre did understand. The more he saw of the communist way, the more he wished he could take Ilonka back to America. But his personal freedom was no longer enough. He wanted Hungary to be free. If Hungary were free, then he could take Ilonka to America and they could come back to visit any time they wanted to. Even thinking such thoughts was dangerous with the increasingly brutal regime at the helm.

"Time to go."

Endre ignored him. He was hoping to spend the evening studying.

"It's five o'clock," urged his dorm-mate.

"Uh-huh," said Endre. Were they serious? Did he really have to attend every meeting? He'd already been to two this week.

"Believe me, you don't want to not be there."

That sounded like a warning. Endre didn't want to ask, or what? Instead, he reluctantly got up from his desk and made his way to the gymnasium, where most of the student body was already gathered.

The band marched in. All the meetings began with The Internationale, the anthem of communism that had replaced the Hungarian National Anthem. Everyone else seemed to know the words already. Endre would soon learn them:

> *"Arise ye workers from your slumber*
> *Arise ye prisoners of want..."*

The third verse was the one that troubled Endre the most:

> *"No saviour from on high delivers*
> *No faith have we in prince or peer*
> *Our own right hand*
> *the chains must shiver..."*

And on to the call to unite the world under the flag of communism:

> *"So comrades, come rally*
> *And the last fight let us face*
> *The Internationale unites the human race!"*

No wonder they banned the playing of the Hungarian anthem, thought Endre. Not only does it reinforce a common national identity around which people might rally, it also opens with a plea for God's blessing on the nation; whereas, the new anthem is perfectly clear in its bold denunciation of any possibility of heavenly help.

The Communist Youth Party leader took the podium. His words rang out like a fiery sermon and Endre couldn't help but make the comparison to religion again. Instead of the Bible, his text was Marx, Lenin, or Engels. Today's theme was freedom, freedom from government. Quoting Lenin, he said, "So long as the state exists there is no freedom. When there is freedom there will be no state." Endre tried his best to follow this logic, but he just could not reconcile it with the most glaring contradiction that communism was, in fact, one of the most controlling forms a state could take. They owned everything: this university, all the factories, even the farms.

Adding his second quote from Lenin, like a preacher might add the second reading from the New Testament, the speaker's voice boomed through the gymnasium, "Socialists cannot achieve their great aim without fighting against all oppression of nations." Nobody would dare say it, but everyone in the room knew it, Hungary was indeed oppressed by the Soviet Union. Yet, somehow, they were supposed to believe they were on a magical path to peace and harmony.

Nothing about this freedom message made any sense to Endre because it bore no resemblance to the reality he had experienced. He had lived in the capitalist America that these speakers regularly condemned. He knew that his parents, operating their own farm, on private property, were much more free and far more prosperous than the farmers in Hungary who were forced to join collectives and robbed of their produce. He knew first hand what no one else in this room knew, that a poor American was better off than most people in Hungary. Ironically, the great exceptions, were members of the communist ruling elite.

The meeting closed with more singing of impassioned political songs and ended with the speaker encouraging them to be good comrades. Just like a preacher, he chose his text, expounded upon it, and finished with the exhortation to go out and live by the holy words. Funny, thought Endre, they say they don't believe in religion, yet they've created their own parallel religion, more fanatical than anything I've ever seen. But, of course, he kept these thoughts to himself.

CHAPTER TWELVE

The leaves turned colors and the crops were brought in. The grapes were picked and Endre helped Uncle Vince make this year's new wine. Most of the apricots and plums were canned but some were used to flavor the *pálinka* brandy. The *zserbó* and *rétes* baking began. It was time for the harvest ball.

The townsfolk were glad to see Endre. The stories surrounding him were confusing. Was he a Farkas cousin? Was he from Arad? Could he really be American like Gombos' goons claimed? Did he and Ilonka really get married? Then, could he still be a cousin? By the end of the harvest ball, most people managed to put together this much information: yes, he was an American student at the university in Budapest; yes, his family was from Arad; and no, he was not Ilonka's cousin. Wasn't it dangerous for Endre to be here, some wondered. Sure it was, but no one was safe these days. Life was dangerous for everyone living in the mad world of communism.

The girls of Markota were ecstatic when they heard that Ilonka's cousin was back, and then disappointed. Anika imagined that he came back for her until she learned that he had married Ilonka.

"I always thought they were more than cousins," she whispered to Rozsi.

Endre danced with everyone at the harvest ball and easily charmed his way back into their hearts. He danced much better without his fake limp. This year he even attempted the *csárdás,* and did a half decent job of the leg-slapping high jumps. By the end of the night, he was firmly established and accepted as a Hungarian boy – a bit more complicated than most – but basically just another Hungarian boy.

Hand in hand, they walked home in the dark and Endre led Ilonka around the back of the house to the foot of the ladder. Sitting on the haybale, with his arm draped over her shoulder, they sat in silence admiring the nearly full moon.

"Come to Budapest with me," Endre said unexpectedly.

"What?"

"Come to Budapest with me," he repeated.

"You know I can't do that."

"I remember you told me once, here in this very spot, that you wanted to go to Budapest and study to become a seamstress."

"Oh, that. That was so long ago."

"Not that long ago," he protested.

"Not that long ago that I told you, but long ago since I thought I could really do it." In the quiet pause, she remembered her brother. "That was when Jozsi was still alive. We were just kids with dreams. Silly dreams."

"I want you to have your silly dream."

"I need to stay here. I need to look after *Anyu*. I need to be here for the boys when they come home on the weekends. Dreams are for children. I have responsibilities now."

Endre wanted to protest but the words that came out made him feel selfish, "I want you in the city with me. I miss you."

"I miss you, too," she said. "I'll be here waiting for you when you come home."

By the start of Endre's second year of university, September 1947, family life had settled into a new routine. Ilonka spent her days working alongside Uncle Vince looking after the farm and caring for her mother. She got together with Mariska a few times a week to work on their domestic projects and to offer each other support while Endre and László were away in Budapest. She budgeted her limited resources very carefully, always making sure there was enough extra food for the weekends when Sanyi and Lajos returned from Győr, and she looked forward to the two weekends a month when Endre came home.

For Endre, life was filled with classes, studying, and long walks on the ancient streets or along the banks of the Danube. He was a good student and rose to the challenges of academia. He loved walking through the historic streets and the castle-ruins of Buda. His initial enthusiasm and sense of connectedness with a thousand years of ancestry never wore off.

Sometimes his walks along the Danube led him across the *Szabadság-hid*, Liberty Bridge, to the Pest side, where it was more built-up and more populated. This is where he felt most keenly the reality of living in a communist state. In contrast to the green hills of Buda, Pest was gray and urban.

He was glad Ilonka was out in the country, and that they still had chickens, pigs, a small vegetable garden and a few fruit trees. The folks in the city seemed worse off. Like that poor man, thought Endre, noticing the beggar dragging his useless legs along the pavement. While Endre was searching his pockets for some loose change, two AVO men appeared and launched an attack on the pitiful figure. They ordered him to stop begging because in communism everyone has all he needs. His behavior was a disgrace to the State.

The beggar cowered, crawled into a doorway and began to cry.

The AVO officers left, laughing.

Endre was moved, "*Apu*, Father," he said, "may I buy you dinner?"

The man was stunned. Acts of kindness towards strangers were rare. In these times, a man could hardly trust his own brother, much less a stranger. More commonly, people just kept their eyes to the ground and their thoughts to themselves. Through his tears, he nodded his acceptance.

Endre helped the man to a table in the courtyard of an outdoor café. Over a hearty bowl of *gulyás*, Endre spoke gently to encourage his new friend to talk to him. The beggar really didn't want to say anything. Talk was dangerous. Yet, this stranger was so kind, and there is that small relief that comes from sharing.

The first thing Endre learned about the beggar was that he was only twenty-nine years old, not nearly as old as he had thought when he addressed him as *Apu*.

His hair was gray and thinning, his cheeks sallow, his skin sagging. "I've aged twenty years in the last eight months," he said quietly.

Endre nodded sympathetically.

The beggar ate some of the beef stew and took a long drink of water, before adding, "60 Andrassy."

Endre understood. 60 Andrassy Ave. was the most infamous address in Budapest, the AVO prison. Formerly, it had been the headquarters for the Arrow Cross Party, the para-Nazi organization that terrorized the Jewish citizens during the war. Now, the AVO had moved in. The political prisoner population was many times what it was when the Arrow Cross resided there. The basement torture chambers had never been so busy. That accounted for the beggar's badly misshapen legs.

He had been beaten, his legs broken, the bones never set and never allowed to heal properly.

Before returning to his dorm room, he left the man with enough forints to buy a few more meals. At least for a while, he wouldn't be beaten for being hungry.

Endre made friends at the university, but the only friend he trusted enough to speak freely to was László. On their trips back to Markota, they tried to make sense of all the craziness around them. Endre told László about the man he met in Pest this week and what he'd seen of the AVO.

"Speaking of the AVO," recalled László, "I wanted to warn you that I saw Gombos in Pest this week..."

Endre bristled at the mention of Gombos' name.

"... wearing an AVO uniform."

"Oh," said Endre, processing that.

"He looked very comfortable in the uniform," added László.

"Yes, I imagine he'd be good at his job," said Endre, with undisguised revulsion. "Did you talk to him?"

"No," said László, "I avoided him. I thought it best not to remind him that Markota exists. I'm hoping he's so full of his self-importance in Budapest that he won't look back."

Endre nodded.

"If he sees you, he'll remember Ilonka. He'll remember that he sent his goons after you, claiming you were American. Now, he'll be proven right. He could get awfully angry at you, Ilonka, or anyone in Markota who protected you. I don't want to see what retribution he might exact in his self-righteous fury, wearing an AVO uniform!"

Endre's blood ran cold at the thought. "No, he can't find out that I'm back. It's best that he forgets Markota altogether."

"I think he mostly has," said László. "And I think Markota is happy to forget him. We certainly don't want to do anything to remind him. Keep your eyes open and make sure you see him before he sees you," warned László.

Endre decided that from now on, he'd limit his walks to the Buda side of the Danube, and if he ever needed to venture over to Pest, he'd do it very carefully.

Endre and László's train arrived at the station. Disembarking, they could see Uncle Vince's horse and wagon. Uncle Vince was pacing.

"What's happened?" asked László, fighting back his rising dread, on seeing Vince's obvious agitation. Uncle Vince was a seasoned war veteran. It would take a lot to rattle him.

"It's Lajos," he began. "Get on the wagon," he ordered them. This wasn't a safe place to talk.

The two men climbed up wordlessly.

Uncle Vince flicked the reins, setting the horse and wagon in motion. The moment he thought they were far enough away from the station, he told them what had happened. "I was expecting the boys home tonight, but only Sanyi came. Where's Lajos? I asked him."

Endre and László waited while Uncle Vince swallowed his fear.

"Then Sanyi told me about the escape."

"Escape?" repeated Endre, immediately understanding. Lajos had often told Endre that he would like to go to America. Sanyi always said he wanted to go too.

Uncle Vince continued, "Apparently a plan was hatched very quickly at the factory this week. Four guys decided they'd had enough and they were leaving. Now! Lajos heard about it and said he'd go with them. Sanyi said he wanted to go too, but not like this. He needed to see his family once more, say a proper good-bye to his mother, so he told Lajos he would see him in America some day soon."

Every time Uncle Vince spoke the word America, Endre braced himself for some recrimination about putting these foolish thoughts into the young boy's head, but none came.

"Sanyi said one of the boys made it back to tell what happened. The AVO found them near the border. Two of them were shot. Lajos and another were taken into custody. The boy who made it back was still under cover of brush when the AVO officers spotted the others. He turned around and ran, reported to work the next day and claimed he had just gone home sick. His pay will be docked for not getting permission to leave but they don't seem to know that he was involved in the attempted escape."

"Okay," said László tracking Vince's account, "then Lajos is in custody now?"

"As far as I know," said Uncle Vince.

Endre said nothing. He was thinking of the man he had dinner with in Pest and was feeling very frightened for Lajos.

By the time Uncle Vince finished telling them all he knew about this, they were arriving in Markota. They stopped talking while they drove through town. At supper, around the Farkas kitchen table, Sanyi answered their questions the best he could. When all was said, they sat quietly looking down at their food, until Mariska broke the silence.

"Oh Lajos!" she cried. "Why couldn't you have been more patient?"

"Well, he wouldn't really be Lajos then, would he?" said László with a small smile, trying to lighten the situation a little.

"No," said Endre.

"No," Vince added, "he was impulsive."

"Yeah," said Sanyi. "Lajos was impulsive but never stupid. I'll bet he talked his way out of getting shot, even though it meant getting captured."

"I'd believe that," said Endre.

"I'm just glad his mother isn't alive to see this," said Uncle Vince. "Katalin adored her boy. If she wasn't dead already, this would have killed her."

"And he adored his mother," remembered Mariska. "If Katalin was here, he never would have left."

"I'm not sure about that," said Vince. "He was still the same Lajos."

Not too much more was spoken about it. There wasn't much else to say and absolutely nothing that could be done. Yet, whenever silent eyes met, it was clear that all thoughts were full of Lajos. No one slept very well that weekend. The dark nights were filled with anxious prayers rising from hearts that hurt for the impetuous sixteen-year-old.

The weekends came and went. The men came home and left again. Day after day, Uncle Vince, Ilonka, and Mariska kept up the work of running their households and their subsistence farms. Harvests were sparse. Taxes were high. Incomes were low.

The Soviet Union had taken over entire industries: electricity, coal, uranium, transportation, and agriculture. Red stars appeared on public buildings and pictures of Stalin and

Rakosi glared at them from everywhere. Private enterprise was demolished. All but the tiniest businesses were nationalized. Farms were organized into collectives, owned by the State. The flag was still the tri-colored, horizontal red-white-green but in the centre – where the coat of arms of the renowned nineteenth century revolutionary Lajos Kossuth had been – there was now a Soviet hammer and sickle. Public holidays were changed. August 20, St. Stephen's Day, when the nation celebrated the establishment of the one thousand year-old Hungarian state, became a day for people to celebrate their 'liberation' by the Soviet Union.

Even Christmas came and went in drudgery. Stripped of its religious significance, it became a secular festival of pine needles. Christmas celebrations with decorations, gifts, and special baking were only memories of times past. This year's biggest luxury was one Italian orange that Endre brought back from Budapest as a special treat for Ilonka.

Ilonka missed the Christmas frills, but even more she missed midnight mass. Although Mindenszentek Church was once the focal point of community life in Markota, no services were held there anymore. The doors were never locked, but still no one dared to step inside. A neighbor might see. Everyone suffered from extreme *csengőfrász* – the fear of the midnight doorbell. When the doorbell rang, loved ones disappeared into the black of the night – often never to be seen again. Having faith in anything other than the State was akin to treason.

Privately, Ilonka prayed while she went about her chores. Her list of petitions was long. She prayed that their basic needs would be met; their daily bread provided; the safety of the men while they were away and as they traveled back and forth; Lajos – God bless him wherever he was; healing for her mother; and peace to come at last. Sometimes she wondered why a loving God would let such things happen in her country, but with Job-like faith she acknowledged that God's ways were unknowable and she put her trust in his ultimate goodness.

Ilonka and Mariska shared their worries while they cleaned their houses and tended their vegetable gardens. On the darkest days, they cried on each other's shoulders. On other days, they encouraged each other to count their blessings. They had each other; they had their husbands, at least on some weekends; they had their families, although they grieved the absence of Lajos; and they still had food enough and a roof over their heads.

The future was uncertain. But why keep thinking it would only get worse? If it could get worse, it could also get better, couldn't it? They waited.

As Uncle Vince directed his horse and wagon to the station, he could see the locomotive pulling away. Either he was late or the train was early. Sanyi was waiting for him, standing next to a skinny boy.

"No! Oh, my God!" exclaimed Uncle Vince, jumping down from the wagon. The scrawny youth ran into his uncle's arms. "Lajos!"

It was the sweater Vince recognized, not the boy. The blue sweater Mariska had knit for him years ago. He had almost outgrown it, but now he'd lost so much weight that he was swimming in it. "Oh, dear God!"

Lajos had no words, just a weak version of the impish smile he was so well known for.

"Lajos!" Uncle Vince exclaimed again. "Come, let's get you home," he said as he helped the boy up onto the wagon. The train station was no place for questions.

On the drive home, Sanyi kept his arm protectively around his friend. Bundled now in Vince's coat, Lajos still shivered in the blast of the cold winter wind.

Uncle Vince couldn't stop looking at him. "Dear God!" he exclaimed again, "I can't believe my eyes."

By the time they pulled into the Farkas yard, Lajos had fallen asleep. "Let's just put him to bed," Sanyi suggested.

Two hours later, Uncle Vince arrived from the train station again, this time with Endre and László. Lajos was awake now and Ilonka was putting the *töltöt káposzta*, stuffed cabbage, on the table. So many questions hung in the air, but with one look at the thin, pale boy, all anyone could say was, "Lajos, I'm so glad you're home!"

For two days they fed him and pampered him. While Lajos slept, Sanyi told them all he knew, which wasn't much yet. When Lajos was released from prison, he was taken immediately to the factory to finish a day of work and to be an example to his co-workers, who might be thinking about escaping. Sanyi said, "hardly anyone even dared to speak to him at the factory. They just looked at him as if he were a ghost walking in our midst."

On Sunday evening, Uncle Vince took the boys back to the train station. He could hardly bear to watch Lajos get on the train. Stay home. Please. Stay for just a few more days, he wanted to say, but he knew that wasn't possible.

Back at the factory, Lajos did his best to make his quota, but in his weakened state he just couldn't manage it. Sanyi made up the extra work for him. His supervisors noticed, but as long as the production targets were being met, they didn't care.

After a second weekend of family pampering and Ilonka's cooking, Lajos was managing to keep up at work most days, putting on a little weight, and starting to look like his old self once again.

On the third weekend, Endre and László were home again. By then, Lajos was feeling a need to talk. "There wasn't much to eat at Andrassy," he said unexpectedly.

Everyone was full of questions, but they waited.

"It was very crowded," Lajos added.

"It sounds awful," said Ilonka.

"They beat people."

Uncle Vince clenched his fist.

"They beat me... more times than I can remember, but not like... not like some of the others. Tortured. I heard the screaming."

Ilonka covered her mouth.

"Enemies of the State. They tortured the enemies of the State. Me... they said I was just a foolish youth who didn't know how lucky I was to be living in this communist paradise, instead of in the capitalist hell I tried to run to."

Again Endre waited for the American recriminations. None came.

"Re-education. They said I needed to be re-educated. They gave me books on Marxism to read. When I could recite enough, they let me go. My reward was that they gave me my job back. I'm supposed to be very grateful... well, I suppose I am grateful to be out of there."

He paused. "The strange thing is, they want to educate you but they make you drink the coffee."

He was met with puzzled looks.

"I don't think the coffee was good for thinking."

"Do you mean drinking? The coffee was not good for drinking?" asked Uncle Vince.

"No," said Lajos, touching his head. "It was not good for thinking."

Oh, now they understood. They had heard rumors about the coffee being laced with sedatives. It helped control the prisoners, and also made them less resistant to the mind-control techniques.

"It made it so hard to read, and hard to remember what I had read so I could answer their questions."

"Because the only lesson they really want us all to learn is that they are in control," said Uncle Vince quietly.

"Did you know," began Lajos, "the problem is not with the communist system, but with the opposition of the people to the system. The system is perfect." Mockingly quoting Marx, he added, "'From each according to his ability, to each according to his needs.' That sounds fair, doesn't it?"

"Yes," said Ilonka, matching his sarcasm, "And our needs are so abundantly met."

No one in town commented openly on Lajos' disappearance or on his reappearance. People were beginning to learn that these things happen. And when they do, it's best to pretend they don't.

CHAPTER THIRTEEN

The cap and gown ceremony was as full of pomp and ritual as it is anywhere in the world. Hundreds of flags fluttered in the wind, military bands played, and Prime Minister Rakosi himself was there to offer his words of congratulations to the graduating class from the engineering department at the Budapest University of Technology and Economics. The graduates were supported by a mob of delighted friends and relatives.

Endre thought about his father and mother. He tried to imagine them in the crowd. Of course, they couldn't be there, but Ferenc and Eva sent their congratulations in a letter and, Endre knew, they were beaming with pride from seven thousand kilometers away.

For Endre, only László was there. Although all of Markota had adopted Endre as their own Hungarian son, Budapest was too far to travel for most folks. Endre knew that Sanyi and Lajos would gladly have made the trip, but they turned eighteen last year and were currently carrying out their compulsory military service. He also knew that Ilonka badly wanted to be there but travel, in her condition, was not advisable. Although they had been hoping for a baby for a few years, Endre was happy it hadn't happened until now. It was hard enough being so far away from his wife while he studied; being away from his wife and baby would have been even more worrisome. Endre couldn't help but smile at the thought, I'm going to be a father!

The band struck up the Internationale. The crowd rose and voices joined in the compulsory communist anthem. By now, Endre had learned the words but he still choked on them.

> *"... So comrades, come rally*
> *And the last fight let us face*
> *The Internationale*
> *unites the human race..."*

At the third verse, he always stopped singing. It was his small act of rebellion. The whole song was repulsive to him, but he absolutely could not bring his mouth to form the words: *"No savior from on high delivers."* Instead, he hummed and joined back in at: *"No faith have we in prince or peer..."*

No one noticed. He had played the role of dissatisfied ex-patriot well enough. In fact, in the valedictorian speech, Endre received special mention: "Although an American by birth, he chose to study here under our superior system. This American is an inspirational role-model to our young Communists!"

Endre held his face expressionless. It was a look he had perfected. After four years in the country, he had still managed to resist all pressure to formally join the Communist Party; although he was required, like everyone else, to attend the compulsory Marxist study groups. The valedictorian didn't mention that.

After the ceremony, László helped Endre clean out his dorm room and move his few possessions home.

As the train pulled into the station they could see the large banner: "Congratulations Endre!" Uncle Vince was there to meet them. The wagon was decorated with a grad cap and brightly colored streamers.

Arriving in town, they were met by a throng of neighbors and friends, and taken directly to the inn, where the party was already underway. No longer did anyone question where Endre came from. Proudly, they celebrated with the first Markota-boy to graduate from university.

Later that night, after the revelers went home, Endre and Ilonka sat beneath the hay-loft ladder. Silently, he looked at her for so long that she finally asked, "What's wrong?"

"Nothing," he answered. "I'm just getting used to it."

"Does that mean you don't like it?" she asked, realizing he meant her new haircut.

"I do like it. It's just so different from your long hair."

"It makes me feel more grown up," she said. "More like a mother."

"I feel more grown up tonight too," he said. "Not a student anymore."

They were on the verge of new beginnings, but tonight was a time for remembering. They had accumulated a grand collection of reminiscences. In addition to the dramatic recollections of the early days of hiding in the loft above, now they also shared four years of married memories.

"It's alright that we don't have much," concluded Ilonka simply, "because we have each other, and soon we'll have our baby."

Endre said he agreed. It wasn't alright, but now was not the time to say it. He agreed that they didn't need more material things to be happy, but he did think they needed peace and security. The AVO was running around the country rounding up good people, who had committed no crimes, and subjecting them to unimaginable horrors. How happy could people be when they lived in constant suspicion of their neighbors? In constant fear of that knock on the door? What kind of world were they bringing their child into?

Ilonka cuddled up beside him, snuggled in a light blanket. On the hay-bale couch, she drifted off to sleep. Endre shifted around and lay down beside her, resting his hand on her enlarged tummy. Those were all things he could worry about tomorrow. None of that could be allowed to intrude on this warm, starlit night, with his wife and unborn baby sleeping in his arms.

Sanyi and Lajos didn't make it home very often these days. Sanyi was serving as a guard on the nearby Austrian border and Lajos was driving transport vehicles all over the country. Rarely were they given leave, so it was a very lucky coincidence that all the men were home on the weekend that Ilonka went into labour.

Mariska handed her another bowl of washed potatoes and carrots. Ilonka set the bowl down, paused, placed both hands on her belly, breathed deeply for a few seconds, then started again to chop the vegetables.

"Are you alright?" Mariska asked.

"Sure," said Ilonka. "It's just…" she stopped talking and started breathing deeply again as the next pain hit her.

"I don't think so," said Mariska, taking the knife and the potato from her hands and leading her into the bedroom. "Go get the mid-wife," she told Sanyi. She sent Lajos out into the yard to find Endre and tell him that the baby's time had come.

Eight hours later, Endre held his son, a beautiful baby boy, six pounds, eight ounces, while his exhausted wife slept.

He presented the infant to Erzsi, "your grandson, *Anyu*."

Erzsi held the precious babe close to her and rocked him gently.

"He looks like you," Lajos said to Endre, smiling at the tiny face peering out at them from inside his swaddling blanket.

Endre smiled proudly.

"I see Janos in him," said the delighted grandmother.

"I do too," agreed Endre.

Ilonka and Endre had months ago agreed on baby names. The chosen boy name was László Janos Kovacs. László was for Endre's best friend; Janos was for the baby's grandfather, who died as one of the first martyrs of Soviet Communism in Hungary.

"Hello Laci," cooed Sanyi at the newborn. "Do you like your new name?" he asked, using the informal version of László, which seemed far too serious a name for this tiny life. Little Laci yawned his approval, then started to cry.

"I think he's hungry," said Mariska, taking him from Sanyi's arms into the bedroom to wake up Ilonka.

The presence of a new life naturally turns everyone's thoughts to the future. Uncle Vince poured a round of *pálinka*, while he wondered what the world would look like by the time this little boy grew up.

The Farkas kitchen table was the one place where they all felt safe to speak their minds, and there was always a lot to say.

Sanyi and Lajos complained about the constant fire-hose feeding of propaganda. "We have two hours a day of Marxist training!" said Sanyi.

"My tongue is sore from biting it to keep from screaming, bull!" added Lajos. "Seriously, such bull. Does anyone really believe this is the best way to run a country? While no one has enough money to heat their shabby apartments and put decent food on their tables, can they really believe that socialism is meeting all their needs?"

The military officer in László was encouraged by what he heard. He was confident that in them he had two loyal soldiers who would fight for a free Hungary if the opportunity ever came. He believed there were many more young men just like them.

Uncle Vince agreed with László and decided that this was the right time to share his secret: he confessed to them that he had been smuggling refugees. "I started doing it soon after Lajos came back from prison. When I saw what they had done to my nephew, I decided that for any refugees who made it as far as Markota, I would do all I could to see them safely the rest of the way to the Austrian border."

"Uncle Vince…" Lajos began to protest.

Vince raised his hand to stop him, "I have to."

"Do you need money?" asked Lajos.

"Of course I need money, who doesn't?" It was well-known that the refugees often emptied their pockets at the border because the forints they were carrying had no value outside the country. "But I'm not doing it for money. It's just the right thing to do."

"It's dangerous," argued Sanyi.

"Of course."

"In that case," said Sanyi, "here are some things you should know." Reaching for a scrap piece of paper, Sanyi drew a rough sketch of the border and marked the guard posts and the patrol routes. "The patrol schedules are varied, of course, but this is where the routes overlap, so there's more traffic in these areas, and not as much traffic here," he said pointing to less protected sections.

"Someday," said Lajos, "I'm going to cross that border again and this time they're not going to catch me."

"Next time, I'm going with you," said Sanyi.

"I understand," said László, "but I hope that not all of our finest and bravest young men will go, or there will be no one left to fight for Hungary."

Uncle Vince knew he'd never leave. He was getting too old to make such a big change in his life. Still, he said, he would gladly die for the chance to defend Hungarian soil from the occupying Soviets. And in the meantime, he would help anyone brave enough to chase the dream of freedom.

All too soon, it was Sunday night again. One of the wagon wheels was broken so the men walked to the train station together. Lajos was headed for eastern Hungary, Sanyi for the Austrian border, László back to Budapest, and Endre to Tatabanya.

With his new civil engineering degree, Endre was put in charge of public transportation in the city known for its coal mines. Tatabanya was only half the distance from home that the university in Budapest had been. Endre accepted this job mainly because he would be able to come home every weekend. Already, he could hardly wait for next Friday night when he could come back home again to his wife and baby Laci.

Little Laci grew quickly, soon walking, then talking, and providing them all with endless entertainment. He loved to kick and throw his big red ball around the yard and the boys were happy to play football with him all day long.

"Good kick!" yelled Sanyi.

"A few more years and you'll be on the Olympic team!" encouraged Lajos.

"Your mommy will be so proud. She was a great football player too, you know?" said Endre.

Ilonka smiled and gave the ball a gentle kick back to Laci.

Hungary was the reigning Olympic Champion in 1953. The 6-3 victory over England was widely celebrated. It was one of the few diversions folks could allow themselves that gave them an outlet for making a lot of noise and openly expressing their national pride.

"The radio will say, 'What a kick! Score! In the net by the famous football player, Laci!!!'" shouted Lajos.

The little boy giggled and kicked the ball back again.

Mariska and László adored and doted on Laci. They seemed destined to remain childless and Laci was the beneficiary of all their longings for a child to love. László brought special treats home for him from Budapest and Mariska knit clothes for him.

He was the apple of Uncle Vince's eye too. When he scooped little Laci up, sat him high on the wagon seat and took him for rides, he looked like a little man going around town about his business.

Laci explored his world with the enthusiasm and eagerness that comes naturally to three-year-olds. Sometimes, he could even persuade his grandmother to come walk in the garden with him. He brought her one shoe, and then he toddled back to the door and brought her second shoe. Even before he could talk the message was clear: Grandma, come play outside with me. Only on her very darkest days was Erzsi able to resist his invitation. As soon as she started to put her shoes on, baby Laci was running towards the door.

In the yard, he watched the little frogs that sat in the grapevines. He tried to catch them, but they were too quick. He loved the big Russian horse. Erzsi was puzzled by his unyielding assertion that the horse was green. He would not be persuaded otherwise. "Green!" he insisted.

"I don't understand," laughed Ilonka, through the kitchen window. "He knows his colors, but he likes to say this white horse is green."

Lajos and Sanyi had been civilians for a year now. Their obligatory military service was completed. America was still on their minds but getting across the border was difficult and dangerous. Occasionally, Uncle Vince transported those who were brave enough to try, but these were usually people who had come to the attention of the regime in some negative way. They had nothing to lose by attempting to make a run for freedom. Lajos and Sanyi could still afford to wait.

Upon completing his service, Sanyi decided to attend the Budapest University and study engineering. Endre helped him with the application. Lajos didn't think he could get into university. Under the communist regime, loyalty to the State was a criteria for admission and Lajos had already made one failed escape attempt. His subsequent compulsory military service might not be enough to forgive that. Instead, his years in the army led him to the discovery that he loved all things mechanical and he was a very skillful driver. He jumped at the opportunity when Endre suggested coming to work for him as a bus-driver in the public transportation department in Tatabanya.

Sanyi received word that he was accepted into the engineering program and he would be starting at the end of the summer. In the meantime he was also working with Endre as a junior clerk in the administration office.

Every weekend, the three men traveled home from Tatabanya together on the train. No one was sitting near enough to hear, so they quietly teased Endre.

"Are you sure it's the State that blessed us with our homes? I know for a fact that it was my great-great-grandfather who built my house," said Sanyi. "But I'll thank the State because I'm sure the idea came from Russia."

As part of the management staff, it fell to Endre this week to lead the Marxist study group because the senior party member was ill.

"I'm sure I didn't use the word 'blessed'," protested Endre.

"No. That's true, you didn't," said Lajos. "Actually, you were pretty good, but you lacked the passion that the boss always brings to these meetings."

"I'll work on that," laughed Endre, discreetly.

Uncle Vince met them at the station. Little Laci, as always, was perched right beside him, joyfully shouting, "*Apuka!* Daddy!" At the first sight of Endre.

"*Napsugar!* Sunbeam!" Endre called back. Little Laci earned that nickname because of the bright smile that always shone on his face.

While little *Napsugar* was smiling and talking more and more each day, Ilonka was smiling and talking less. Endre took notice of that on his last few weekends home but he hadn't had a chance to ask her about it yet. He was determined to find some time, for just the two of them, this weekend.

After supper, Endre packed a light picnic and a bottle of wine, made from the grapes in their yard, and together they walked down to the Keszegér.

It was nice to have a quiet moment alone, just the two of them. For most of the week Endre was gone away to work, and when he was home so was everyone else. Ilonka loved having all of them home, but she also needed some time alone with her husband, and since the baby was born it was even more difficult for the two of them to find time to themselves. Just being out in the countryside on this late July evening felt like freedom.

Sitting on the old log at the boys' favorite fishing hole, Ilonka leaned her head on Endre's shoulder and whispered, "I love you."

"I love you, too," he said, as he pulled her closer.

Ilonka turned and rested her back against Endre's chest. He wrapped his arms around her and together they watched the river wind its way around the bend. Time stood still until a fish jumped and broke the trance.

Endre moved to unpack their picnic. Ilonka basked in the magic of the summer evening. She felt like she had the best husband in the world and moments like this proved it. This little picnic was just what they needed.

As Endre poured the wine, and handed the glass to his wife, he saw the sadness still in her eyes. "What's wrong?" he asked.

Ilonka looked inside the deep red liquid, searching for words, "It's just... well, everything."

Endre waited.

Turning her head cautiously, she looked in all directions, even though there was no one around for miles. "It's this cursed communism! I hate it!"

The floodgate broke and the litany spilled out. "We work so hard and we have nothing. It's okay for a young couple to have nothing when they're first starting out but you have an education, a good job, and still we have so little. Right now, we have Sanyi helping with expenses. One day, he'll find a wife and they'll start a life of their own – as they should – but we'll have even less than we do now and they, too, will have nothing. Everything is so expensive. The salaries are so low to start with and then they take off all those deductions for Communist Party insurance and for donations to every kind of party and AVO cause they dream up to collect for. During the days I listen to the radio, to the Voice of America broadcasts. They say the same things you say about life in the west. On one salary, families can afford to buy clothes, cars, even their own homes. Here, I know couples with two jobs and no children who can barely afford to rent an apartment and buy food."

Endre knew this was true. He thought about one young couple that worked for him. Both of them worked ten hours a day and still only scarcely made ends meet. Endre knew his wife was not seeking anything extravagant, just a decent living.

"They tell us this is socialism where we have all we need, but we don't. We have food shortages. The damned collective farms are just an efficient means of stealing the crops from the farmers. Only the high-ranking Communists can afford to shop in the stores. For us, things are much worse than they were before the war. They say this is a classless society but that's nonsense. There are still those who have and those who have not. How much you had used to depend on how hard you worked; now it's based on your position within the party.

"Endre, I'm not talking about luxuries, but I would like to be able to buy a new dress once in a while. I wanted to buy you a watch for your birthday last year but I could not scrape together enough money. And Laci, he's only three so he doesn't need much to make him happy, but it would make me happy to be able to buy him a new toy once in a while. Anyway, he won't be three forever. Soon, he will need clothes and shoes to go to school.

"The very idea of him going to school has me worried. I hear from the other mothers what the children are taught in school! They're teaching our children to speak Russian! Their textbooks are full of Marxist propaganda, and that is all they are taught. They come home and tell the things they've learned. Parents are shocked but dare not speak up to correct them – afraid to teach their own children! Afraid because the children are asked directly about what their parents tell them. 'Do your parents have Stalin's picture hanging on the wall at home?' Every family does, of course, for fear the child will answer innocently and the father will disappear one night and never return. No one dares speak his mind even to his neighbor because he may be an AVO spy.

"Mariska was telling me this week that Anna's little girl came home and announced that God is dead! Her ten-year-old told her that only old fools rely on God. Enlightened, modern people know that salvation comes from the State. The State meets all our needs. That's what she learned in school. Imagine a generation with no God!"

Ilonka shook her head. "And about Cardinal Mindszenty, they teach the children that he is a traitor to Hungary.

"Cardinal Mindszenty! I remember when they arrested him, in 1948, and charged him with treason for crimes against the State because of his opposition to communism and his unwavering support of religious freedom. Now the school children are being taught that he confessed to a long list of crimes, but those of us who remember his impassioned radio broadcasts know that these 'confessions' were the result of years of imprisonment and torture."

Sadly, she said, "Even I... even I pray for Laci but I never pray with him. I guess that's my mother-instinct not wanting to hand him something dangerous, but it scares me to death. Remember when we had him baptized? It was a secret ceremony and he was too young to ever know whether he was baptized or not, unless we tell him. But we can't tell him; he'll blurt it out. He's three. He talks all day long about whatever enters his innocent little head. He's so curious about those little green frogs but I can't teach him about the God who made them. No one ever goes to church in Markota anymore. Everyone is afraid his neighbor will see him and report him and he'll be shipped off to a re-education camp."

Silently, Endre put his arm around his wife's shoulder.

"Oh Endre," she sighed loudly, "What's happening to our country?"

Looking around once more to make sure they were still alone. "It's that damned Rakosi!" she said naming the Prime Minister who had made such horrific use of the powers of the AVO. "Ever since he returned to Hungary, right after the war, there has been nothing but trouble. He has led us into this brutal Stalinistic regime. Endre! People are disappearing daily! What kind of world have we brought our little boy into?"

Ilonka was silent for a long time after that. Finally, Endre asked, "Do you want to leave?"

She searched the dark red wine again. "I have to admit I've been thinking about it… but, is it right?"

"What do you mean, right?"

"Maybe this is crazy but I think Hungary is special. I imagine everyone feels the same way about their homeland, but we have a thousand years of history. We survived 150 years of Ottoman occupation before the Islamization of Europe was finally halted at the Gates of Vienna. Next, the Germans – 150 years of Habsburg occupation – until we formed the Austro-Hungarian monarchy. That fell apart in the first world war and then we lost most of our country through Trianon. Now, it's the Russians… Hasn't my homeland suffered enough?"

After another long silence, she said, "I'd feel like a traitor, like I left my country in its time of need. Do you think that's crazy?" she asked.

"No," Endre shook his head. A part of him felt that way too.

"But at the same time…" she continued, "I don't know that my being here is doing any good."

The quiet evening down by the river had worked its therapeutic magic. Around mid-night, they walked back under a cloudless starlit sky. They had solved none of the country's problems, but they felt like they could face another week.

CHAPTER FOURTEEN

Suddenly everybody was talking politics – quietly, with carefully chosen words – but they were talking to each other about political matters for the first time in years. Stalin was dead and, little by little, information about his reign of terror was becoming known. "They're saying the blood of twenty million is on his hands," said László to Endre, in a quiet corner of a Budapest cafe. "Even the Kremlin is trying to distance itself from the name of Stalin."

"Incredible," said Endre. "Even Rakosi is considered too hard-line for the Soviet Kremlin now."

Once again, the country was thrust into a time of massive changes. Imre Nagy replaced Matyas Rakosi as Prime Minister and he introduced a program, which he called the New Course. By western standards, Endre knew that Nagy was still considered a communist, but his vision was for a kinder, more humane socialism. During his two-years in office, he freed thousands of political prisoners and ended the mass arrests, but the AVO still operated. More of the large, ugly, block-style apartment buildings were built. The units inside were tiny, poorly ventilated, and inadequately heated, still the Communists boasted about their provision of affordable housing to the masses. People still went to the black market for medical and dental services, if they could afford to, because the state doctors pushed their patients out the door with the injunction to get back to work. The medical instruments were old, sometimes even rusty. Food prices continued to rise while wages remained the same. Practicing religion could still be considered an act of treason. Special stores were still only for the favored communist elite. There was some movement towards private enterprise as some farmers were allowed to leave collectives and sell their own produce. Everything didn't change overnight, but people began to have hope.

In 1955, Rakosi rallied to regain power but Moscow feared an outright revolution if they reinstated the unpopular Rakosi. Instead they installed Andras Hegedus, but retained Ernő Gerő – Rakosi's fervent deputy – in the position of General Secretary. Once more, the population was disappointed. The small hope faded again to dark despair.

Magyar Radio, broadcasting from Brody Sandor St., was the voice of daily propaganda. The host was interviewing a guest, allegedly just returned from America. He was describing the atrocities in the west. "Capitalists abuse their workers. The laborers do all the work but it is their bosses who get rich. The owners of the big corporations are the only ones who are rich in

America. The proletariat slaves labor without reward to keep their bourgeois masters in luxuries. Unlike here. Here, the people own the factories they work in, or the collectives they farm in. We all work together and we all profit together. The capitalist corporations are…"

"Oh shut up!" snapped Ilonka as she punched the off switch.

Little Laci looked up from the toy truck he was pushing across the kitchen floor. "What's a corporation?" asked the six-year-old.

"Nothing," said Ilonka, "and don't use such big words ever again!"

Laci looked away, feeling hurt and confused.

Ilonka reprimanded herself silently. *Oh, God! I'm an idiot!* She sat down on the floor beside her son and drew him into her embrace. "I'm sorry, darling. You didn't do anything wrong. You just heard a word on the radio. The thing is…" What was it she wanted to say to him? "The thing is, that's not a nice word so you should not say it, okay?"

"Okay," agreed Laci with childlike faith in whatever Mother says.

Ilonka held him close, and solemnly vowed to herself that she'd never again listen to these broadcasts when Laci was around. *I can't have him going around and blurting things out. Someone might think we're raising him to be a capitalist-sympathizer. After all, his father is an American.*

Little Laci, forgetting by now what all the fuss was about, wiggled his way out of his mother's embrace and went back to playing with his truck.

Uncle Vince knocked once and opened the kitchen door. He was heading to the train station and wondering if Laci wanted to come. The question wasn't even out of his mouth before Laci was running to the wagon.

"I guess that's a yes," laughed Vince.

Ilonka smiled as she closed the door behind them and watched the horse-drawn wagon turn out of the yard before returning to her dinner preparations.

At the train station, Uncle Vince and Laci met Endre and Lajos returning from Tatabanya. While they waited for Sanyi's train, Endre and Lajos took turns swinging Laci in big circles and pretending to lose foot races to him. An hour later, they heard the distant rumble of an incoming train on the tracks stretching towards Budapest. Laci jumped up and down yelling, "Sanyi, Sanyi, Sanyi!" Endre held his hand tightly as the train approached but let him go when he caught sight of Sanyi dismounting. The affectionate little boy ran straight to Sanyi and was scooped up in a big hug.

"What a wonderful welcome home," said Sanyi to the beaming child. This was the end of the first week of classes in the fourth and final year of his studies.

That evening, after Laci was tucked snugly into his bed, the adults shared a bottle of homemade *pálinka* at the kitchen table.

Uncle Vince told them about his week. "Two couples came from Budapest. One of the women had blisters on her feet so bad she could hardly walk. I kept them here for two days to try to give her feet some time to heal. Even after that, I could see she was still in a great deal of pain, but they wanted to go to the border as fast as possible. The two men had recently been released from prison and they were terrified of being sent back.

They told me they were forced to work up to sixteen hours a day. They said most of their meals were nothing more than stale bread and smelly water. When they were given vegetables, they were near-rotten. On little sleep and inadequate food, they were expected to meet production quotas and beaten if they failed to achieve their targets.

Endre shook his head and topped up the *pálinka* glasses.

"To add insult to injury," continued Vince, "even in prison they were subjected to lectures on the virtues of communism. They were told it was a great system that paid its laborers, even in jail. It didn't take advantage of their forced labor like the capitalists."

Ilonka remembered the radio program from this morning. *I guess they think we'll believe their lies if they tell them often enough*, she thought.

"So, I asked them if this was true," said Uncle Vince. "I asked them if they were paid for their labor."

A skeptical snicker worked its way around the table.

"Oh! They were paid alright," said Vince, "the same fair wage they would have been paid at the factory down the street. That all sounded good, except that they were also charged exorbitant rates for room and board. For crowded, cockroach infested cells and barely enough food to stay alive, they paid their full month's salary. But this way, the Communists could go on the radio and tell the world that they pay their prisoners a fair wage for the work they do. That's why they were in such a big hurry to move on. They were afraid of getting caught and jailed again for trying to escape. Just as well, I don't like to hide anyone here any longer than necessary."

"It's just too dangerous," said Lajos, worried about the chances Uncle Vince was taking.

"Especially when you never know who anyone really is!" said Ilonka.

"AVO are everywhere," agreed Endre.

Uncle Vince was quietly wondering whether or not he should tell them the rest of the story. He started with, "I took them to the border on Thursday. Two guards stopped us…" Then, he paused to take a swig of *pálinka* before continuing. "I think we might have been able to talk our way out of it."

He tapped his fingers on the table. "Anyway, we'll never know. One of the guys was very quick to draw his gun. I didn't even know he had a gun. Pop! Pop!" Vince gestured like he was shooting a pistol. "Two shots; two dead guards."

"Russians or Hungarians?" asked Sanyi.

"Hungarians," answered Vince.

"They wouldn't have shot you," said Sanyi.

"Well, you wouldn't have when you were a border guard, but who knows about these guys," said Vince. "Anyway, I wouldn't have shot them either, at least not at that point, but I never had the chance to make that decision."

"Then what happened?" asked Endre.

"Then," continued Vince, "they just wanted to get going over the border as quickly as possible.

"No doubt!" said Lajos.

"But I made them help me hide the bodies first. We just dragged them into some taller grass off to one side," said Vince. "I didn't want their comrades to come upon that scene and start shooting in revenge at anything that moves. This way, maybe I'd have time to make it home at least."

"Good thinking," agreed Lajos.

"I'm getting too old for this much excitement," said Vince, looking tired.

Endre reached for the *pálinka* bottle and topped up the glasses again.

"My week," began Sanyi, "wasn't nearly so dramatic, but it was interesting."

All eyes turned to Sanyi.

"I joined a secret club," he said.

Ilonka looked worried.

Endre put his hand on Ilonka's.

"It's called the Petőfi Circle," he said.

"A poetry club?" asked Ilonka. Everyone knew that Sandor Petőfi was one of Hungary's most famous poets and his poetry was an inspirational force of the 1848 revolution, in which the Hungarians fought to free themselves from the Habsburgs, eventually resulting in the establishment of the Austro-Hungarian Empire. His poems continued to inspire patriotic sentiments.

"Not exactly…," said Sanyi. "It's a university debating club, originally formed by the Communist Youth Organization. That part isn't secret. The cautious debate of Marxist philosophy is permitted, but the debates are becoming more pointed, for example, debating the exploitation of Hungarian uranium by the Soviets."

Ilonka raised her eyebrows.

"The students are making increasingly bold statements about freedom and the need for political change."

"Like Petőfi did…" she said.

"Yes." Sanyi began to recite:

"Talpra magyar, hí a haza !
Itt az idõ, most vagy soha !

By the third line, all the men had joined in:

"Rise up, Magyar, the homeland calls!
The time has come; it's now or never.
Shall we be slaves or be free men?
By the God of the Magyars,
we swear unto Thee,
We swear unto Thee –
that slaves we shall no longer be!"

With each line, the recital grew louder and Ilonka looked very afraid. "Shhhh!" she commanded. "What if someone hears you?"

But they would not be shushed. Partly it was the *pálinka*, but mostly it was the breaking loose of a nationalism too long suppressed.

"Sanyi, please…" she began again. Turning to Uncle Vince, "Please tell him not to do this! You know the AVO will squash these students and their little club!"

"They might," agreed Uncle Vince.

"Endre, please…" Wouldn't anyone listen to her?

"Ilonka," began Endre. "You said yourself that you don't want your son to grow up in this hell."

"I know, but…" she began. She remembered the radio broadcast incident and how she had silenced Laci. Her son was six years old and she was afraid to teach him about her own values, her family's values, Hungarian values. Instead, she trained him to survive. Always say this; never say that! These children will become nothing more than communist robots. No, she admitted, this was not the way she wanted to raise her son. This was not the world she wanted him to grow up in. But could anything really be done to change it? Or does everyone who tries, die?

"Okay," she conceded. "Tell us about this club."

"It's an underground group on campus. People are fed up with the lies they've been told. Any idiot can see that the average worker is not well off. Hungary's resources are raped. Hungary's workers are paid slave wages. The profits all go to Russia. That's not right. We want a form of government that is Hungarian controlled, with Hungarians as the beneficiaries. The profits from our labors should stay in Hungary, not go to lining the pockets of the fat hogs in Moscow!"

"That sounds like a step in the right direction," said Ilonka.

"It would be," agreed Sanyi, "but even more important is freedom. Hungarians should not be ruled by Russians. We want our government to be made up of freely elected Hungarians. We want freedom of the press, freedom of religion, and the immediate release of all political prisoners."

"Exactly," said Ilonka. "Without those liberties, it doesn't matter what economic system a country has."

"That's right," agreed Endre.

"We need freedom from being told what to think all the time. Even at the bus station, the posters of Marx and Stalin stare at us constantly," Lajos spat their despised names.

"Even in my own office," admitted Endre, "I have to display a picture of Stalin."

"We need freedom from terror," added Vince. "People must be free to speak their minds without fear of retribution. These days you can be thrown in jail not only for what you said but even for what someone thinks you meant by what you said!"

"There should not be any political prisoners. No thought police, no Russian thugs, no AVO," agreed Lajos.

"I'm with you," Ilonka said to Sanyi. She couldn't help adding, "but please, please, be careful."

Lajos initialed and dated, October 23, 1956, on the sign-out board at the back of the bus station and picked the corresponding ignition key off the adjacent panel. He had one more trip to make before he could call it a day. On this run he would transport the afternoon-shift workers to the coal mines and return the exhausted early shift to their base camp.

"*Jó nappot, Péter!*" Good day, Péter," he called to the driver of bus number six.

"Shhhh!" answered Péter. "Are you hearing this?"

Lajos stopped his preparations and joined Péter and the other drivers who were glued to the radio broadcast:

"An unruly mob has gathered at Bem Square. The rebels say they are peaceful protesters, supporting the workers in Poland who are revolting against Mother Russia. Fear not, Hungarian comrades," the radio announcer's voice assured them, "police are on hand to subdue the rebels and the public will not be in any danger. We don't want anyone to be alarmed."

"Nice to know they're protecting us from the rebels,'" said Lajos sarcastically, defiantly ignoring the possibility that there could be AVO ears in their midst.

"They started marching this morning," said Péter. "From Budapest University to Bem Square. Veres – from the Writer's Union – gave a speech in front of General Bem's statue and they all started reciting Petőfi."

"From the university? The students?"

"It started with the students," said Péter, "but as they marched other people joined in."

"Alright! All of you, on your buses and get going! Comrades are waiting on you to take them to work!" shouted the shift supervisor.

They almost turned away from the radio and boarded their buses when the announcer said, "They're marching again. The demonstration is being led by a group of rebellious university students who say they're going to Parliament. The crowd has grown to about fifty thousand. They are flying Hungarian flags with the Soviet crest ripped out, and shouting *Ruszkik Haza!* Russians Go Home!"

"This is it!" exclaimed Lajos. "Today is the day we take back our country!"

The bus drivers looked at him, stunned at first, and then all at once every face was illuminated with the same realization.

"We're not getting on our buses!" shouted Lajos. To a man, every bus driver followed him in the spontaneous protest strike that grew amongst the bus drivers of Tatabanya.

The supervisor turned back in confusion. He couldn't stand with them, could he? It was his duty to get them back to work. He shouted again, "On your buses!"

Péter answered him by cranking up the volume on the radio.

Drowned out by the electronic voice, the supervisor was flustered. What else could he do? He went upstairs to the administration offices to report the drivers. Endre Kovacs, the

Transportation Engineer, was in his office. Relieved, the supervisor handed the problem up the chain of authority.

Endre tried to listen to the frazzled supervisor, but the full-volume electronic voice booming from one floor below really said it all.

Endre went downstairs. By now the drivers had made placards, some were of the Hungarian flag without the Soviet crest in the middle, others contained bold and dangerous slogans like *"Ruszkik Haza!"* And "Gero into the Danube!" The radio was turned up loud and the hypocritical assurances of the electronic voice – that the dangerous rebels would soon be put down and Hungary would be safe again – only spurred on their new-found courage to fight.

Endre walked straight to the radio and adjusted the volume to a more tolerable level. Mixed reactions rippled through the crowd. With the appearance of an authority figure, some started to walk back to their buses; others, defiantly, took up the chant on the radio, *"Ruszkik Haza!"*

Endre went over to Lajos and tried to speak quietly and reasonably to him in private, but Lajos would not allow it. "Come on Lajos," said Endre, "I have to get you guys back to work."

"Forget it. The revolution has begun. This is not a day for driving people to work at slave labour mining jobs. This is the day to free our country!"

The radio announced that the crowd had begun to call for the return of Imre Nagy to the government. The drivers' chant changed to "Imre Nagy! Imre Nagy!"

Lajos was right. The revolution had begun.

"I'm with you," said Endre. The uprising broke out in Tatabanya in support of the students in Budapest. First the bus-drivers, then the workers from the coal mines. The intoxicating buzz of revolution was in the air.

"To Budapest!" yelled Lajos.

"Take the buses!" ordered Endre, "and take everyone who wants to come!"

Lajos and Endre knew that Sanyi and his Petőfi Circle group were already in the thick of this, and they had heard of the growing multitude on the radio. Still, they could not believe their eyes as they neared Parliament. The crowd was now two hundred thousand strong, calling for Imre Nagy, calling for the ousting of the Russians, calling for freedom!

As the sun set, darkness enveloped Kossuth Lajos Square. The red star on Parliament's dome spire was illuminated, casting its eerie crimson glow over the crowd. The reaction was immediate:

"Turn off that damned star!

"Turn it off! Turn it off!"

Extinguished. Cheers of victory.

Then total darkness. All the lights were put out.

"Guess they want us to go home," someone said. But no one left.

People began making torches out of newspaper. It seemed like everyone had a copy of today's *Szabad Nép*, Free Nation. Endre and Lajos rolled up their newspapers and lit them on fire. Thousands more did the same. Newspaper torches burned amidst continued chants, "Imre Nagy! Imre Nagy!"

The lights came back on.

Word was getting around that Gero had been on the radio this evening denouncing the demonstration, calling them a revolutionary mob.

"Gero into the Danube!"

"*Ruszkik Haza!* Russians, go home!"

"We want Imre Nagy!"

"Give us back our uranium!"

The crowd continued to press their demands, but the protest remained peaceful.

Finally, Imre Nagy appeared on the balcony. "Dear comrades," he began to address the crowd, but the protestations to the objectionable communist term 'comrades' drowned him out.

"My fellow Hungarians," he began again. Now they had a leader they could rally around. He led them in the hymn, which is also Hungary's national anthem. It had not been heard in public for many, many years:

Isten, áldd meg a magyart...

God bless the Hungarian with good cheer and abundance
Stretch toward him your protecting arm when he does battle with the foe
Long has misfortune been his fate; bring now joyful years
The nation's suffering has already atoned for the past and for the future.

Voices rose together in the words of the anthem while tears streamed down the faces of the gathered multitude. Could victory have come? Yet, there stood Imre Nagy, proof that Hungary's fate was about to change. Hungary would be run by Hungarians for the good of Hungarians.

Jubilation and optimism pulsed through the crowd. "Imre Nagy! Imre Nagy!"

"Sanyi!" Lajos shouted with no chance of being heard over the throng. He grabbed Endre's arm and began pulling him through the energized masses towards the spot where a moment earlier he had caught sight of Sanyi.

"Come on!" he called, keeping his eye on the spot where Sanyi alternately appeared and disappeared with the pulse of the crowd.

As they got closer, Lajos could see that Sanyi was part of a group that was leaving the square.

"Sanyi!" he called again, finally catching up.

"We're going over to the radio station," said Sanyi without stopping. "We have a delegation there already, but they haven't been allowed to broadcast yet."

"Broadcast what?" asked Lajos.

"Our manifesto. We want the whole country to hear it."

Throughout the day, everyone had heard at least some of the sixteen points that the students had drafted:

1. The immediate withdrawal of all Soviet troops
2. The election by secret ballot of new officers for the Hungarian Worker's Party
3. A reconstituted government under the leadership of Imre Nagy; immediate dismissal of all Stalin-Rakosi criminal leaders
4. Public trial of Matyas Rakosi and his associates
5. General elections by secret ballot throughout the country to elect a new National Assembly and for workers to have the right to strike
6. Re-adjustment of Hungarian-Soviet and Hungarian-Yugoslav relations

with no interference in each other's affairs

7. Re-organization of economic life in Hungary to protect the vital interests of the Hungarian people

8. Re-evaluation of our foreign trade agreements in respect of reparations that can never be paid; disclosure of information about the uranium deposits in our country; Soviet exploitation and concession regarding these resources; and the right to sell our uranium freely at world market prices to obtain hard currency

9. An immediate adjustment of wages including a minimum wage for workers

10. The rational use of produce and the equal treatment of individual peasant farms

11. The re-examination of all political and economic trials by independent courts and the immediate release and repatriation of prisoners-of-war and of civilians deported to the Soviet Union and elsewhere outside Hungary

12. Freedom of opinion and expression, freedom of the press, free radio, free daily newspaper

13. Removal of the statue of Stalin, symbol of tyranny and oppression, and replacement with a memorial monument in honor of the freedom fighters of 1849

14. The replacement of the existing foreign coat of arms with the Hungarian Kossuth arms; new uniforms for the Hungarian Army consistent with Hungarian national traditions. March 15 (1849 Habsburgh revolution) to be declared a national holiday and October 6 (1849 execution of thirteen Hungarian military generals) to be a national day of mourning with school closures

15. The students of the Technological University of Budapest unanimously declare their solidarity with the students and workers in Warsaw and the Polish national independence movement

16. The students of the Technological University of Budapest will organize local branches of the Hungarian Federation of University and College Students' Associations (MEFESZ) and all the nation's youth shall be represented by their delegates

By the time they rounded the corner onto Brody Sandor St., a large crowd was already assembled at Magyar Radio. Long-suppressed anger about the daily propaganda broadcast from here was suddenly unleashed in shouts of, "No more lies!"

A delegation of students had made it inside the building but they were detained by the AVO, whose presence heavily guarded the building. Amidst fears of violent outbreak, calls rose to let the students broadcast.

Shortly after 9:30 p.m., reports began to reach the crowd at the radio station of the events on Dozsa György St. The Joseph Stalin statue was down! The students had pulled with ropes, but the sturdy figure resisted their efforts. Then the metal workers arrived, and the giant communist icon was no match for their acetylene torches. The ugly iron dictator lay on the tram tracks.

Victory shouts echoed through the streets and, encouraged by the achievement of one of their sixteen goals – the removal of the Stalin statue – the students pressed on.

Gero's broadcast from two hours ago, still rang in their ears. He had called them reactionaries and hostile elements determined to disrupt the political peace of Hungary. Enough of the deception! They would listen to no more propaganda!

Renewed calls for the student broadcast were still not met and concern for the students inside the radio station continued to grow. Rumors began to circulate that they had been shot. Again, the crowd's fury rose.

The AVO deployed tear gas in an attempt to subdue the protesters. Half-blinded, with stinging eyes and tears streaming down their faces, they stood their ground. The AVO opened fire. With the first bullet, the revolution exploded.

Soldiers from the Hungarian Army were dispatched to bring order to the scene. Once there, László – and the men under his command – tore off their red stars and sided with the students. The moment László had been waiting for had finally arrived. He had the loyalty of his men and they were fighting for Hungary, not for their Soviet masters. As news spread of the AVO firing on unarmed protesters at the radio station, Hungarian army units everywhere began distributing weapons and ammunition to the protesters.

The crowd turned on the murderous AVO. For all their heinous acts of brutality they would pay, starting today. The AVO was surrounded and running out of fire power. They attempted to smuggle in a re-supply of weapons and ammunition in an ambulance, but when the crowd cleared to let the ambulance through and it failed to stop to assist the wounded, the students caught on to the ruse. They stormed the emergency vehicle and appropriated the delivery. The armed protesters began returning fire on the AVO. They could almost touch freedom. There was no turning back.

By the early morning light, Lajos and Endre made their way through the city streets to where the Stalin statue used to stand. Only his boots remained, and a Hungarian flag was flying from them now. The people had spoken.

When the sun came up the next morning, October 24, 1956, factories were shut down all over the country. Word of the revolution had spread and workers went on strike in support of the freedom fighters in Budapest. Red stars, Marxist posters and other public symbols of communism were vandalized and began to disappear. Communist books fed spontaneous bonfires. Hundreds of political prisoners were released. The tri-colored Hungarian flag was popping up everywhere, often with a hole cut out of the middle where the Russian coat of arms had been.

At regular intervals the radio announced that fascist and reactionary mobs had launched armed attacks against the citizenry and the government. The announcements were openly mocked. Suddenly people were infused with the courage to challenge the propaganda. All public assemblies were forbidden, but no one paid any attention.

Later repeats of the announcement explained that, "Soviet soldiers are risking their lives to protect the peaceful citizens of Budapest." This brought laughter.

When the announcement concluded with, "workers of Budapest, receive our friends and allies with affection," the laughter turned to scorn.

And when the big news broke that Imre Nagy had become Prime Minister, the cheering crowds could not be quelled. The new Prime Minister announced that the AVO would be disbanded and that several of the students' demands would be met – in particular, negotiations for Soviet withdrawal would commence immediately.

Meanwhile, Soviet tanks rolled through the city streets, taking up positions, but holding their fire.

On October 25, 1956, Russian tanks snaked their way through the streets of Budapest. They had been filing into the city all night long. Everyone who had a radio opened his windows, and the city was filled with the electronic voice. The radio blared continued assurances into the streets: "Our Soviet friends and allies are here at the request of our government to help us put down the reactionary forces and restore order to our country."

"How could Nagy have appealed to the Soviets?" many asked.

"He didn't!" others responded. "It's a lie!"

"He said he was negotiating for the withdrawal of Soviet troops."

"Then why are more tanks coming?"

Russian speaking students pled their case to the Russian soldiers. "Don't shoot! We're Hungarians, students, workers, farmers. All we want is a free and democratic Hungary. Don't shoot!"

Throughout the city, there were violent encounters between student groups and the AVO.

Imre Nagy was heard on the radio urging an end to the violence and an end to the strikes, along with further promises that negotiations for Soviet withdrawal were underway.

A crowd was gathered at Parliament. Soviet tanks ringed Kossuth Lajos Square.

"Long live Imre Nagy!"

"*Ruszkik haza!*"

Lajos and Endre were half a block away, tired and hungry but driven by the adrenaline that surged through the city.

Endre spotted movement on the rooftop. Men with guns. He stopped abruptly, causing Lajos to follow his eyes. He saw them too.

The AVO officer raised his weapon and fired. Did he aim for the Russian tank? Or just happen to hit it?

The Russian T-34s, believing themselves to be under attack, began firing into the crowd. Many in the crowd were armed with weapons provided by the Hungarian army, but they were no match for the tanks and the roof-top snipers. Parliament square was awash in blood.

The fighting escalated through the night. Steel-helmeted soldiers fired rounds from their sub-machine guns, tanks rattled through the streets, civilian freedom fighters overturned cars to create barricades and fired back with whatever weapons they were able to get their hands on.

Imre Nagy pleaded on the radio and continued his calls for cease fighting and to return to work. Assurances about the withdrawal of Soviet troops were falling on deaf ears when the Soviet tanks were right there – in the heart of the city – firing on them.

Men, women, and even children joined in the fight to drive out the Russians. Lajos and Endre arrived at Corvin Cinema to witness the astonishing sight of teenagers assembling Molotov cocktails. "What are you going to do with those?" asked Lajos.

"Come with me," said a young girl, following a slightly older boy of about sixteen. "And bring these," she added, handing them each a gasoline bomb.

They moved out along Ulloi Rd., to find a tank coming upon one of their barricades. The tank stopped. The young boy took a paving stone in his hand and began to crawl towards it. "What's he doing?" asked Lajos, alarmed. "He's going to get shot!"

"No. No, he's not," she said almost calmly, "he's staying in the tank's blind spot. They can't see him."

Endre and Lajos wondered if they should try to stop him, but it was too late. The young boy wedged the paving stone into the caterpillar tread. When it started to move forward again, the tread popped off, bringing the mighty Soviet T-34 to a dead stop.

The boy ran back to them. "Now we wait," he said, breathlessly.

They didn't have to wait long. The hatch popped up and the first soldier flung himself through the opening. Without a moment's hesitation, the boy pumped three bullets into him, while the girl lit the fuse on her gasoline soaked rag and tossed a perfect shot into the immobilized tank. The explosion was immediate.

The young freedom fighters had devised many tricks for stopping the tanks. Besides creating barricades, they also placed fake land-mines on the streets that the tank drivers would be afraid to drive over. Other streets, they doused in soapy water causing the mechanized monsters to lose traction. And sometimes, they lured the tanks down narrow streets into corners where they could not maneuver. Eventually, the air supply ran out, the hatch was opened, and the Molotov cocktail was launched. Burned out tank hulls smoldered all over the city.

Hungarian soldiers continued to tear the communist badges off their caps and uniforms and join the fight on the side of the freedom fighters. Soviet flags, red stars, and other Soviet emblems burned in fires all over the city. Shop windows were plastered with "*Ruszkik Haza!*"

The hospitals were full. Women took wounded into their homes to nurse them. Along with the tri-colored flags, black flags were flown in windows to honor the dead.

Food was becoming scarce. Mothers risked their lives standing in line-ups on the violent streets trying to gather enough rations to feed their children.

The Russians began to get hungry. Their supply chain was breaking down.

Lajos and Endre cautiously picked their path around the bizarre tangles of downed telephone and electrical wires. Fatigue and hunger made them quiet. Endre thought about Ilonka. When would he make it back to Markota?

Gunshots reverberated through the streets, returning Endre's thoughts to Budapest – to the increasing violence, the growing Russian presence despite the promises on the radio, and the still-rising wave of patriotism that pulled every last citizen to his feet to advance the desperate bid for freedom.

"It's Uncle Vince!" shouted Lajos.

A very excited crowd had grown rather suddenly. Food! Fresh produce! Farmers were bringing wagons full of fresh food into the city to give away to the freedom fighters. Endre and Lajos pressed their way through the crowd towards Vince.

After hugs and relief at finding each other safe in the midst of so much chaos, news of home was exchanged for news of the battle. Vince told them that everyone was safe in Markota and said he'd be happy to go back home and tell them that the boys were safe also. "Have you seen László?" he asked them.

"Not today," said Lajos, "but we saw him yesterday. He's with his unit. They're fighting on our side."

"I'll keep looking for him," said Vince. "I don't want to go home without good news for Mariska too. And Sanyi, have you seen Sanyi?"

"The last time we saw him, he was at the radio station.

While they were talking the fresh produce disappeared from Vince's wagon, but Vince had stashed a secret supply under the seat: four separate bags. He gave two bags to Lajos and Endre, and kept the other two in the hope of finding László and Sanyi.

Energized by fresh food and the sight of children defeating tanks, the revolution rolled on boldly. "*Ruszkik, haza!*"

Walking by an open window, they heard the radio again urging an end to the fighting, talking about establishing relations between Hungary and the Soviet Union as equal partners, raising the wages of all the workers, pledging amnesty to all the fighters, and negotiating a withdrawal of Soviet troops. "But," Lajos noted, "the tanks are still barreling through our city."

"What's going on there?" asked Endre, looking straight ahead at an angry mob of about sixty people.

"He's AVO! I know him. He arrested my father," the woman screamed.

The AVO had removed their uniforms, but as the personal dispensers of years of terror, their faces were not soon forgotten.

"Killer!"

They punched; they kicked; they spat.

"Torturer!"

They tied a rope around his neck and strung him from a lamp post.

"Murderer!" one last call.

Leaving the gruesome scene, the crowd dispersed quickly, suddenly very quiet. It had to be done, but it couldn't be celebrated.

Lajos and Endre turned away too.

Endre picked up a newspaper, suddenly there were newspapers everywhere, springing up overnight, some only a page or two in length. The lead story was an exposé on the privileged lives of the hated party leaders: villas on the Balaton, nannies for their children, special stores to buy food for their families.

"I thought we were all supposed to be equal," said Lajos.

"You didn't really think that, did you?" asked Endre.

"No, but it's what they always said. That's what they told us socialism meant. But what about where you're from – America – are people equal there?"

"Depends what you mean by equal. Economic equality? No. America doesn't promise that. There are rich people and there are poor people but, I can tell you this, poor families in America are better off than most families in Hungary."

Endre and Lajos walked on, each one thinking that it would be nice to find a place to lie down and sleep for a bit. Everyone they passed looked just like they felt: ragged, unshaven, sometimes blood-spattered, vacillating between dead tired and revolutionary adrenaline rush.

CHAPTER FIFTEEN

Intense optimism electrified the air. All over the country, labour unions were quickly forming and negotiations were moving towards safer working conditions, shorter work-weeks, and fair wages. Plans were being made for restructuring collective farms, either as private enterprises, or to remain collectives but with the profits being shared amongst the farmers instead of being exported to Russia. Municipal governments were going down without a fight, replaced by democratic local councils. Change was energizing.

There were no AVO uniforms to be seen anywhere. Former officers were either trying to pass in civilian clothes, hoping not to be recognized, or they were hiding in whatever holes they had crawled into. Overnight, the AVO simply disappeared.

Imre Nagy moved into his office in the Parliament building and his continued calls for ceasefire were finally being heard. The Russian tanks were rolling out of Budapest. Peasants spat on them as they passed by and there was no retaliation. Freedom rose from the ashes of revolution.

Nagy continued to press his demands for equality between Hungary and Russia as sovereign states, for Hungary's neutrality, and for withdrawal from the Warsaw Pact. Suddenly, there was free speech, freedom of the press, and freedom of assembly. On the streets of Budapest, lay dead Hungarian civilians and Soviet soldiers, but the fighting had stopped. Women were no longer standing in dangerous lines for meager rations and making fearful dashes back into their homes. Overnight, the shops were filled with fresh vegetables, and bread, and meat! Farmers, whose crops were no longer being diverted to Russia, brought wagonloads of late autumn harvest into the city.

Neighbors talked to each other. Speech, repressed for decades, broke lose. Husbands and wives freely shared their thoughts once again. People talked more openly with strangers than they had spoken with their closest friends in years. Parents and teachers began to speak honestly to children. Out poured words that, only a week ago, they were afraid to even think, much less speak.

They had forced the collapse of a tyrannical government. Imre Nagy was president and the Russian tanks were leaving Budapest. Infectious euphoria intensified every moment. David slew Goliath. They won.

But it was rumored that fresh Russian tank columns were entering the country, crossing the eastern borders with Slovakia, Ukraine, and Romania.

The church in Markota was full for the first time in over a decade. Little Laci sat with Ilonka, Erzsi, and Mariska inside the building he had walked by many times but had never been inside – that he could remember. After the service, Ilonka took Laci to the baptismal font and told him, "This is where you were baptized." Baptism was only one of the mysterious new things Laci learned about that day. Ilonka shared her faith with her son for the first time in his life and delighted to answer his many questions about this strange new place. She promised him that they could always go to church on Sundays from now on.

The new religious freedom solidified: Cardinal Mindszenty, the Head of the Roman Catholic Church in Hungary, was released from captivity. He was first arrested in 1944 for his opposition to the Nazi Arrow Cross government and then freed in 1945, when the Soviets 'liberated' Hungary from the Nazis. He was re-arrested in 1948 for his opposition to the oppressive communist regime. Upon his release, he gave a statement to the press praising the students, the workers, and the peasants, publicly siding with the revolutionaries.

His release symbolized the rebirth of religious freedom for all and it was met with the thunderous approval of the masses shouting, "Freedom for Mindszenty!"

Laci tried to repeat the shouting he heard on the radio but had difficulty with the pronunciation of Mindszenty.

Ilonka hugged him, and feeling her worry beginning to rise – despite her joy – reassured both herself and her son, "Daddy will be home soon."

"For the Survivors," read the sign on the donation boxes on street corners in Budapest. They were stuffed full of forints, yet nobody stole from them. The shop windows were broken, but there was hardly any looting.

"Nobody wants to taint our fight," said Lajos.

Schools reopened, so did barber shops, bakeries, and newspaper stands. Convoys of food continued to arrive in the city. The Red Cross brought medical aid. The gypsy music played at Parliament Square and people gathered to share their stories amidst dancing, singing, and celebrating. Hungarian flags fluttered on the breezes.

Radios continued to blare through open windows and Imre Nagy's speeches were applauded by all. He declared the expulsion of the old regime, gave assurances of Soviet troop departure, and promises of withdrawal from the Warsaw Pact.

The AVO had vanished and the Russians were leaving. People walked the streets with a lightness in their steps that switched easily to dancing whenever they heard music from a radio in someone's window or one of the street celebrations that had sprung up on every block.

The AVO had good reason to remain in hiding. The lynchings continued. The brutality with which they had terrorized the people was not so quickly forgotten, but shame began to grow, and the lynch mobs got smaller.

"We weren't trying to start a revolution. We just wanted to have better lives," Endre heard the student tell the foreign journalist.

The BBC sign on the side of his car filled them with hope. Surely, they had won. The world was watching. There could be no turning back now.

The MiGs appeared at the break of dawn. Endre heard the rumbling. There was no time to seek shelter. In an instant, the city went from triumph to chaos.

On November 4, 1956, Budapest woke to the sound of Russian fighter planes roaring overhead, the whistle of falling bombs, the detonation of explosives, followed by the crumbling of buildings.

Since the ceasefire and the troop withdrawal, Soviet Communism in Hungary appeared to have been defeated. For one week the nation revelled in victory. Unfortunately, Moscow did not accept this defeat. Contrary to what he told Nagy, Khrushchev intended to squash the revolution. Columns of Soviet tanks poured into the city.

The cries of the wounded mixed with screams of terror and began to fill the damp, cold early morning air.

Endre looked at Lajos, "Are you alright?"

"Yeah, you?"

The celebrations had started to slow a little as people grew tired and started going home to sleep but now, roused from their beds by the bombs, the people spilled back out onto the streets. Terror stiffened back into hardened resolve: the Americans will be here soon, they told each other. We will hold our ground! Immediately, the search for wounded began and make-shift medical brigades of women dragged the injured off the streets and did what they could to ease their suffering.

When the bombs started falling again, multitudes sheltered in cellars. Spaces quickly became crowded. Dripping pipes, poor ventilation, diminishing food supplies, lack of adequate toilet facilities rapidly turned hellish the safe refuges they sought.

Meanwhile, tank after tank rattled down Ulloi Street towards Kalvin Square. The nearby Corvin Cinema became the focal point of the battle. Anything that moved was a target. Many of the buildings in the central-Pest district were linked by underground tunnels, dating back to the days of the German occupation. The revolutionaries made good use of these tunnels, both for strategic deployment and as escape routes.

Once more, children made Molotov cocktails. Again, with sticks, stones, and simple gasoline bombs they fought against armored T-34s. They knew how to stop the tanks in their murderous tracks. Young boys and girls ran under the guns and wedged bricks and steel pipes into the treads. They had already learned how to use overturned trams as barricades, how to make counterfeit landmines to deter the tank drivers, how to soap the roads so the tanks would lose traction, and use the narrow city streets to their advantage.

Once the armored beasts were brought to a stand-still, they knew that all they had to do was wait. The occupants were trapped. Eventually, the hatch had to open – or sometimes it was pried open by bold young hands – then a volley of gunfire was showered inside and the job was finished off with the home-made gasoline bombs.

But this was a different week. The Russians had learned some lessons too. This time, the tanks didn't stop arriving. One thousand tanks rolled into Budapest. Also, this time, heavy artillery was stationed atop Gellert Hill and firing into the city, supporting the strafing and bombing by the MiGs.

The Hungarian Army units fought for their country. Hungarian tank units turned their guns on the Soviet tanks. Army officers supplied the freedom fighters with guns, bullets, and grenades.

Russian troops peppered the crowd with machine gun fire. The massive tank deployment, supported by air power, was overwhelming and devastating. Buildings crumbled to the ground, piles of rubble, tangled wires, broken glass.

Endre and Lajos made their way to Kilian Barracks to re-supply their ammunition. They found László's unit there and joined the fight alongside his men. Many others were doing the same, especially the factory workers.

In a brief moment of extreme clarity, in the midst of all the mayhem, Endre saw the irony: these workers were the very people that communism said it benefitted the most, the common man. Yet, despite their hard work, they were pitifully poor and they hated the system that enslaved them.

The further irony was in the ferocity of the youth. The average age of the Hungarian Freedom Fighter was sixteen to twenty-one. It was these youthful hearts that the Communists most actively sought to win. On the blank-slates of this new generation the Communists hoped to build their utopia. Yet it was the youth who spat in Mother Russia's face. Although they had known nothing but communist propaganda, and although they had no other first-hand experience to compare their lives to, their hearts knew they were not free people.

They fought on. Even when the bodies started piling up in the streets, they bolstered each other with brave words. One thousand were dead, and the sounds of mourning and weeping were coming from every home... two thousand dead, and the black flags hung in the windows.

Journalists from the free-world were everywhere. Rumors swirled that the United Nations and the Americans were coming. At any moment, the freedom-seekers expected fighter jets, paratroopers, arms and munitions supplies to support their desperate bid to throw off the yoke of communism and join the free world. Only more Russians came. The foreign journalists were bombarded with questions, really only one question: "When is help coming?"

It seemed like an eternity but, in less than a week, the Russians had regained control of the city. The death tally rose. Sporadic defenses were still attempted, but the Soviets had begun the mass arrests of tens of thousands of citizens. Still, the body count climbed... three thousand were dead, and an additional twenty thousand wounded.

On the road back to Markota, Endre, Lajos, Sanyi, and László looked like all the other travelers heading for refuge across the Austrian border. Mothers carried children, some were crying; others were wide-eyed at the adventure, but sensing their parents' fear, remained quiet. Fathers carried everything they could salvage from the homes they left behind. The travelers wore six or seven layers of clothing, partly for warmth but also as a way of transporting their limited wardrobes. The road was rough especially when shoes wore out, and feet blistered and bled.

Thankfully, for the most part, the passing Russian military convoys ignored them. Nobody knew how long that would last. The very sight of anything Russian caused them to hurry just a little bit more. They might open fire. They might close the borders. Perhaps they were already closed. Rumors circulated. Still, they kept walking in the hope that they could make it out of the country without getting shot. What lay ahead? They didn't know, but behind them Budapest was burning.

László looked past the trail of humanity and wished himself to be in Markota already. He wondered what to tell Mariska. He had betrayed the Soviets by leading his army unit in support of the revolutionaries. He dreamed of making this journey home to tell his wife about battles fought that ended with the liberation of Hungary, but they didn't. They ended with the deaths of thousands and the return of the Soviets.

After the euphoria of the past week, it was tempting to think they could re-group, launch another attack and win next time, but what seemed possible a few days ago – when the Russians were in retreat – seemed like silly, wishful thinking now.

"The battle is lost," he said simply. László was proud of the valiant young heroes who fought the military might of the Soviet Union with their bare hands.

As if to finish his thought, Sanyi added, "Bravery wasn't enough."

The tiny country was severely out-gunned by the super power to the east. The Hungarians knew that on their own they could not defeat the Soviet military. Realistically, their objective was to hold their ground until the West arrived with support. Initially they had great momentum. They sent the Russians packing, formed a new government, breathed free air for about a week, and even put up a good fight against the massive assault that followed.

"If the United Nations had shown up," said Lajos, "it might have been different."

It was well past midnight when their tired and swollen feet shuffled along the dusty Markota road. Coming up to Lajos' house, they could see the light was on. Uncle Vince was still up. They bid Lajos good-night and carried on. Next door was home for Sanyi and Endre. László continued alone wondering how to make his entrance without frightening Mariska.

Endre and Sanyi opened the back gate and went in through the kitchen door. All was perfectly still. Nobody heard them come in. Sanyi went straight to the couch and fell asleep the moment his head touched the well-worn cushion.

Endre went in to peek on his son, sleeping soundly. He kissed him lightly and crept back out again.

Very quietly, he opened the bedroom door. Ilonka. "My beautiful Ilonka," he said softly, and she stirred.

Gently lifting the covers, he eased his aching legs into the bed beside his wife.

She woke to the sound of his voice whispering her name. In the dark, she smiled, and thought she must be dreaming. She turned to face him and wrapped her arms around him, delighted to feel his body in the bed next to hers.

"I'm so glad you're home." She exhaled a deep sigh of relief. "Never, never leave. I was terrified I'd never see you again."

He didn't answer.

"Endre? Endre, promise me you'll never leave again."

He was fast asleep.

She snuggled herself up close against him, and kissed him. "Good night, Darling."

Ilonka didn't sleep for the rest of the night. She lay in the dark, quiet bed, moving her hand gently along Endre's back from time to time to reassure herself that he really was there beside her. Her heart was grateful and immeasurably relieved that he was safe and home. Ever since he left, she had been glued to the radio continuously monitoring the events in the city. Thousands were dead. Was there any chance at all that he was safe? She held her fears at bay by keeping busy. Fortunately, keeping busy was easy, thanks to Uncle Vince's unending procession of refugees.

While the boys were fighting in Budapest, Uncle Vince was leading a steady stream of migrants to the border. The money they gave him was passed on to Ilonka and Mariska, who used it to purchase extra food, which they cooked for the next wave of freedom seekers. A pot of *gulyás* or a hot breakfast of scrambled eggs was ready for anyone who wandered into Markota enroute to the Austrian border.

The radio was constantly on. The nation sat on pins and needles, listening for word of what was happening in Budapest. Khrushchev had replaced Imre Nagy with the puppet government of Janos Kadar, in blatant disregard for the expressed demand of the people. Because Nagy refused to support the Kadar administration, he was deported to Romania. Ilonka cried when the announcer said that Cardinal Mindszenty was forced into hiding. He was given political asylum at the United States embassy. For one Sunday, they were free.

These thoughts circulated in Ilonka's head and denied her any further sleep. Once more she ran her hand along Endre's back and kissed him lightly on his shoulder, before she eased herself gently out of bed. It was time to feed the animals and start cracking some eggs. Vince and his refugees would be here for a hot breakfast before setting off for Austria.

Endre woke to the sound of the bustle in the kitchen. Vince was here with the family of five travelers who had spent the night at his house. Each wave of refugees brought more bad news. One said there were thousands of bodies lying dead in the streets. Another said that there are now at least a hundred thousand Russian troops in Budapest. An American journalist was travelling with this group, documenting their flight. While Ilonka served the eggs, Endre grilled the American on one of the biggest questions on the nation's mind: Where are the Americans, the United Nations?

The American journalist said simply, "They're not coming." With downcast eyes, he added, "I'm sorry."

"But why?" prodded Endre. "I am an American. I fought in WWII for Europe's freedom. Voice of America broadcast the alluring vision of freedom into the farthest, darkest corners of communism. The Hungarian people rose up to grasp that freedom. As one American to another, tell me why couldn't we stand with them."

The journalist put his hand on Endre's shoulder and said, "Walk with me."

The two men rose from the table and went outside for a candid talk.

Clouds Over Markota 329

"How long have you been here?" asked the Journalist.

"Since the war," replied Endre.

"A lot has happened in the world since then," said the Journalist. "You probably don't get all the news here."

"No, I'm sure we don't"

"America is occupied right now with the Suez Canal crisis."

"Oh come on!" said Endre. "We're Americans! We can manage more than one crisis at a time, can't we?"

"I'm inclined to agree with you," said the journalist. "I think the real issue is the east-west power balance. It's only a decade since the end of the second of world war. The world is not ready for World War III."

"Who said anything about World War III?" said Endre. "We're just talking about supporting a tiny country's bid for freedom."

"Freedom from the Soviet Union," added the journalist. "That's the problem. To side with Hungary would be to start a war against the Soviet Union."

"I see," said Endre.

The journalist continued, "Since you've been here, nuclear weapon proliferation has become the major global security issue. The Russians and the Americans have missiles pointed at each other. The Hungarian-Soviet conflict is not winnable with a limited, strategic deployment of Special Forces to support the uprising. The Russians, as you saw for yourself, brought out all the muscle. To win this, the Americans would have to match that strength. If the Russians upped the ante, we would have to match that also. The fear is that the escalation would eventually lead to the use of nuclear weapons. The stakes are too high."

"Okay," conceded Endre, "I can appreciate that rationale, but I've seen young boys – and girls! – fighting tanks with their bare hands. If this wasn't a revolution deserving of the support of the free world, I can't imagine one that is."

"I can't either," he agreed.

The next day the journalist set off with his group of refugees to witness and record their decision to leave behind homeland and loved ones in their quest for freedom.

As one group of refugees left, another arrived. Their reports grew increasingly dismal. One man said the AVO was back. Another added that special police had begun arresting those who had any involvement in the revolution. This was to be expected, eventually. For Lajos, Endre, Sanyi, and László this news forced an immediate decision. It was only a matter of time now before their names would turn up on arrest warrants.

Lajos made his decision on the spot. Turning to Uncle Vince, he said, "Tomorrow, I'm crossing the border."

Endre pulled Ilonka away from her busy kitchen and said, "We have to talk."

"I know," said Ilonka, untying her apron and following Endre out to the yard.

At the foot of the hayloft ladder, they made the decision that would define the rest of their lives. Ilonka needed no convincing now. She had borne the pain of having to lie to her child. She had experienced her father's brutal murder and the living-death that her mother walked in ever since that horrible day. Now, she knew, her husband was in danger because he stood with the freedom fighters.

"I've already spoken to *Anyu* about it," said Ilonka. "She said she has already lost one son to the war, *Apu* to communism, and she does not want to lose her grandson too. She wants us to go to America."

"Are you sure?" asked Endre, remembering that concern for Erzsi was Ilonka's main reason for not wanting to leave earlier.

"Yes," said Ilonka. "I've also spoken with Mariska and Vince. They'll look after *Anyu*. They want what's best for Laci, just like we do."

László said he would be staying. He thought he was safe enough, given his role with the Hungarian Army. He reasoned that the Russians couldn't afford to prosecute every Hungarian soldier or they wouldn't have any domestic army left at all.

Sanyi also said he would stay. László advised very strongly against that. As a member of the Petőfi Circle, he would surely be a target for retaliation. He said, "Maybe. Or, maybe I'll live to fight another day. Besides, I'm in my final year of studies. The Russians still need engineers."

Early the next morning, Ilonka crept out of the house and walked down the empty street to the little church. She pushed the door open. It was never locked. The building had fallen into a state of disrepair, but it was still always open to anyone who dared to enter. In the sanctuary she knelt to pray. She looked at the Christmas crèche, set up even though hardly anyone would step inside to see it this year. There was Mary with baby Jesus, and Ilonka remembered that Mary had known what it was to flee for the sake of her baby's safety. She took courage from that and prayed for safe travel. She prayed for her mother, Sanyi, László, Mariska, and Uncle Vince who would stay behind. She prayed for her country, that somehow – soon – a way would be provided for Hungary to be free.

When Ilonka opened the front door to her house, she was welcomed by the smell of freshly brewed coffee. The household had awoken and, to everyone's surprise, Erzsi had begun the breakfast preparation. Mariska and László were here bright and early with a food basket for the travelers to take with them on their journey. Sanyi was at a loss for words. His sister, brother-in-law, and beloved nephew were leaving, probably forever. If that wasn't enough, his best friend since childhood was going with them. He wished them well and tried to be strong, but he couldn't keep the tears from pooling in his eyes when he hugged Lajos for the last time.

Immediately after breakfast, Uncle Vince brought the horse and wagon, loaded up the travelers and began the journey to the Austrian border. He had made this trip many times before, but always for strangers. This time was different. This time he was taking people he loved, including his own nephew. Lajos had been a handful as a young boy, left in his care after Katalin died, but he had grown into a fine young man, of whom he couldn't have been more proud.

Vince looked at the six-year-old little man sitting beside him. This was his last wagon ride with Laci as his co-pilot. The beautiful boy was one of the few bright lights in his life, and even he was leaving. Vince was always careful about the safety of his human cargo but never more so than on this trip. They passed Hungarian border guards who passively waved them through.

At the bridge, the little group bid Uncle Vince a somber farewell, crossed the border into Austria, and made their way to Andau, the nearest town. The tiny Austrian town was converted into a hospitality center with the entire population dedicated to welcoming and assisting the flow of refugees. Here, they began the immigration process that eventually landed them in Camp Kilmer, New Jersey.

In Austria, Endre asked an American journalist to send word to his parents. Eva nearly dropped the phone in her excitement. They'd been living from one news report to the next, waiting anxiously for word of what was happening in Hungary. They were up to date on the national matters but had no idea what had become of their family, until they heard the news that they were onboard an airplane that had departed from Vienna an hour ago.

Eva and Ferenc drove in from New York and were there in time to see the airplane land. They hadn't taken processing time into account in their haste. Many of the refugees spent weeks at Camp Kilmer before obtaining all the necessary medical clearances and arrangements for moving on. The fact that Endre was already an American citizen, with his parents waiting outside, helped considerably to expedite the process for his party of four, and they were cleared within a few hours.

Most of the other refugees would be starting from scratch, building new lives in America, but Endre, Ilonka, Laci, and Lajos had a family and a home waiting for them. Through the crowd, Ferenc was the first to spot them. He was overcome with emotion and couldn't stem the tears when he laid eyes on the little boy sleeping on Endre's shoulder. Time reversed. Just for a moment, Endre was six years old again and Ferenc was carrying his sleepy boy. Little Laci was the perfect miniature image of his father. Their family was home at last.

Christmas was still six weeks away, but Eva already had every gift she could hope for. Not only was her son home but now she also had a daughter-in-law and a beautiful grandson.

Christmas 1956 was eye-popping for Lajos, Ilonka, and Laci who had never seen Christmas trees with so much glitter, shops so full of food, and sweets, and clothes, and toys. Little Laci was introduced to Santa Clause. He sat on his knee, but had no idea how to answer the question of what he would like for Christmas. No one had ever asked him that before. Who was this magic man who could grant him a wish?

Little Laci understood very little English, so Daddy stood nearby to translate. Laci was stumped. What did he want for Christmas? Santa helped him out with some suggestions and they settled on a train set. Endre reminded him of the one he'd seen in the store window. Was that what he wanted?

"Oh, yes!"

The snow fell, but it was winter unlike any that Lajos, Ilonka, or Laci had ever known before. They had good coats and boots that didn't leak. The house was toasty warm and the heat wasn't lost to drafty doors and windows. The hot food and baked goods poured endlessly out of Eva's kitchen.

On Christmas Eve, they went to the Hungarian church. At least here, the newcomers weren't lost in the language. In the midst of the many things that were so different in their new world, church had a comforting familiarity to it.

"That's Mary and Baby Jesus," said Laci, pointing to the nativity scene.

"That's right," said Ilonka. It dawned on her that not too long ago – when Mindszenti was first freed – she had promised her little boy, in the sanctuary of the Markota church, that they'd be able to go to church every Sunday. Now, she'd be able to keep that promise. In the soft glow of candle light, the congregation sang Silent Night and little Laci fell asleep on Daddy's shoulder.

Laci woke to the sounds of Grandma making breakfast in the kitchen. He made his way down the big, wide staircase, much larger than any he'd ever seen before. He didn't make it into the kitchen because he was stopped in his tracks by the sight of the Christmas tree. He gasped at the mountain of the presents.

He ran back upstairs and shook Lajos awake. "There are millions of packages under the tree!"

His excited shrieks were heard all over the house and everyone was awake now.

Eva tried to get them all to the table for breakfast first, but Laci was mesmerized. "Okay," she offered, "you – only you – can open one gift before breakfast."

Laci accepted the deal. He chose a package with his name on it. Christmas up till now, had meant a special orange. Never had he unwrapped a gift before. Endre told him it was alright to rip the pretty paper. And there inside was his train set!

"Santa Clause!" What a wonderful magical land this was, where a little boy could tell his wish to a jolly bearded man and it would appear under the tree!

There was no getting him to the breakfast table now, so Eva gave up. He could play with his train set while the adults ate. Enthralled as he was with his train set, little Laci soon wanted to know what was in the rest of the packages, but those would have to wait until the adults were finished eating and brought their coffees into the sitting room.

Eva insisted that the next gift to be opened would be Ilonka's. Eva had noticed Ilonka's simple wedding band and knew immediately what her first gift to her daughter-in-law would be. When she and Ferenc married they didn't have money for fancy rings either, but when their farm prospered Eva received a beautiful diamond ring for their tenth wedding anniversary. She never took it off, until now. Ilonka opened the smallest gift under the tree. With her own diamond ring, from her hand to Ilonka's, Eva welcomed her new daughter to America and into her heart. The glitter of the diamond multiplied as it refracted through the tears of joy in Ilonka's eyes.

The new year brought new beginnings for all of them. Lajos moved into the city and began English language studies. He sent letters back to Uncle Vince and Sanji describing America. He wrote, "It's just like they always said it was on the radio."

Ilonka sent letters back to Mariska and Erzsi. She wrote all about their new life in America. She told about how she struggled to learn English, but how quickly Laci had picked it up at school. She wrote how supportive her mother-in-law was of her sewing and of her long-forgotten dream to become a seamstress, and that she was planning to return to school next fall to study fashion design.

Endre took a job as an engineer and, each year, he used his summer vacation time to help his father with the farm work. Laci loved coming out to the country to help Daddy and Grandpa look after the animals and work the crop fields. It reminded him of the green horse back in Markota.

CHAPTER SIXTEEN (EPILOGUE)

The muscular rottweiler jumped to his feet and growled protectively.

"Hush," she commanded. "It's only the wind."

Okos stopped growling and sat back down.

Reaching for the cheap plastic clip, Mariska concentrated on the task of manipulating her fingers into tying her thinning silver hair back from her face. "They'd still be here if that pilot hadn't fallen from the sky," she told the dog.

Steadying herself on her cane, she began to pick her steps across the yard. Another loud bang shot through the air as the wind slammed shut the neighbor's gate. Okos growled again. "Lajos' bells," she said, and the dog settled down.

"Sixty years, it's been at least sixty years," she mumbled. Lajos. He was only ten or twelve years old at the time. "He lived for those airplanes," she told Okos. "And anything else that could make a loud noise." The banging in the wind reminded her of the young boy's prank. "Do you want to hear the bells of Dusseldorf?" he used to ask. Almost everyone fell for it. Then he'd slam the biggest rock he could find against the heavy metal lock on the gate of the nearest house, terrifying everyone within earshot. After all, there was a war on. Sudden loud noises made people jumpy. But Lajos would laugh, and declare with childish glee: the bells of Dusseldorf!

"I think he just liked the sound of the word Dusseldorf," she said, once again addressing Okos, who had trailed her all the way to the gate.

"Stay," she commanded. Okos halted. Mariska went through the gate, turned slowly to pull it closed behind her, and twisted the rusty skeleton key to lock it. That was probably unnecessary. No one would dare to enter her yard with Okos standing guard, but at ninety-one years of age Mariska was not about to change her ways, and the habit of keeping the gate locked dated back to more dangerous times.

This Sunday morning, like every Sunday morning, Mariska was headed for church. Since 1752, Mindenszentek Church had been the center of community life in the town of Markota, except of course during the Soviet years when going to church was illegal. She pushed back the dark memories and turned her attention to walking carefully. Mariska's back was so curved that her balance was affected by the unnatural weight distribution above her feet, but she was undeterred. She carried a thick cane to steady herself. Her steps were slow, but what did it matter? The church was only a block away. She would get there soon enough. She always did.

The autumn wind ruffled her faded peach housedress as she made her way along the dirt road, past the empty houses with overgrown, untended gardens. The main street that had once bustled with small town life was quiet now. She heard the clopping of hooves. Cars had long ago replaced the horse and buggy in the cities, of course, but in Markota a good horse or a bicycle was still better than a car. She knew who was coming just by the cadence of a horse's step, the squeak of a wagon's wheel, or the jangle of a rusty bicycle chain. Her once bright brown eyes had dimmed, but she didn't need to be able to see very far to navigate her withered world.

Just as Mariska shuffled through the open doorway, the church bells began their call. She smiled softly. Again she thought about Lajos and his bells. The rhythmic ringing welcomed the parishioners. There weren't many to welcome anymore. Everyone who could leave, left Markota years ago. Some in 1956; that's when Lajos left. Many more left in the 1990s. With the eviction of the Soviets from the country, there were new opportunities for entrepreneurs to prosper in business and for young people to study. Those opportunities were in the cities like Győr, Debrecen, and especially Budapest. Mariska had nowhere to go, so she stayed.

She eased herself down gently onto the green and yellow floral print of the thin pew cushion. She remembered sewing these cushion covers. They were her gift to the restoration of the church after the fall of communism.

By the time she sewed these covers in 1991, she had already been a widow for thirty-five years. Participation in the revolution on the part of a senior officer of the Hungarian army was unforgivable. László was amongst those who were executed in the weeks after the uprising. In 1956, he finally had his loyal army of Hungarian soldiers. They made their bid for freedom and lost, and Mariska lost the only man she would ever love.

For his part in the Petőfi Circle, Sanyi was arrested and sent away for re-education, which had become the popular euphemism for torture. They hurt his body, but his body healed. They failed to change his mind. He completed his studies in engineering and continued to hope for the day he would see freedom in his country. He often thought about those who left.

In 1991, after communism had collapsed and it was safe for them to return, Endre and Ilonka came to visit, but it was too late for them to see Erzsi and Uncle Vince. They had died while waiting for their world to change. By then, Sanyi was sixty years old, with a lovely wife, two daughters who'd grown up to be successful young women, and three grandchildren. Sanyi had built a reputation as a well-respected business manager of an engineering firm who found innovative opportunities emerging in the new economy, and his hobby wines were known to be the finest in the region.

Over in America, even little Laci had grown up. In 1991, he was a forty-one year-old man with two teenaged girls of his own. Endre and Ilonka brought photos.

They also brought that American news article, Mariska remembered. It was from January 1957 when Time Magazine featured the Hungarian Freedom Fighter as "Man of the Year." The young man in the picture always made her think of Lajos. He didn't have Lajos' blonde hair or blue eyes, but there was something about him, maybe it was his sad-determined look, she thought.

After going to America with Endre and Ilonka, Lajos had continued in his passion for all things mechanical and loud. Much to Endre's delight, Lajos became an international airline pilot. Mariska suspected that even if he'd been born in peaceful times, her nephew would not have been content inside any border. Lajos was one of those souls whom destiny called to adventure. He desperately longed to fly a commercial jet home to Hungary. Unfortunately, in 1982 at the young age of fifty-one, he died of a cancerous brain tumor. Although he always carried his beloved homeland in his heart, he never made it back to Markota because he didn't live long enough to see the Iron Curtain fall.

A lot had happened since 1956. At ninety-one years of age, Mariska's memory was still sharp. It seemed like some of these things happened only yesterday. Horrible memories, like the rapes. All those terrible rapes. How many lifetimes would it take to forget that? Women hid. Looking around the church, she remembered that a group of young women had been given refuge in a church in nearby Győr. When the Russian soldiers came demanding to have them, the Bishop tried to protect them, but the Russians wouldn't let the cost of a bullet come between them and what they wanted. Senseless violence. She shook her head silently. So much senseless violence.

Father Matyas brought the communion to Mariska, so she wouldn't have to get up. "The body of Christ," he said.

"Amen," she replied.

Mariska remembered the horrors but she also remembered the heroism. That December – after they killed László – the radio reported that twenty thousand women, dressed in black, held a silent protest march through Budapest in honor of those who lost their lives in the revolution. The Russians were everywhere by then. Those women were very brave, she thought.

She remembered Imre Nagy. Despite the people's demand for a government led by Nagy, he was never able to regain any political influence in Hungary. Instead, Kadar had him prosecuted in a secret trial and executed for treason in 1958. Thirty-one years later, in 1989 on the anniversary of his execution, he was finally given the hero's funeral that the nation felt he deserved. There seemed to be some justice in the fact that Kadar lived just long enough to see his arch-rival honored; he died three weeks later. Mariska remembered hearing on the radio that more than a hundred thousand people were at Nagy's re-burial ceremony. She would have liked to have gone, but Budapest was a long way from Markota. Still, she thought, I'm glad they honored him.

It's shameful that they killed a man who tried to help our country, but then Kadar was evil, she remembered. Nagy's death wasn't the only sorrow he was responsible for. It was because of him that she lost her one true love. It was Kadar who ordered the execution of her hero too.

Mariska remembered Cardinal Mindszenty. After the uprising, he spent fifteen years in asylum at the United States Embassy in Budapest. At seventy-nine years of age, in September 1971, he was finally released when the Communists allowed him to leave the country. He died four years later in Vienna.

Following the 1956 revolution, the country was terrorized by mass arrests and executions, and two hundred thousand refugees fled. Still, the dream of freedom continued to live in the hearts of the Hungarians who stayed, although it was thirty-three more years before the Iron Curtain finally fell.

Reflecting on a lifetime of changes, Mariska looked around the old church. Her eyes fell on the baptismal font. It's been a long time since any baby was brought here for baptism, she thought. Mariska herself had been baptized here. Almost everyone she knew had been baptized here. Oh! Her eyes opened wide at the memory of the scandal. Katalin's baby boy had been baptized here too. Of all those who left in 1956, Lajos was still the one she missed the most.

Mariska turned her attention back to the altar. The mass was ending.

Father Matyas raised his hands in blessing over his tiny congregation, "Go in peace."

For more about Markota and other books by Kathleen Hegedus, please visit http://CloudsOverMarkota.blogspot.ca

Made in the USA
Charleston, SC
01 June 2016